PAT GRIFFITH

ITERATION

I0545512

The DPA Declassified Files

www.thedpa.us

Editing
Scott Alexander Jones

Cover Design
GetCovers.com

Typesetting & Layout
Abdul Moiz, Fiverr(**abdul_moiz**)

DPA Logo Designed by:
David Landry, **The Anomaly**

Copyright © 2022 Pat Griffith
All Rights Reserved.
ISBN(Ebook): 978-1-7332626-5-1
ISBN(Paperback): 978-1-7332626-2-0

Venture Forth Publications
Where to next?

77 Van Ness Avenue, 1920
San Francisco, CA 94102
www.ventureforthpublications.com

DEDICATION

To Pauline, Kelly, Sophie, and Heather
for all your love and support through this entire series.

ITERATION

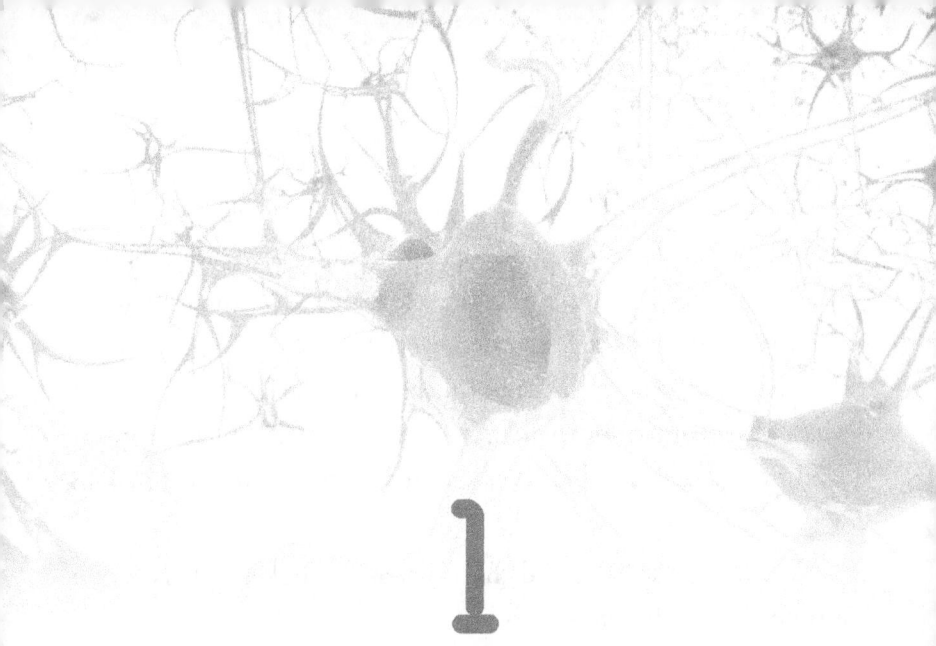

1

CENTRAL LOS ANGELES, CA

1000 hours PST

Lysandra Carlisle pushed the baby carriage out of the handicap stall. Its lopsided center of gravity caused it to wobble drunkenly on its cheaply constructed suspension as she parked it next to the wall. She washed her hands in the sink, examined her outfit, and frowned. The garish light of the bathroom brought out the puke-green leaves on the floral pattern of her flouncy, off-the-shoulder top. The lemon-yellow slacks did not fare any better. At least no one would recognize her; she barely recognized herself. Turning her head, she pulled back strands of dark-brown hair to look at her ear. The earpiece could hardly be seen. Only the most observant person would notice it, even if it were visible.

With a resigned sigh, she dropped the sunglasses from the top of her head over her eyes. They looked to be an ordinary pair of protective wear, but they recorded everything she saw. Any sound would have to come from her earpiece. The transmission of both devices was recorded somewhere in the parking lot. Where Eriksson sulked in a surveillance van that shouted "spy van" to anyone who saw it.

"Waste of time," she said cheerfully as she looked at herself one last time in the mirror.

Time to head back out. She went to the baby carriage and pulled back the corner of the bear-covered blanket that covered the top of it. Inside, all the pieces of highly classified DPA equipment were still present and accounted for. The last four days had been mostly spent fending off the curious strangers from trying to ogle her imaginary child. More than once it had come to firm wrist grabbing and whispered threats of violence at soccer moms and shop clerks.

The general din of the mall came into full effect as she left the bathroom. Lysandra backed through the bookstore doors and headed over to the magazines and newspapers. She picked up today's copy of the *L.A. Times*, a wide shot of the crowd plastered across the cover. Signs lofted above the sea of angry faces as people shouted their demands. Alpha Cortex, Edward's company, was in hot water for tainted drug treatments. There was nothing wrong with the drug's ability to fight neural deterioration, but somewhere between the drawing board and pharmacy shelves, something had gone wrong.

Lysandra thought it was unfair to blame Alpha Cortex. Had she been in charge of the investigation, her questions would have been: who manufactured the actual doses? Who packaged it? Who shipped it? Had the factory, or wherever they make drugs, been inspected and the employees questioned? If the science was solid—and it had to be, if it had been released to the public—that meant sabotage. Any one of those stages was an opportunity for sabotage. It was a competitive industry where millions of dollars were at stake. Not to mention a seething black market ready to take advantage of a pharmaceutical giant's downfall. And if it meant taking out a competitor with massive market share like Alpha Cortex, that would leave the field wide open for smaller research companies to swoop in on Alpha's territory.

She made a note to herself to look up Edward's competitors. He probably had people, Nolin, who already did that. Best offense is a good defense sort of strategy, but she knew to look in not-so-obvious places, like Dark0de and DeepBay type places. Well, at least she knew people who knew about that sort of thing. Did Edward employ hackers? The government did. If for no other reason than as a defense against other hackers. If Anonymous didn't like what you were doing, then you would get a world of trouble for it.

The bookstore was a good location for another reason. Research. She had never been a good student. School bored her to tears, with its routine and predictability. But knowledge was power—that she had figured out at an early age. Ignorance was not bliss. It meant being taken advantage of. Being gullible was a liability. Social sciences, conspiracy theories, anything that had to do with activism, modern revolutions, industrial pharmaceuticals, and geopolitics—all of these rolled into her search for a way to help

Edward. Without him knowing, of course. The currents of history and society were often from the most unlikely of places. She felt in her gut that Alpha Cortex—and by proxy, Edward—was being targeted specifically. She wanted to get to the source if at all possible. Once she had a few theories, she would talk to Nolin and see if he and his team had come up with any leads.

In her earpiece, she heard Matt's voice give his coffee order to a barista. She took a quick glance to each side of her to make sure no one was paying attention. She was essentially alone.

"How's it going over there, shark bait?"

Matt Holloway sank uncomfortably into an under-stuffed chair with the sports paper in his hand. A cup of mocha-latte-something-or-other cooled on the table in front of him. Indie band music crooned louder than necessary from the speaker system. For four days, he had taken up residence at the bustling cafe watching people come and go, all the while pretending to be reading.

"This is such bullshit," he said under his breath and sank lower into the chair.

"Buck up, champ." Lysandra's voice in his ear sounded unusually cheerful. "I nearly had to knock out three people today who wanted to see my baby. Why don't people mind their own damn business?"

While he had been holed up in the coffee house, Lysandra had been on patrol disguised as a mother. For four days now, as she had wandered around the mall with a covered baby stroller, he sat in the cornerstone coffee establishment as a decoy waiting for Elbie enthusiasts or hosts to approach him. So far, nothing had happened. Other than buying coffee, throwing it out at the end of the day, and spending the whole day wishing he could be doing anything else. "If I had known this was why Kristy had been sent away—"

"She wanted to leave. What happened next was no one's fault. All of this is the Department trying not to repeat the mistakes of the past."

"Look who's defending the government monster organization now."

"Reminder." Eriksson's voice crackled on the line. "I can hear you. If either of you has a problem with this assignment, you can address me directly. For now, focus on your surroundings."

"Yes sir," Lysandra replied from across the mall somewhere.

"Is this seat taken?"

Matt looked up from his paper. A pretty blonde leaned toward him, one hand on the matching chair next to his. "No, go ahead." Matt forced a smile and sat up.

It had been a week since Kristy had left on her next tour. She had been out and about playing ambassador for the Department of Planetary Affairs for months, and he just found out that she had an armed escort with her wherever she went because her appearances tended to bring out others who had had contact with Elbie, people previously unknown to the Department of Planetary Affairs. And the encounters were not always friendly.

At least when she was on base, he could protect her himself, but out in the world, there was nothing he could do for her. And the fact that Commanders Eriksson and Draegg had not ever once mentioned it to him made him mad. So mad he had considered leaving the organization for the first time in his life.

"This is a waste of time," he whispered.

"Excuse me?" The bronzed female next to him looked at him with expectant eyes.

"Sorry." Matt shook his head. "Just talking to myself." He reached for his cup and took a sip. The lukewarm sugar concoction nearly made him gag, but he forced it down to keep his dignity. Spewing liquids in front of this woman would leave the wrong impression, to say the least.

"I do that all the time." The woman leaned toward him on the arm of her chair with her elbows, rolling her drink between both hands. "Confuses the hell out of my roommate sometimes."

"Oh." Matt ran a hand through his hair. She was actually interested in him. It had been years since he talked to someone not affiliated with the government. He could hardly believe it was happening. "That's cool. How many roommates do you have?"

"There's five of us. We're all actresses."

"Five. Wow. The bathroom must get pretty crowded in the mornings."

The woman knit her eyebrows and pressed her lips together.

"I mean, I only have one sister, and growing up, I could never get in there. She made me late to school every day of my life."

The woman laughed and took a sip of her blended pink drink. "It can be a problem."

"Ask her out," Lysandra's voice whispered loudly in his ear. Matt involuntarily flinched, resisting the urge to pull the device out of his ear.

The woman smiled and took another sip of her drink, still squarely turned toward him. A question came into his brain: what would Derek do?

Derek never passed up the chance to talk to anyone. Matt had nothing to lose and only time on his hands. He cleared his throat. "What's the most interesting thing you've auditioned for?"

2

GLENDALE GALLERIA

1130 hours PST

Waiting for something, anything, to happen, Lysandra perused the business magazines. In all her reading, she noticed that Edward Drake never appeared on a cover. Nor did he do close-up, stand-alone shots. If Alpha Cortex Pharmaceuticals was a featured story, there would be a picture of one of the drugs they produced or the team of engineers who made it. None of the photos were of individuals. Always groups. Edward only took photos with his team members (he never called them employees). How much of that was an Elbie's affinity for groups or Edward's constant mission to exalt others around him, she couldn't tell.

She took a break from reading current affairs to watch groups of patrons come and go out in the corridor between storefronts. Over the last four days, Lysandra had seen a thin woman with a pointy chin and sharp cheekbones lead groups of uniformed workers through the throngs of shoppers at a clipped pace. Huddled together, the workers kept their heads down, looking up only long enough to see where they were walking. Each day it was a different group of people. Mostly women, but a few men too. These little groups of people being escorted through the mall never happened at the same time like a shift change. Given how much Lysandra walked around the mall, she probably was only seeing a few instances when this procession was happening. Each time, an oversized guy in regular street clothes followed along behind the group, hanging back a few yards.

Lysandra had worked for one kind of crime network or another since she was fifteen. Everything about this woman, her wards, and the rear guard screamed organized crime. Given that the uniformed workers in this instance had dejected looks and that they were in Los Angeles, this would most likely be a case of forced labor. Most criminal enterprises came in clusters. It would not be surprising to discover a money laundering or drug ring hiding in plain sight, but human trafficking was one crime she could not ignore.

Throwing the magazine aside, Lysandra grabbed the stroller and headed out into the crowds. She quickly spotted the group of workers and their guardians and tailed them. In her earpiece, Matt continued to make awkward small talk with what sounded like a couple of people now. This whole stakeout was a waste of time; there were no Elbie hanging out in this mall.

As she followed, the crowds thinned out, forcing her to track the group from a greater distance. The group turned down a side corridor where there was almost no foot traffic. They continued to the end of the corridor. No windows, no exits. Lysandra quickly ducked into an empty piano store just as the rear guard turned around. There was no way the group could leave from down there, so she waited a few minutes before going back out into the corridor.

Leaving the shelter of the piano store, Lysandra pushed the stroller ahead of her, walking at a casual pace. The burly guard who had been following the group now sat slouched in a deserted seating area, facing the store as he stared hard at his phone. As Lysandra strolled by, humming softly, she made sure to keep her eyes on the walls, but from the corner of her eye, she could see the guard watching her. She stopped momentarily at the very last storefront at the back of the dead end. Black vinyl letters stuck to the marble above the entryway read "A2Z Personnel Services."

Personnel service my ass, she thought.

She took a casual survey of the strangely quiet corridor. The white noise of the mall sounded miles away from here. The guard glared at her over the top of his phone. Lysandra pushed the stroller into the establishment. Behind a lattice privacy screen and water feature was a reception desk and plain waiting room. The woman who had led the group of workers was seated at the reception desk. She stood suddenly, as if caught off guard by a prospective customer.

"Good afternoon." She smoothed her hair. "How can I help you?"

"Yes, hi," Lysandra said in a slightly higher pitch, hoping it made her sound cheerful and not shrill. "I'm so glad I saw this place.

My husband and I are in desperate need of a new agency for our yard and housework. Do you offer that sort of thing here?"

The woman's shoulders visibly relaxed. "That's exactly the sort of thing we do here."

Lysandra gave an exaggerated sigh. "What a relief. I'd love to speak to any of your candidates you think may be suitable. I'm really not that picky."

Eriksson's voice crackled in her ear. "Sitrep, Carlisle."

Lysandra had to resist the urge to pull the earpiece out while talking to the woman.

"I'm afraid it's a new recruit day and not many of them speak very good English at the moment. We usually give English lessons the first several weeks, along with customs and cultural training."

"So thorough. That's wonderful. Do any of the new recruits speak Spanish?" It had been years since Lysandra had spoken Spanish. Hopefully she could remember enough of it to find out what was going on in this place.

After a pause, the woman responded, "Yes. Most of them."

"Fantastic. I've got time right now. It really would mean so much to me if I could just get this one burden off my shoulders." The lady started shaking her head no. "I can pay whatever your fees are—in cash, if needed. I need to get some help for the house before I go crazy."

The woman studied Lysandra for a moment. The offer of cash had caught her attention. She was probably trying to decide how much she could ask for without risking Lysandra walking out. With a tilt of her head, the woman gave Lysandra a professional smile. "Let's see what we can do for you. If you could complete the application while I round up some candidates for you." She handed Lysandra a clipboard and pen. "If you have any questions, my name is Judith. I'll be right back."

Judith disappeared down a hallway and out of sight. Lysandra flipped through the pages. She hastily made up the house address and family details, along with the services they were interested in.

"What the hell are you up to, Officer Carlisle?" Eriksson's voice burst in her ear. His voice was so strained it sounded like he had swallowed a handful of gravel. "What's your location?"

Lysandra did a visual sweep of the room. It was the most boring waiting room ever. No effort had been made to create ambiance of any kind. If this place was a cover for criminal activity, they would probably have hidden cameras, but none were immediately visible. She covered her mouth, pretending to think about her answers for the application. "In the mall."

"Doing what?"

"Checking out something suspicious." Lysandra checked the opening of the hallway.

"It had better be a secret faction of rogue Elbie."

"Just give me a few minutes." Lysandra pulled the earpiece from her ear and quickly slipped it into her pocket.

Judith came out with a big smile on her face. "All ready for you." She held out her hand. Lysandra handed Judith the clipboard. She scanned the application. "Mrs. Edwards."

Judith led her down the narrow hallway with way too many turns, passing several doors. As was her habit, Lysandra looked for exits and possible escape routes, but there was none of the required signage. So far, only the main entrance up in the front of the space was the only way in or out.

"Your baby is so quiet." Judith looked over her shoulder at Lysandra.

"He's been teething. I bring him to the mall for walks. It's the only thing that puts him to sleep. I've spent hours here lately." Lysandra hoped that was accurate. She had no idea when babies got their teeth, nor how old her apparently male and also imaginary child was.

Judith ushered Lysandra into a cramped office with a desk and two chairs. The desk had a monitor and keyboard but no mouse. It was also free and clear of absolutely anything else. A middle-aged woman with dark skin and black hair pulled tight into a bun sat in one of the two chairs near the door. She wore the dark-green polo Lysandra had seen the group sporting before, with "A2Z" emblazoned in white thread on the left shoulder. Maybe these guys were legitimate.

"This is Maria," Judith announced. "Maria, this is Mrs. Edwards."

Maria stood, her eyes darting to Judith and then to Lysandra for a split second before she turned her gaze to the floor. *"Buenos días."*

"Buenos días," Lysandra started confidently, suddenly very aware of how many years it had been since she last spoke Spanish. Maria kept her head bowed, shifting her weight from foot to foot.

"Don't mind me." Judith attempted an air of casualness. "I'll be working on this." She indicated the clipboard and sat behind the desk.

Lysandra sat in the only other seat. The stroller with all her DPA equipment fit only between the desk and door, leaving little room to move around. Maria took her seat. Lysandra had hoped she would be alone with the candidate. Having Judith in the room would hinder her.

Lysandra cleared her throat and searched her brain, willing any Spanish she once knew to reappear now. *"Perdón."* She smiled at Maria apologetically. *"Mi español... está un poco... malo."*

Maria nodded, holding her hands tightly in her lap, her eyes going to the door often.

Lysandra reached out to the stroller and started rocking it gently. It really did help to give her hands something to do. *"¿Tiene... experiencia li... limplando casas?"*

"Si, señora." Maria wrung her hands and stumbled through a list of places she had previously worked, mostly resorts. Her responses were very rehearsed, as far as Lysandra could tell. And having Judith watch them like a hawk despite pretending to work on the computer did not help. Maria's eyes went to the stroller. *"¿Qué edad tiene su bebé, señora?"*

Lysandra easily recognized the word for baby and year. *"Mi bebé is uh nueve...* months. *¿Tienes experienca en el cuidado de niños?"*

Maria smiled and shook her head. Even with direct questions her eye contact with Lysandra was brief. *"Sí señora, ayudé a mi mamá a cuidar a mis hermanos."*

Lysandra nodded, feigning comprehension. *"Mi bebé está dormir ¿le gustaría ver una foto?"*

Maria looked over at Judith, her eyebrows raised in a question.

"*Está bien.*" Judith waved her hand at them and went back to faking work.

Lysandra took out her phone. "Oh. I've missed a few texts. Just *un minuto.*" Lysandra had several missed calls from Eriksson. There were texts, too, but there was no way she was going to check those. She started a text to Matt and typed out, "*¿Necesita ayuda? ¿Está siendo retenido contra voluntad? 911.*" Lysandra wasn't sure the 911 part would mean anything to someone not from the US, but she figured it couldn't hurt to add. She faked some actions on her phone, making sure the screen was visible only to her. "*Aqui.*" Lysandra turned the phone so that only Maria could see the text.

Maria stiffened in her chair. Her countenance faltered for a split second. The twisting of her hands increased, and she nodded. "So... pretty," Maria said in faltering English.

"*Gracias.*" Lysandra glanced at Judith.

Judith glowered at the two of them, a deep frown frozen on her face. "Mrs. Edwards, I can't find your address on Google Maps."

"How much?" Lysandra stood up and started searching her pockets for her wallet with her free hand.

"How much for what?" Judith asked, her scowl deepening.

"For Maria. Two thousand? Five?" Lysandra dropped her phone. "And all her papers too." The phone fell face up, revealing the text message. Judith looked from the phone to Lysandra. Judith probably couldn't see what it said, but it obviously wasn't a picture of her non-existent kid.

Lysandra grabbed the phone and shoved it in her back pocket.

Judith started around the side of the desk. "Who are you? I demand you tell me this instance."

Lysandra grabbed Maria's hand. "*Vamanos.*" Lysandra pushed the stroller into the hallway.

"Stop!" Judith shouted.

Maria's hand tugged from Lysandra's grasp. Turning around, Judith held Maria by the sleeve of her branded polo shirt. "You can't take my employee."

Lysandra squared off with Judith. "She is *free* to leave at any time, isn't she?"

Judith's gaze hardened as she let go of Maria's shirt. Maria was visibly shaking now. Judith straightened her shoulders and relaxed her face. "Of course." Her voice was a gentle coo.

Lysandra turned her attention to Maria. "*Quieres venir conmigo o….*" Lysandra couldn't remember the Spanish word for "her," so Lysandra just pointed at Judith.

Tears started to streak Maria's face. The terror in Maria's eyes made something inside Lysandra's head snap. All the tears and pain she had suffered at the hands of her abusers and users, starting with her father, filled her with rage.

Pushing the stroller down the narrow hallway, Lysandra stopped at the next door. She tried the handle. It was locked.

"Get out!" Judith yelled, rushing at Lysandra.

Lysandra took a step back and kicked the door handle. With the help of a telekinetic burst, the hollow door split open. Inside, a shocked group of people in green polo shirts huddled together.

"Go!" Lysandra waved at them to leave.

A sudden weight on her back dropped Lysandra face down on the floor.

"Security!" Judith shrieked as she leaned all her weight into Lysandra's shoulders. For such a small woman, Judith was surprisingly heavy. A few pairs of feet from the liberated room rushed past Lysandra. Getting her arms under her, Lysandra pushed up, flipping the two of them backward. Judith grunted as Lysandra fell on top of her.

The hulking figure of a man filled the hallway and towered over the two of them. His beefy hands hauled Lysandra to her feet. A solid kick to the groin buckled him to his knees. Leaping over him, Lysandra kicked in the next available door. She caught a glimpse of surprised and confused workers inside. She moved on to the next couple of doors, kicking as she went. "Run. Go. Leave," she shouted at the groups of startled people in green polo shirts.

The end of the hallway neared, leading down to more hallways. She would kick in every door she could find. A few people had pushed past her to escape, but only a few. Then she saw the bright red-and-white fire alarm pull station. She ran for it.

A sharp crackling noise burst to life behind her. Lysandra glanced over her shoulder. The groin guy lurched toward her with a stun gun in his hand, the electric arc firing. She reached the end of the wall and pulled the lever on the small red box. The fire alarm started to flash and blare. A strange sort of relief washed over her. Everyone would have to leave, and there would have to be an investigation.

Electricity bit into her side. The pain ripped across her ribs and into her stomach. Every muscle in her body seized up, and she fell against the wall. Before she could fall over, Groin Guy pressed her against the wall with his forearm, brandishing the stun gun in her face.

"Freeze," someone shouted from down the other end of the hallway, in the direction she had been trying to go. Groin Guy blocked Lysandra's view of whoever it was.

She tried to shift her legs to prepare for another kick. An electric pop snapped in the air behind Groin Guy. His body jolted, his eyes went wide, and he collapsed to the ground. With him out of the way, she could see several mall security guards crowded into the hallway. At the front, Matt was on one knee, lowering a DPA-issued stun gun. Eriksson was easy to spot at the back of the group, his eyes boring into her.

Lysandra slid down the wall, exhausted. Eriksson was going to chew her out later, but she didn't care. Knowing that all the people held captive could get help now made the reprimand worth it.

Matt strolled up to her and offered his hand. "You're the one who's supposed to be protecting me. Not the other way around."

She took his hand and pulled him down. "Yeah, well, I'm still getting a hang of this good guy thing." He settled on the floor next to her, their shoulders touching.

Lysandra leaned her head back against the wall. The pain from the stun gun was gone for the most part, but her muscles were still stiff. "How did you find me so quickly?"

"Well, we were already on our way here because of your 911 text."

She laughed. "I must have sent it by accident. And the GPS in the phone led you to my location?"

"You betcha." A smile spread across his face.

"What?" She wanted to punch him. He probably wouldn't mind. It would only encourage him anyway. "What?"

"Nothing." He shook his head and looked down at his feet.

"That was something."

Police had arrived at the scene, and the hallway was getting busier as the place was searched. Orders were being shouted back and forth. The fire alarm had been turned off, but the blue light still flashed.

Matt pulled his legs into his chest, to allow people space to walk by them. He looked at her, his eyes shining with eminent tears. "You reminded me of Brendan just now. For a split second, I felt like I was back in high school. Before all of this, we were just kids doing our best to avoid boredom and parents." He stared at the floor, sniffling.

Lysandra held her tongue. She thought a lot about how things could have been if she had grown up with her brother. That line of thinking always ended with a mantra about not dwelling on a past you can't change. After all the fantastic things she had seen, changing the past was still outside of her reach. Introspective pity parties were a waste of time. Looking forward was the only thing that had kept her going through all those years.

"I asked her out."

"What?" Lysandra looked over at Matt.

"That woman I was talking to at the cafe. We're going out on Friday." Matt turned away from her, his cheeks flushing red.

Lysandra smiled. "That's awesome. What are you guys going to do?"

Matt shrugged. "You know, the usual. Dinner, dancing, world domination."

"World domination, again?"

Eriksson walked up, wearing street clothes but with his Department ID in plain sight. Only the second occasion Lysandra had seen him out of uniform. The last time they were both in traditional East Indian garb. He stopped directly in front of them, his broad shoulders casting a looming shadow over them. "You finished playing vigilante superhero?"

"Yes sir," Lysandra and Matt answered in unison.

"Let's go." He waited for the two of them to get up and started walking. "Lysandra," Eriksson said solemnly, "I appreciate your swift action here today, but as a member of a special branch of government, we need to leave ordinary problems to ordinary authorities."

"Human trafficking is not an ordinary problem. I had to do something."

They came out into the waiting area, where there was a lot more room. Scattered around the waiting area, police officers tried to talk to some of the "employees" of A2Z Personnel Services.

Eriksson circled them up at the far end of the room. "Your primary objective was to protect Matt." He crossed his arms.

Lysandra's attention was drawn back to the hallway, where a couple of police officers escorted Judith and a few other people out in handcuffs. Once upon a time, Lysandra would have been the one taken away in handcuffs. It was almost fantastical being on the flip side of the law. Judith glared at Lysandra, her thin lips in a tight frown, until she was taken out of sight. Lysandra's rage returned. Her father had used her as currency for his illicit activities from a very young age. She had had no one to protect or defend her from her father's exploitations. If there was anything she could do to protect others from the same kind of abuse, she would.

"You're right, I know that, but when I saw those people, every day, being led in here like cattle, I just… I had to do something." She knew too well the powerlessness and fear that could hollow a person out. It had taken her years to get back any sense of self-worth.

"Lysandra." Eriksson put his hand on her shoulder. "I'm not saying your instincts were wrong. L.A. has an entire department dedicated to this specific issue. If it's not related to our main mission, we let the local agencies handle it." The frustration had drained out of his voice by now, taking on a more teacherly tone, similar to Commander Draegg.

"Yes sir, I get it." She met his gaze. He had been so hard on her in the past. She wasn't sure who was changing, him or her. Maybe a little of both.

"Good." Eriksson dropped his arms. "Once you give your statement to the police, we'll leave."

Matt pulled out his earpiece. "Since my backup is probably no longer welcome at that mall, does this mean that we are going to try another coffee place?"

Eriksson shook his head. "No. I've determined that trying to lure hosts into the open is a waste of resources."

"I would have said deceptive." Lysandra watched the police and victims talking in small groups. Even if Eriksson was being nice, she didn't have to agree with his methods.

"Be that as it may," Eriksson growled, "we are looking at other ways of being proactive when it comes to finding hosts."

"I thought that was what the covert ops division was for." Matt took out his phone for the first time.

"What?" Lysandra took a step back. "The DPA has an official covert operations department?"

"Of course it does. They're called field agents." Matt didn't take his eyes off his phone as he scrolled through social media. "Haven't you ever read the website?"

"Why would I do that?"

"Don't you research a company before you go to an interview?"

"I've never been to a job interview in my life, and neither have you, Matthew."

"I have too. Once. When I was in high school."

Lysandra turned to Commander Eriksson. "Field agents, what do they do?" Anything had to be better than basic security. "How come no one has ever mentioned this before?"

Matt snickered. "If you'd read the handbook or kept up with the job board, you'd know that they exist."

Eriksson shook his head. "It's a very small team. There are only a few of them, and they usually work alone."

"Sounds ideal to me." This was the first time Lysandra was excited about anything to do with the DPA.

Eriksson grimaced. "If today was an example of your work, then I think you're better suited to your current position."

Lysandra bit the inside of her cheek. Eriksson was right, of course. She could practically hear Matt's unspoken thought: *Zing.* Or: *Burn on you.* Then again, maybe it was her own inner critic chiding her. Hardly the caliber of a professional like herself. In her own private defense, this was the first time she had been trying to stop a crime rather than committing one.

Matt clapped her on the back. "Cheer up. It's Skype night."

Lysandra groaned. "Already? I'll be busy."

"Come on. You can't spare one hour to talk to Derek?"

She sighed and leaned against the reception desk. "Derek is your friend. All he talks about are digital neural nets and ubiquitous cloud connections. I know more about machine learning than anyone not in the field should. It's boring."

"He's excited about his job. Today you actually have something to tell him about your job." Matt smirked as he typed something.

"Only if you tell him about your new girlfriend."

"Deal!" He called her bluff. "Of course, I'd tell my best friend something like that."

"Perfect." Lysandra looked around the waiting room. The police were totally wrapped up talking with other people. "I just want to get out of here. Can I just write out my statement on a piece of paper?" She started to look around the desk.

"Holy crap!" Matt looked at Lysandra.

"What?" She stopped her search.

"You have to see this." He shoved the phone into her hand.

On the screen, a breaking news story: "Edward Drake, CEO of Alpha Cortex Solutions, has been shot." Her stomach dropped before she had finished reading the headline. She scrolled through the bulletin. It had only been a couple of hours. The proclamation of "critical but stable condition" did nothing to quell the storm in her chest. The Mayflower Coalition claimed responsibility with no apology. She handed the phone back to Matt, a tremble in her hand.

"Lysandra." Matt put his arm around her.

"I'm fine." She forced herself to breathe slowly. It had been a few months since she had last seen Edward, and it was not her most shining moment. So much so, she had been too embarrassed to face him again. She had missed so much with her brother while he had been alive. Because of her stubbornness and pride, she had also cut out Edward, the one person who truly knew her.

"What is it?" Eriksson asked.

"Esben was shot by some activists." Matt held the phone in front of Eriksson to read.

"Don't call him that." Lysandra gripped the edge of the desk.

Matt put the phone away. "Sorry, I forgot. It says Mr. Drake will recover."

Lysandra nodded. Precisely because Edward was a host, he would be okay; she would not accept any other conclusion. The Mayflower Coalition had been on her list of organizations campaigning against Alpha Cortex Solutions. Claiming responsibility was the stupidest thing they could have done. Now she knew who to hold accountable.

Eriksson said, "Once we're done here, we'll get an update on Edward's condition. I'm sure Commander Draegg will know more."

"Thanks." Lysandra nodded, wanting to sink to the floor. What she could use right now was a hard drink and some time to sort through her feelings.

3

PASADENA, CA

2348 hours PST

Lysandra parked the SUV with government plates in one of the handicapped spaces and ran into the hospital. She figured no one was using the space, and government business took precedence. She followed the signs to the ICU. It was almost midnight and fairly quiet. Maybe that was what freaked her out the most: hospitals were always so solemn.

One lone nurse sat at the nurse's station, which blocked the entrance to the ward. Many of the lights were off, casting the hallway into shadow.

Lysandra leaned on the aqua Formica countertop. "I'm here to see Edward Drake."

"Are you family?" the nurse asked without looking up from her monitor.

Lysandra bit her lip. *Stay calm.* "Family?" she asked quietly. "Edward Drake doesn't have any immediate relatives."

"What's the password?" Still no eye contact.

Lysandra took a deep breath. "Are you effen kidding me with this shit," she whispered loudly. "I'm the goddamn girlfriend." She stabbed a finger down the hall. "I demand to see him now."

A security guard came over to the counter. "Ma'am, I'm gonna have to ask you to leave now. Visiting hours are over."

Lysandra pressed her lips together, breathing through her nose. She held a finger up: one minute. From her pocket, she pulled out the cell phone that Edward had given her. "Observe." She held up the phone. Holding down the 1 button she waited until Edward's name popped up on the screen and stated it was "dialing."

The guard shook his head, "Ma'am, seriously—"

"Listen." She handed him the phone.

Rolling his eyes, he took the phone and put it to his ear. After a few seconds, he handed it back to her. "That doesn't prove anything. How am I supposed to know that's not a published number?"

"You think Edward Drake has his personal phone number publicized?" Lysandra had abandoned whispering now.

"Now I'm asking nicely, ma'am, please leave." He reached for his radio.

A figure appeared in the hallway from one of the rooms down the hall. Nolin passed through a pool of light, his left arm in a sling. His eyes lit up with recognition the moment he saw her. "Lysandra. You came?"

"You say that like I had a choice. Why didn't you call me?"

The nurse jumped from her chair. "This woman says she is part of your group, but she's not on the list you gave me."

That stung. She shoved the security guard off. "Tell them, Nolin."

Nolin sighed heavily. He did look exhausted, almost as if he were Elbie-free.

"Nolin, what are you waiting for?" Staying calm was getting harder the longer he hesitated. Nolin's chief function was to protect Edward. But she was the last person to be a threat to him.

He looked at the nurse. "Give me a minute." He took Lysandra by the arm and led her aside. Lysandra shot a look of triumph at the guard. "You've been totally MIA the last few months. Why now?" he asked in a low tone.

"Why now!?" Lysandra looked at him in shock. "Why now! Uh, because he almost died. That a good enough reason?" She glanced at his injured arm.

Nolin leaned near her and kept his voice low. "When was the last time you two talked?"

Lysandra crossed her arms. It was true—contact with Edward had been sporadic at best. Her feelings toward him were too conflicted. It was easier to ignore him than to deal with their dynamic.

"How do you know he wants to see you?"

The mere suggestion of it rankled her. "Intuition."

Nolin shook his head, a smile breaking through his tiredness. "You sound like L'heilh." Lysandra did not respond. He took her arm again, and they came back into view of the hallway. "Officer, thank you for your service. Nurse, please add Miss Carlisle to the list."

"Relationship?" the woman asked.

Nolin glanced at Lysandra, then the nurse. "Significant other."

The nurse hesitated as she evaluated Lysandra. The nurse's eyes flitted in Nolin's direction for final confirmation before she wrote Lysandra's name.

"Come on." Nolin waved at Lysandra and started down the hall.

It seemed this hall had been cleared of any other patients, no doubt some sort of privileged security measure since Edward Drake had been under threat of bodily harm and death threats for the last few weeks. The two of them stopped in front of a door. "Go on." Nolin gestured toward the door. "We're just across the hall if you need anything."

"Thank you." Lysandra nodded in appreciation.

Pushing the door open, she peeked her head inside. The room was dimly lit, and Edward lay in the bed, an oxygen tube taped to his face, bandages wrapped around his chest and stomach under the open gown. The green line on the heart monitor jumped at long, regular intervals. Except for the IV and bandages, he looked totally normal. The wads of gauze, in sharp relief to his darker skin, made her heart skip a beat. Reading about what had happened was one thing; seeing it with her own eyes was more of a jolt than she was expecting.

Silently she crossed the room and stood at the side of the bed. She had not seen him for a couple of months, not in person anyways. He had a habit of showing up in her dreams. Then someone tried to assassinate him. If he had died... She shoved the thought back.

Most likely, he had not been anywhere near death. The accelerated healing abilities that came with being a host made a person hard to kill, but what if they had gotten him in the head? Her eyes burned at the thought of it. Some injuries were too much for an Elbie to heal. Though she had lived without him all this time, the thought of him dead filled her with dread.

Leaning against the edge of the bed, she wrapped her fingers over the top of his hand. He was warm. Placing her free hand against his cheek, she leaned close to him and whispered in his ear, "Esben, what are you doing in there? Tell Edward I'm here to see him." She waited for a response. She did not like using his Elbie name—she preferred Edward without his Elbie—but he would never give it up. Having been a host, she understood how very separate they were. The body may be in one state while the mind is in a totally opposite one.

"If you wanted to see me, you could have called." She teased.

She smiled at him, waiting for his eyes to flutter open. Only the steady rise and fall of his chest.

Her head dropped on the pillow next to his. Why had she come? This was the stupidest thing she had ever done. There was no future for her here. She kissed his cheek and stood up. He was alive and would live. She could go back to ignoring him now. As she prepared to leave, Edward-Esben gripped her fingers.

Heart beating in her throat, she leaned against the bedside. With his free hand, he pulled the oxygen tube off, and his eyes cracked open. "Going somewhere?" he whispered.

"You need your rest." Lysandra swallowed hard.

He tugged on her arm and drew her closer. "I need you." He wound his arm around her waist and pulled her onto the bed.

Unable to resist his delirious request, she allowed herself to settle next to him, very aware of how small the bed was and how close their bodies were.

"I've missed you." He breathed onto her neck and kissed it.

Lysandra lay beside him, her heart beating so hard in her chest she thought it shook the bed. This was the last thing she wanted, exactly because she wanted it so deeply. He had to feel how tense she was, how uncomfortable. What if someone walked in? Months of ignoring these feelings gave them the power to overwhelm her. Disarmed by her own emotions, her hand went to the bandages around his waist. "We'll have matching scars now."

"True," he agreed groggily, resting his head in the crook of her neck.

She ran her hand through his black hair. It had been cut shorter since the last time she had seen him. "New hairstyle?"

Edward-Esben nodded. "L'heilh thought I needed updating."

"I think you looked better with the curls you had before."

"Noted," he whispered. With his arms wound around her, he was asleep again.

Lysandra forced herself to relax. Awkward as it was, she found peace in the moment.

4

HUNTINGTON HOSPITAL

0300 hours PST

Edward Drake woke with a chill. That had happened only one other time in recent years.

Lysandra shifted next to him; her arm rested across his stomach and her head in the crook of his arm as she slept. In the time since the Department of Planetary Affairs had moved its base of operations to downtown Los Angeles, the two of them had seen each other only on a handful of occasions. It was like they were both warming up to the idea of being together, but neither of them was willing to be the first one to talk about it openly.

Edward held her tight, euphoric at the opportunity to be with her even under such intense circumstances.

As his arms tightened around her, an urgent ache to have her close to him overwhelmed him. A sensation not experienced since India. The last time he was Elbie-free. He turned his focus inward, looking for Esben's presence. Like the phantom pain of his missing finger, Edward sensed the emptiness of something that should be there and wasn't.

He gently touched Lysandra's cheek with the back of his hand; she was burning up.

"Esben," he whispered into her ear. No response. Her eyes moved back and forth in REM sleep. "Esben!" He tried for a more curt tone.

Lysandra's eyes snapped open. "Yes."

Even in the low light of the room, her blue eyes glimmered. This was the first time ever that Esben had left Edward of his own volition. The only time they had ever been fully separated was when Xander had forcibly removed Esben. "What are you doing in there?"

"I wanted to ensure the events from India were still locked up safely." She reached up, brushing his cheek.

Edward took her hand and sat up. His injuries were completely healed, not even any residual muscle pain. "You should have consulted with me first."

"Everything looks good." She sat up with him, so that they stayed eye to eye. "In case you were wondering."

"I appreciate your diligence. Now come back to me." He put his hand on her neck, expecting the immediate transfer of heat.

Esben-Lysandra slid her arm around his neck and pulled him in for a kiss. His stomach dropped as their lips touched and her tongue gently caressed his own. It had been so long since she had touched him in this way. But it wasn't really Lysandra doing it.

He gently pushed away from her. "What are you doing?"

"You both want this. I'm just trying to speed things along." She leaned forward for another kiss.

Edward held her back but her shoulders. All he wanted was to be with Lysandra, and if she felt the same, this was not how he wanted their relationship to develop. "If that's true, then you don't need to do this. Just come back."

A smile curled on Esben-Lysandra's lips. "I like it in here." She combed his hair with her fingers. "Draegg thinks that she is like them now. A good little government employee."

Edward did not like this behavior from Esben. They had been of the same mind for so long and now… He took her hands and held them. "Esben." It was so strange, confronting a part of himself in another person. "Please tell me you haven't changed anything."

Her smile twitched. "I've changed nothing."

Edward bowed his head with a sigh. "Good. Now come back to me and we can discuss this later."

"Yes, of course." Esben-Lysandra kissed him again.

This time heat moved from her hands into his neck. A slight lightheadedness made him sway a bit. Lysandra crumpled into him. Lying back down with her asleep in his arms, Edward-Esben rehearsed how he would tell her what had happened and hoped she wouldn't hate him for it.

Edward-Esben buttoned up his pink dress shirt in the cheap bathroom mirror. The metal sides of the hospital bed creaked again as Lysandra turned in her sleep. She had done this several times already; she would be awake soon. He lassoed a gray silk tie around his neck and began looping it.

"Ez." Lysandra's voice echoed from the room, still heavy with sleep. She had never called him that to his face. He liked knowing she had a secret nickname for him.

He stepped out from behind the bathroom door. "Good morning, Miss Carlisle."

Still tangled in the blanket, hair in her face, she squinted up at him. "Oh, hey." Finally, she sat up and stretched her arms over her head. "I take it you've recovered from the attempt on your life?" She combed the long strands of her dark-brown hair with her fingers.

He adjusted the tension of his tie as he walked over to the bed. "I am. How are you?" He sat down next to her. "You seem disoriented."

Lysandra rubbed her temples. "Just really weird dreams, is all. But I'm good." She threaded her arm into the bend of his elbow and leaned against his shoulder. "I'm glad you're okay."

See, she's fine. As I said, Esben chided Edward.

Edward wanted to believe him, but she was being so… sweet. He liked it, but it was a departure from her usual demeanor. He couldn't be sure Esben hadn't nudged her into a more amiable state.

It was the thought of your death and nothing else, I promise, Esben responded to Edward's silent accusation.

Lysandra lifted his arm over her head and encircled his waist with her arms and squeezed.

"What's going on with you?" He tightened his arm around her. He should tell her what Esben had done, but he didn't want to ruin the moment. If she didn't have any recollection, maybe it didn't matter, and he could keep this one to himself.

Lysandra sighed heavily. After a moment, she finally confessed. "I'm sorry I've been avoiding you."

"Would you like to tell me why that is?" He had his theories but wanted to know hers first.

She tilted her head back to look up at him. "Embarrassment, probably. I was not my best self that last time I saw you."

Thanks to Nolin and L'heilh, she had escaped a hospital visit from alcohol poisoning. Why she had practically drunk herself to death had most likely been a subconscious response to the repressed memories Esben claimed to have been checking on a few hours ago. So far, the secret she was keeping from herself was still safely buried.

Edward-Esben found her hand and held it to his chest. "Perhaps not, but I wished you'd mentioned it sooner. I would have told you that it didn't matter. That I'd rather see you than not. We all make mistakes, and I don't care what you've done. Just don't shut me out."

She nodded, a sadness dulling the light in her eyes. "I wanted to let you know it wasn't because of anything you had done." She rested her head against him and sighed. "Do I have to go back? Eriksson is going to be so mad at me. I'm already in enough trouble as it is."

Edward-Esben laughed. "I thought you liked it that way."

"Yeah, well, after he took a bullet in the chest for me in India, I can't help wanting to impress him. No matter how hard I try, impressing him is impossible."

"That's how work life goes sometimes."

"Lysandra Carlisle has a freaking day job with the government. Unbelievable." She laughed. "I don't think I can deal with living a normal life."

"I would say not." This was not the reason for her dissatisfaction, but the mind must have a reason. Humans created stories to explain everything that happened in the universe. Edward-Esben struggled to keep his gaze on her eyes and not her lips. "Nor should you. Come work for me."

"What?" Lysandra pulled away from him. "You can't be serious?" She stood up.

"I absolutely am." Edward-Esben stood too. If she was going to make a hasty retreat, he wanted to be ready for it. "I want you with me." There. He said it. He had wanted to say it ever since their return from India. After everything that had happened there, he wanted nothing else but this: to live his life with Lysandra.

"I have to go." She started for the door.

Edward-Esben reached for her and pulled her toward him. "Don't go."

"You don't need me."

He put one arm around her waist, drawing her in as close as she would allow.

She looked down. "You're one of the most successful men in America. You have everything you need."

She's looking for an emotional way out. She doesn't think she's good enough for you. Esben informed him. *You have to convince her otherwise.*

"I'm afraid you're wrong, Miss Carlisle." Edward-Esben lifted her chin to look her into her eyes. "I don't need the money or the accolades. I have found them to be hollow if you're not around."

Lysandra leaned forward, planting her forehead at the center of his chest. "You know that's absurd, right?"

"I don't care if it makes sense to others, it makes sense to me."

Lysandra lifted her head and searched his gaze. It was the honest-to-god truth, and he hoped she believed him.

She believes you. She can't accept it for herself yet.

Edward forced his focus on Lysandra by combing strands of her hair away from her cheeks. The corners of her mouth twitched. A sensation flooded into his chest. A swirling of want, desire, happiness, and belonging, but they were not his emotions. Unable to resist any longer, Edward-Esben bent his head down to Lysandra and gently touched his lips to hers. A promise from him to her that he meant what he said.

All the tension left her body. Her hands slid over the top of his shoulders and around his neck as she pressed her body against his. Her lips parted, inviting him in. The tips of her fingers tickled the back of his neck as they drank in each other.

Crickets chirped from Lysandra's back pocket. Reluctantly she pulled away from him. They looked at each other in the brightening room, the morning sun burning behind the sterile white curtains. Light in her eyes, cheeks flushed. She pulled out her phone. He could see that it was a text that consisted of one word: *Report!* Lysandra pushed away from him. "I really do have to go now."

She started for the door again. Edward-Esben caught her arm as she turned and drew her back. "When can I see you again, Miss. Carlisle?"

"I'll have my people call your people." She gently peeled his fingers off her arm and went to the door. With her hand on the handle, she stopped and looked sidelong at him. "See you soon, Mr. Drake." She opened the door and walked out.

Edward's smile faded as the door closed. *Do not ever do that again.* Edward thought at Esben. *Whatever you learned about Lysandra while you were in her mind, keep it to yourself.*

My mistake. Esben retreated from Edward's mind into the coursing activity of his nervous system.

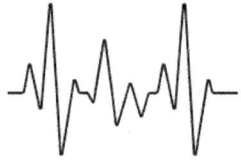

Lysandra closed the door behind her. The corridor echoed with conversation suddenly cut short. Nolin and L'heilh stood near one another in the doorway across from Edward's room, looking at her. Lysandra always thought that they were an unlikely pair. Nolin's hair was in a constant state of bedhead, while L'heilh, no matter the time of day, looked like she had stepped from the pages of a fashion catalog. As long as she had known them, they had been inseparable.

"Cheerio," Nolin said in an overly cockney accent and saluted at her, smirking.

L'heilh smiled with a knowing glint in her hazel eyes. "Morning."

We're all adults here. Besides, nothing happened. The thought of them talking about her made her cringe. Had Edward told them everything? They were a tight group. Maybe they would just know, as you do with people you spend your life with. You get to learn the subtle signals of body language, tone of voice, and glances when you spend so much time together, and those three had been together for years.

"Nolin. A word." Lysandra started walking toward the exit.

Nolin easily caught up with her. "How may I be of assistance?"

"Do you have any leads on who pulled the trigger?"

Nolin did not respond right away. "We know the organization behind it."

Lysandra stopped walking. "Know or suspect?"

He examined her face as he massaged the hand of his injured arm. "We can't be sure until the gunman is caught, but we have strong evidence to support our conclusions."

"Is it the Mayflower Coalition?"

His eyes hardened. "Why are you so interested?"

"If it wasn't them, you would have said no. Thank you for your cooperation." She pressed the down button for the elevator.

Nolin grabbed her elbow. "Lysandra. This is an internal matter. The proper authorities will take care of it."

"That's a first."

"Yes, well, things have evolved."

"Meaning it's too public for more covert means."

The elevator door opened. Lysandra pulled her arm from him.

Nolin put his hand on the door. "Meaning, we'll take care of it."

She pressed the button and crossed her arms. "Fine. I'll leave it alone."

"Good." He smiled and released the door.

They began to slide shut. "For now!" Lysandra yelled through the doors just before they closed. She caught a split second of Nolin's face as he heard her, his lips bunched with aggravation. As head of Edward's security, he probably took it as an insult to his management of the situation. Or maybe he just didn't like his momentary victory being taken from him. A win for her in either case.

5

HIDDEN HILLS, CA

2200 hours PST

dward-Esben sat on the couch in the suite to the side of his room reading documents. This was his habit most nights, just before bed as he wound down from the day. After reading for a short time, he would go to sleep, or at least let his body sleep. The phone on the coffee table buzzed.

He looked at the message. From Miss Carlisle: "Knock, knock."

Esben's presence faded from the forefront of Edward's mind.

As it formulated a response, the familiar flare of white light from a portal illuminated the main part of his bedroom, beyond his line of sight. It could only be Lysandra. The portal anchor that was linked to her watch was kept in the nightstand next to his bed so the portal would be only a few feet from his bed.

Lysandra sauntered around the corner into the suite. She was dressed in pajama shorts and a tank top. Without a word, she walked straight over to where he sat, pulled the papers from his hands, and straddled his lap. With her arms loose around his neck, she touched her lips to his with a light kiss. She tasted like red wine.

"What happened to your people calling my people?" Edward-Esben asked, dizzy from the sudden rush of adrenaline and endorphins.

"Too many people," she whispered in his ear just before her tongue swirled around the ridge of his ear and she nipped him lightly on the lobe.

Tingling ran down his spine. "Lysandra," he said with difficulty and put his hands on her shoulders. "Lysandra, please, wait."

The kisses down his neck stopped. After a second, she sat up and looked at him. "Yes?"

"Lysandra, why are you here?"

Her hands rested on his chest. "You want to talk about this now?"

"Absolutely." He let his hands fall to her waist and waited.

"I thought about what you said after we got back from Australia. I think that even though what I feel about you is due to some powerful suggestions, they wouldn't have worked if there wasn't some truth to them. And after India, I know you are honest about your feelings for me. The only time I ever feel any true sense of happiness is when I'm with you. Good enough?"

He had concerns that she would always harbor resentment toward him for his part in her brother's death and blatant brainwashing. She had pronounced her forgiveness towards him, but he still wasn't sure how deeply she meant it. But this was different. She was not deceiving herself or sugar-coating anything that had happened between them in any way. After all this time, she was finally admitting to herself that she was attracted to him from the start.

Lysandra's presence in his life had been unexpected, as was his need to be with her. He had never felt this way about anyone. There was no pretense between them. No secret agendas. Each knew the worst about the other, and it didn't matter. She wanted to be with him, and he wanted nothing else but to be with her.

"Well?" Lysandra moved her hands up his neck.

Edward-Esben shook himself. Getting lost in thought had been a problem for him ever since India. "I... I'm honored. And relieved."

"I have to say, that is the least sexy thing that you could have said right now." Her knees tightened around his hips.

He laughed. "So sorry. I'm just amazed that you're here."

"So, amaze me." She leaned into him, her lips lingering near his. "Let's see what you're made of, Mr. Drake."

Gripping her hips, he bucked and flipped her onto her back. She screamed in surprise at the sudden turn. Her legs tightened around him and he pressed his body onto hers. "My pleasure, Miss Carlisle."

Their lips met hungrily for each other.

6

DPA HEADQUARTERS

2300 hours PST

Even though it had been several months since the relocation, Eriksson was still adjusting to the DPA's new headquarters. Unlike the previous facility, the new building had multiple floors. The bottom levels were dedicated to administration and security, the middle floors for medical treatment and research, and the top levels for living space. The DPA was not technically a paramilitary organization, but they operated similarly to one.

Moving from their isolated location in the Angeles National Forest to downtown Los Angeles came with its own challenges and advantages. The increased public contact meant much more security but greater transparency. It had made a huge difference for the medical division. Patients appreciated not having to travel so far for treatment and testing. It also meant more protests. But all these things came with being part of a government agency.

After checking the logs for who had come and gone for the day, Eriksson used the elevator to get to the top levels, where officers of the DPA lived. Not all of them, but many officers choose to stay onsite for the convenience of it. Technically, Eriksson lived onsite as well, but he split his personal time at Eva's home. She traveled a lot for her job. While they had spent more time together since the DPA relocated, they still had very busy, individual lives.

Eriksson had not made it a point of knowing the specific location of everyone's rooms, but he was unsurprised to find Lysandra's room was located close to the nearest exit. He had no reason to believe she was planning on leaving the organization anytime soon, but old habits die hard. When reviewing the daily logs, he discovered that Lysandra had gone out a second night in a row. It was a rare occasion when she left late at night. Based on the late hour, he surmised she would not be back tonight.

Commander Draegg was waiting for him outside Lysandra's room. It was department protocol that any searches of private quarters had to include both of them. "Evening," Eriksson greeted his co-commander as he took out his access card.

"Evening." Draegg stepped back from the door to give Eriksson room. "Are you sure this is necessary?"

Commander Eriksson swiped his card and punched in his access code. "I'd rather be safe than sorry."

The door slid aside, and they quickly stepped inside her room. As commander, Eriksson took his responsibility seriously. Those under his command were free individuals to spend their time as they wanted, but Lysandra was the most unpredictable person he knew. Something was going on with her, and he did not want to be blindsided by anything.

A quick visual sweep of her room confirmed her private habits remained the same. Since officially joining the DPA, she had improved on many levels, but this was not one of them. Clothes scattered around the room. Piles of newspapers and current affairs magazines piled on the nightstand. The order imposed on her by a steady work schedule had done nothing to tame the chaos of her life. This time, however, there was the addition of something he had not seen before.

They both went directly to the standard issue desk that everyone had in their quarters. Lysandra's desk was stacked with books and handwritten notes. Newspaper articles cut out and glued to them.

Commander Draegg picked up a few of the books and opened them to pages she had marked with sticky notes. "I see what you mean."

Eriksson shuffled the stacks of magazines and dozens of printouts, all of them about current activist organizations and the identified people tied to them. Another pile had timetables for trains and ferries, maps, and lists of establishments. Nothing explicit was laid out, but one thing was clear: Lysandra was on a mission. She spent too much time on this for it to be a passing interest.

Eriksson sat down at the desk and turned on the computer terminal. First, he sifted through her internet browser. Not much there. She knew enough to clear it. He would have to have IT pull the records from her IP address.

Eriksson looked over at Commander Draegg and watched him as he read through some of her notebooks. "She hasn't said anything to you about this?"

Commander Draegg shook his head. "To be honest, we haven't spoken much lately. I'm sure this is why."

Eriksson did a quick survey of her email. There, he found several exchanges between her and Matt. Being alone was her preferred method of spending time, but Matt spent most of his free time with her. He needed the human interaction more than she did. Matt had sent her several articles complete with sources. Why Matt let her boss him around that way, Eriksson could not understand. He had seen Matt stand up to Brendan on several occasions, but when it came to Lysandra, he gave in every time.

Commander Draegg replaced her notes and faced the wall behind the desk. "Any idea when this all started?"

Eriksson turned off the monitor. "I only noticed after we started the stakeout at the mall. The protests over at Alpha Cortex have been going on for a few weeks now."

Eriksson examined the wall as well. It had become a collage of drawings that Jyot had sent Lysandra over the last several months. The two of them exchanged letters and gifts often via DPA official mail. Their adopted brother-sister relationship was the cornerstone relationship between DPA US and DPA India. Lysandra Carlisle had come far in a relatively short time. Criminal to ambassador. A role she took to easily, to his surprise.

Commander Draegg took in everything on the desk and floor. "If this is only a few weeks of work, we really are underutilizing her potential."

Lysandra's involvement with the DPA and Elbie had not been by her design but by someone else's. After all was said and done, she had been given a choice to stay or leave, and she chose to stay, entangling her life even further with the DPA and, therefore, Elbie. Her brother, Brendan, had not been given that choice. The whole purpose of the DPA was to protect the public from Elbie, and she had dived into it headfirst while Brendan had been pulled under by the forces of history.

Eriksson had often wondered: if Brendan had been given the option, would he have stayed? Perhaps if his first encounter had been a positive one, then everything would be different now. Eriksson's first encounter with Elbie had been just as traumatic as Brendan's, and here he was working with them on a daily basis.

Commander Draegg sat back on the desk. "You said there was something else you wanted to talk about."

Eriksson leaned back in the chair. "Yes. Lysandra's at Edward Drake's house tonight."

Commander Draegg rubbed his chin in thought. "Not surprising, given the assassination attempt."

"They'd seen each other on several occasions right after we got back from India but then stopped suddenly. Do you know what happened?"

Commander Draegg shook his head. "I never asked and she never said. I have my suspicions, but it's only conjecture. What's on your mind?"

Eriksson weighed his words carefully. He knew that what he was about to ask could be taken the wrong way. He had no evidence to support anything he was feeling. All he had was instinct that something was not right. "Given what you know about Edward

Drake and Esben, is it possible that they could be manipulating her in some way?"

Commander Draegg stood up. "Alex, what are you suggesting?"

Eriksson met his partner's bewildered gaze. "Edward, Esben, nor anyone in his circles have ever registered with us as hosts, which in my opinion is a kind of passive-aggressive act of sedition."

Commander Draegg sighed. "Alex…"

Eriksson sat up. "Hear me out. Lysandra is a government employee with official levels of clearance that could be useful to them."

"But to what end?"

"I don't know. I'm trying to anticipate threats. That's part of what we do."

Commander Draegg bowed his head and pinched the bridge of his nose.

Eriksson stood. "The way Edward, Esben treated Brendan before his bionic implants is a precedent. If they are after something, they will not hesitate to…"

"You're not wrong. But that was a long time ago. A large part of what happened to Brendan predates Edward. Besides, I would be absolutely shocked if Edward meant any harm toward Lysandra."

"Edward. What about Esben then?"

Commander Draegg thought for a moment. "A large part of what drove Esben was Doctor Li's obsession with Brendan's gifting. Edward carried that for a little while, but that was ages ago. There just isn't any motive to use Lysandra in that way."

Eriksson knew Draegg was right. Perhaps he was so used to being on the defensive he couldn't let himself believe disaster wasn't around the corner. "I don't know. Maybe."

"Alex." Commander Draegg put his hand on his shoulder. "Are you sure this isn't your own bias getting the better of you?"

Commander Draegg had always been the voice of reason, as had his previous host Miranda. It had taken Eriksson a couple of years to adjust to his partner being a host because of his negative experiences. Eriksson dropped his head. "I hope you're right."

"I'll check in with her this week. If I suspect anything, I will let you know."

Eriksson nodded. "I'd appreciate that."

Until Lysandra or Edward-Esben did something overt, he could not take any action. Eriksson could not dictate who she associated with or stop her from leaving the premises, but he did have his concerns for her safety outside of the base. She was under his command and, therefore, his protection. She was scheduled to work tomorrow. If she didn't show, he knew who to call. Until then, he would keep a watchful eye on the situation.

7

DRAKE ESTATE

0800 hours PST

Edward lay on his back, looking up at the four-post canopy above his bed. He had gotten a few hours of sleep, but with an Elbie that was all he needed. He pondered the feeling that he was forgetting a dream. Hosts could not dream, so it was a feeling he had not had for some time and did not miss. The chaos of dreams had always bothered him. During his imprisonment by Xander, separated from Esben, Edward had dreamed profusely, but all of that stopped after he had Esben back. Maybe he had dreamed. He did a quick search for Esben. Esben ebbed closer into Edward's mind, letting Edward know that he was indeed where he should be.

A beam of sunlight breached the break between the heavy curtains, hitting the bed, illuminating Lysandra's peaceful face. With a stretch, she rolled away from it and wrapped herself around him. Edward had slept soundly after they had tired each other out, but he was hyper-aware of her presence next to him.

"Good morning." Turning toward her, he ran his hand down the curve of her back, cupped her ass, and gave it a light pinch.

Lysandra shuddered. "Not fair," she said groggily and threw her arm over his, pinning them.

Pulling his arm free, he stroked her hair. "Would you like breakfast before going back to the DPA?"

Lysandra groaned and opened one eye. "Had to mention work, did you?"

"I have better coffee."

"It's a low bar, trust me." She rubbed her eyes and repositioned herself next to him. "Ten more minutes." After a light kiss on the cheek, she buried her face in the side of his neck.

They had had sex before, but this time was different. She had confessed freely and passionately her need for him, and it was equal to his own need for her. He didn't know it was possible to feel this… happy. He had not been unhappy. Work accomplishments gave him a sense of pride and were a source of satisfaction. He did not have a single thing to complain about in his life. But all of that paled in comparison to what he had with Lysandra right now.

Stretched out next to him, she ran her fingers up and down his ribcage, her eyes closed and a faint smile on her face. He took her hand in his. "Lysandra."

"Hmm." She was starting to fall asleep again.

"I rescind my offer from yesterday."

She opened her eyes, searching his face. "Excuse me?" The tone she used was playful, and she feigned hurt feelings, but he caught the confusion in her expression.

"I don't want you to work for me." He cupped her face. "Marry me."

"What?"

Her body went rigid.

"I want to wake up every morning with you here."

She propped herself up on one elbow. "Whatever for?"

"You said it last night. This is where you're happy. Why be anywhere else?"

"Because it's insane." She sat up, wrapping the sheet around her.

"How so?" Edward-Esben sat up.

"We have nothing in common. We come from totally different backgrounds."

"I don't see how any of that is relevant."

Lysandra shook her head. "I'm not going to talk about this, and neither are you." She got up from the bed and stomped into the bathroom, shutting the door behind her.

Edward-Esben sat in the reverberating silence, reviewing the conversation in his mind. Equating his desire to build a life with her to insanity was an extreme reaction he did not understand. After last night's discussion, they should be in agreement. He stared at the closed door between them, wishing to talk about this. One thing he did know, when Lysandra was upset it was best to leave her alone until she was ready to talk. Until then, this discussion would be off the table.

8

DOWNTOWN LOS ANGELES

1500 hours PST

Lysandra watched the steam from her coffee swirl in the afternoon sunlight. The Formica table they sat at looked like it had been stolen from a fifties drive-in diner. The small mom-and-pop cafe was directly across the street from the Department of Planetary Affairs building. Her mind turned over all the possible explanations for the consistent smell of boiled cabbage that permeated the tiny establishment.

"So..." Matt sat down across from her with his usual glass of whole milk and a warmed chocolate chip cookie.

When the DPA had first moved into the neighborhood, people were alarmed by their presence. The imposing uniforms with classified weapons, an association with government intelligence, and the mystique of dealing with aliens unnerved people. Lysandra imagined this must be what it was like to be a cop, a strangely contradictory position for her. The nervous looks and the way people moved out of the way for them wherever they went. She had never liked giving the authorities deference, and she certainly did not like receiving it.

But after a few months, the area workers and residents had gotten used to them, and the interactions with the public were usually positive. Putting names to faces with the mysterious members of the DPA really helped people feel more comfortable with their presence. Most officers had gotten used to the impromptu question-and-answer sessions from citizens.

Matt cleared his throat.

"Sorry." Lysandra shook herself and took a sip from her coffee. "What were we talking about?"

"We weren't. You've been suspiciously quiet all day."

"What's suspicious about it? You're the one who usually does all of the talking."

"Am I more talkative than you? Yes. But today it's like you're not even here."

"Sorry, I'm distracted."

"By..."

"It's nothing."

"Uh, I wouldn't call staying out all night nothing."

Heat rose in her cheeks. If he knew she had been off the premises all night, did others? Did it matter? She had never cared what people thought about her before, but it could make for awkward working relationships. The last thing she would want is for Matt to have to make excuses for her.

"You noticed that, huh?" She took a quick sip of her coffee.

"It was game night."

"Shit." Lysandra put her cup down. "I'm so sorry. I totally spaced it."

"I know you were worried about Drake. It's fine."

"I should have let you know, at least. Really, I am sorry."

Matt waved off her apology. "Is he okay?" He took a drink of some milk.

"Yeah. Fully recovered." Lysandra nodded. She started to pick at the cup sleeve, contemplating her next words. She didn't want to think about what had happened with Edward this morning, but she needed to process it. Matt was really good for that sort of thing. "He, uh, asked me to marry him."

Matt gagged on his milk and started coughing violently. Lysandra jumped to pat him on the back.

After a few minutes, Matt regained his composure and cleared his throat. "Are you serious?"

Lysandra nodded solemnly.

"What did you say?"

"What any sane person would say. 'We're not going to talk about this.'"

"Uh-huh." Matt held his milk at arm's length, silent and unmoving.

"Speaking of which, how was your date?"

"No changing the subject." He relaxed again and looked at her. "What are you going to do?"

"Do? There's nothing to do."

"Well, you have to give him an answer."

"No, I don't. Where's the rule on that?"

"Lysandra. Come on. The guy is—"

"Is what, Matt? Being vulnerable with me? Going out on a limb? Exposing his soul? What are you going for here, buddy?"

"Okay, sarcasm is your defense mechanism. So for whatever reason, this is hitting a raw nerve. But yeah, all those things. This is some serious stuff."

"Okay. Now we're not going to talk about it."

"Hey, woman, you're the one who brought it up."

"True. But only because you're supposed to agree with me. You're my friend, on my side, partner."

"Friends don't let friends act stupid unless it will be hysterical."

"I'm not Derek." Lysandra tapped the table with each word. "You don't get to make jokes at my expense."

"There's nothing wrong with wanting to be with him. And honestly, I don't like the guy, but I think he's good for you."

"Why don't you like him?"

"For all the same reasons, you shouldn't like him either."

Esben was the Elbie, not the man. Esben had been the worst of them all and caused all of them the most suffering. Edward, as a host, had not come onto the scene until well after the damage had been done. Being allied with the worst Elbie of them all did not help his case in the eyes of Matt and his friends.

"You mean you don't like his Elbie."

"I don't like either of them, but as a host, Edward has really tamed that Elbie, and I'm sure the world is a better place for it, even though he refuses to register or cooperate directly with us."

Lysandra drew doodles in her cup sleeve with her thumbnail. Edward and Esben were very distinct entities that happened to work well together. She, of all people, had reasons to hate them both, but Edward at least had displayed genuine remorse and shown her true affection.

"You're smiling."

Lysandra looked up. "What?"

"I said, you are smiling."

"Shut up." She sat up in her chair and took another sip of coffee. Matt broke off pieces of his cookie, watching her. "Fine, Matthew. I'll think about it."

"There ya go." He gulped down his milk in triumph.

She knew what Matt wanted to hear. She also knew that despite her feelings of dread around Edward's proposal, she would be unable to stop thinking about it for a long time.

9

DRAKE ESTATE

0030 hours PST

Lysandra's head rested against Edward's bare chest as she listened to him breathe. She had hoped the rhythm of his breaths would help her get to sleep. It didn't.

Earlier that day had been a real struggle. The usual routine required of her from the DPA and Matt's chatter had not been enough of a distraction to help her forget the argument with Edward that had started her day. Instead, she forced her thoughts onto Edward's attackers and the organization behind his attempted murder. The group was not headquartered in Los Angeles, but they had at least a temporary base of operations while they waged war on

Edward's company. Nolin's investigation had narrowed down their specific location to two places. He was forced to work with law enforcement. That was too slow for her.

The attack on Edward's life had backfired on the group, getting him only sympathy. To play the big bad corporation card worked with most of the public, but Edward's company focused on drugs that helped people with Parkinson's and Alzheimer's and were brilliantly successful at it too. It was hard to bash a company that had contributed so much to advancement in those areas.

Around and around her thoughts went, but at the end of her shift, sitting in the quiet of her empty room, there was only one thought that filled her mind. To be with Edward. After a short text to him, she left the DPA via the portal in her watch. Since she still had the watch on her, this meant that getting back to base had to happen through more mundane means. This morning it had been Edward's private car, and she imagined it would be the same tomorrow too.

Dinner was cut short by their desire for each other. That had concluded an hour ago or more, and now she lay wide awake staring into the dark, unable to quiet her mind. It was then, in that moment, that a familiar sensation seeped into her skin. An uncomfortable heat moved from where her hand rested on Edward's chest. The wave of heat moved fast up her arm, across the back of her neck, and oozed into her skull. Her senses quickened. The scant light in the room brightened slightly. Edward's deep breathing grew louder to her now heightened hearing.

A slight panic quickened her pulse. She knew from unfortunate experience that an Elbie could transfer to a human without their immediate knowledge. She sat up, trying to decide what to do.

Unless something had changed, there was only one Elbie between them, and she knew that Esben had not switched hosts since finding Edward Drake. For Esben to be so forward about his presence meant he wanted her to know this action was intentional.

Images from newspaper headlines she had seen flashed in her memory. The headline: "Activist Organization Mayflower Coalition to Blame." The first line started off: "Mayflower Coalition claims responsibility for the attack on Edward Drake, CEO of Alpha Cortex Solutions."

Bile burned at the back of her throat. She did want to get them back. *Retribution.* So did Esben. It was a common goal between them. Esben needed a body to exact revenge. Considering her availability—that is to say, direct physical contact with Edward and a working knowledge that could get her into seedy places—it was a match made in heaven, as far as Esben was concerned. *Act now.*

Lysandra watched Edward sleep as she gathered all her clothes from around the room and went into his walk-in closet to get dressed. Even though the racks of clothing would absorb any sounds, she took extra precautions to be quiet.

He's in a deep sleep. Nothing will disturb him.

She wanted to shush the Elbie, but she knew that vocalizing was not needed. She only had to think it.

It was not the first time she had been a host, but this time felt different. She watched herself with heightened self-awareness. Like in a dream when she is both the observer and participant. Her view of the world was from the perspective of her own eyes, but she was annoyingly aware of the limits of her field of vision. If being completely and fully aware of her surroundings had not been distracting enough, now the voice in her head talked at her in the tone and inflection of Edward.

Once her shoes were on, she went to the doorway to make sure nothing had changed. Assured that Edward was still asleep, she went to the nightstand on his side of the bed only a few feet from him and pulled the drawer open at a painfully slow rate.

Inside were six portal anchors. About the size of a credit card, they looked like simple remote controls with only two buttons. Each had neatly printed labels: Office, Caribb, NYC, Seattle, San Fran, and Miss Carlisle. The last one linked to her watch. This would be her ticket back to the house. She also took the one labeled "Office." This would take her to the Alpha Cortex office in downtown L.A. She could take one of the cars in the garage, but this would be faster, and time was what they needed most if they were to succeed.

Lysandra went into the bathroom and closed the door behind her. As she passed by the mirror, she jumped, thinking there was another person in the room. It was only her reflection. Staring at the reflection of the woman in the mirror, she felt a complete disconnect. It might as well have been a stranger.

She broke off her contemplation and continued through to the door on the other side of the bathroom and stepped into her bedroom. Making sure the doors to the bathroom and the hallway were shut and secure, she opened the closet door and switched on the light.

With a hard stare, she looked into her own eyes. "Does Edward know about this?"

The voice in her head kept silent.

"Esben." She glanced over her shoulder, paranoid that Edward would walk in on them.

Time is short; we should hurry.

"Answer the question," she told her reflection sternly.

Take a seat.

Lysandra sat on the corner of the bed. "Now what?"

Close your eyes.

Lysandra waited. The need to get even with Edward's assassins pressed on her soul like a great weight. As she sat, there was a falling sensation. She gripped the blankets under her to keep steady. Everything felt surreal and… floaty.

Open your eyes.

Heavy red velvet curtains hung on both sides of her, and a lifeless movie screen in front. Above her head dangled the art nouveau chandelier that illuminated suffocating confinement with horrible yellow light. This *place* was a construct in her mind to contain her while someone else did the driving. The last time she was trapped inside the tiny theater, Brendan had been alive. On more than one occasion, the image of it showed up in her dreams, and she hated it every time.

"Lysandra."

She stood up from the cushioned theater seat and turned around to see Edward Drake in the door-less room. He was dressed in her favorite suit. She had never vocalized that to Edward. How much effort did it take for Esben to find that fun fact somewhere in her brain?

Esben pulled his hands behind his back. "Edward and his company are at the center of this thing. They have to play nice with the police; otherwise, it will look like they are guilty of everything these people are accusing them of."

"I get that, but did he, at any time, actually think that he wanted to get back these people?"

"He wants justice. Anyone would."

Lysandra started pacing. From all her research, she knew that this organization was in California only for the purpose of harassing Alpha Cortex. The extra step of taking Edward's life only showed the depth of their conviction. They would not be going away anytime soon. "I still don't think he'd want me involved. Not to mention, I'm a government employee." What would Commander Draegg say if he found out? And Matt?

Esben touched her arm lightly with his left hand, stopping her. "You're the one with piles of books back in her room. Can you honestly tell me that you did all of that research to do nothing?"

Lysandra paused. "Not nothing, but through legal channels. Give the police the info and let them take care of it."

"You, more than most people, know how easy it is to evade the police. You did it for years."

"So you've been thinking about it because Edward has been thinking about it. Or is it the other way around?"

Esben slid his hand up her arm and leaned closer to her. "We take these guys out, get them to leave, and Edward will be safe."

Lysandra looked at his hand and then his face. Edward's face drew her in. She had been attracted to Edward from the moment they met, but she had chalked that up to pheromones and mutual attraction. "How are you doing that?" She took a step back so that his hand fell from her arm. It was then that she noticed he had all five fingers. Edward had lost his pinky finger because of her. This was not Edward. This thing in front of her was just a mental image of the man she loved.

"Doing what?" He pulled his hands behind his back with a slight smile.

She crossed her arms and cocked one eyebrow at him.

He met her gaze, but the look in his eyes was distant. He had checked out for just a second. With a blink, he returned. "Memories are powerful. I'm borrowing from your most potent encounters to evoke your emotions."

Even his honesty couldn't be admired. Even though he was in her head, hiding a lie was still possible. What a bastard. Her aggravation made the yellow light in the room flare white for a second. "Stop it right now or this whole thing is off."

Esben's entire demeanor flipped from charming to stoic. The warmth in his expression switched to calculating executive. "Our time is short."

Lysandra shook her head. "See, this is why this is a bad idea. The charm bullshit didn't work so now it's the ticking clock."

Esben turned away from her, and he balled his fists. "What will it take then, Lysandra?"

Lysandra stared hard at him. He could read her thoughts. Could she read his? She tried to look for them, but it was so abstract she had no way of knowing if she was doing anything at all.

Esben looked down at his feet. "Edward never explicitly said anything. But it's there. Under the surface, like most emotions. He is a mature adult, so he will let the authorities deal with it. But if someone tried to kill you, what would you do?"

Lysandra started pacing again. Killing them right back, of course, would be her initial reaction, but that was a figure of speech. As a mercenary, she had been an infiltrator, not an assassin. Killing was reserved for life-and-death situations. But let it go? Never.

"Exactly," Esben said.

She drew herself up. "Okay. Let's see what we can do."

Esben smiled. "Excellent."

"But"—she walked up to him—"this is a collaborative effort. If I find myself in this room, locked up, with no say or control, we'll both regret it."

"Shared control." Esben nodded in agreement, his face devoid of expression.

"And if I think for one second that you are trying to manipulate me, I'll see to it that you are extracted permanently one way or another."

"I would expect nothing less."

She searched his face again, trying to find his thoughts in her own head. "For Edward then."

"For Edward." He nodded once.

With new resolve, Lysandra sat in the lone velvet covered theater seat and closed her eyes.

As she opened her eyes, the plan, Esben's plan, formulated in her mind. First things first. In the drawer of her dresser was her most prized possession: a brushed nickel Jericho .45. It irked Eriksson that she had a personal firearm; Edward didn't care, so she kept it at his place.

She threw together a practical outfit from the piles of clothes around the room. Putting the shoulder holster on, she loaded the gun, made sure the safety was on, and concealed it under her jacket. They had no plans to use it, but she hated being caught off guard without it. It was a source of comfort for her in dangerous situations.

They set the portal anchor labeled "Miss Carlisle" on the nightstand for the return trip. In the dark of her room, she pressed the button on the portal anchor labeled "office." A disc of iridescent light burst into the center of the room. She set the office anchor next to the other one and stepped through the portal. On the other side she found herself in Edward's office at Alpha Cortex Solutions' main office. Finding the matching half of the anchor was in the top drawer of his desk. She pressed the button and closed the bridge between the two points.

Lysandra walked out into the hallway. Most of the time, she arrived at the building from the outside. To get her way around, she would need to rely on Esben to direct her as they went. There would be a few cameras, but he had her maneuver through the building in a way that would not trip security, and where security was a concern, he could use Edward's pass codes to override it. Once outside, they hailed a cab.

From her hours of extensive research, she knew a few members from the activist organization that had been persecuting ACS spent their time at a club in Hollywood. Social media had made being an activist a popular hobby among the young and the chaotic atmosphere of a nightclub, combined with drug and alcohol intake, made these kinds of places excellent recruiting grounds for new followers. At least of a certain kind. Numbers were far more valuable than actual ethical values for some causes.

Lysandra was not dressed for clubbing, but she was female and with an Elbie—extra persuasive. As the cab careened toward

Hollywood, Esben made one thing clear: she could not be linked to anything that was about to happen. Lysandra was just a vessel to get Esben close enough to their victims. Once the people they were seeking were located, he would take care of the rest.

10

HOLLYWOOD, CA

0245 hours PST

hird time's a charm, she thought as they climbed out of the taxicab. Each ride from one club to the next had led them farther and farther out of the city limits. Surrounded by rows of nondescript warehouses, one stood out with flashes of light behind obscured windows, music pounding from behind the metal and walls. This had to be the place. After almost three hours of talking to people at other clubs, Esben and Lysandra had learned that the person they were seeking went by the code name of Robin Hood.

While she had a legal right to carry her weapon of choice, guns were not allowed in nightclubs for obvious reasons. This being their third time in this situation Lysandra had the routine down. Upon approaching the door check guy, she stumbled and fell into one of them. Esben transferred immediately. Being with humans for years had taught most Elbie how to transfer undetected and take swift control with shocking fluidity.

Lysandra showed her ID but the door check guy, now an Elbie host, barely registered the information. Even if the man's eyes looked it over, Esben would make sure any memory of it was lost in a kaleidoscope of IDs from the night. After reclaiming her ID, the doorman waved a metal detector wand around her. When it went off, he announced "BELT!" immediately and passed her through into the dark interior.

Inside the cavernous warehouse was an ocean of people bunched together in the semi-darkness. Only a few stage lights, random Christmas lights strung around, and glow attire on the patrons lit the place up. Lysandra shouldered her way between clumps of blissed-out ravers and packs of people shouting at each other to the edge of the bar and ordered the most innocuous drink available, some premade vodka mixer from an aluminum can. The heavily eye-lined bartender cracked the can and poured it over glowing ice cubes for her. Hardly a skill, but she tipped him all the same.

With a raver drink in hand, she kept it close with her hand over the top of it, and she turned her back to the bar to wait for Esben to make his way back to her. In his journey from the doorman to her, he would attempt to pass through as many people as possible to gather all the information he could. Together they would build off what they knew and decide from there the next step.

Lysandra had been in plenty of nightclubs, but she had never been into the rave scene. The electronic music lacked depth, and the fog machines and glow-in-the-dark accessorizing made no sense to her whatsoever. She took a sip of her drink and immediately regretted it. Staying sober would be easy tonight.

From out of the jumbled crowd, a tall woman glided between the crush of bodies heading directly toward Lysandra. Lysandra checked her watch. If this was Esben returning to her, he had done it in record time. While the woman's snug pleather crop top and neon fishnet leggings helped her to fit in, her stature made her stand out like a lighthouse in the fog. Her squared shoulders and confident stride were more akin to a corporate lawyer than a raver.

With just a passing glance at Lysandra, the woman leaned provocatively over the edge of the bar, called the bartender by name, and ordered a side car. Not a raver drink. Lysandra took a quick peek. The woman's jet-black hair sprouted atop her head from a gold band and cascaded down between her shoulder blades as a perfect shining swath from a Pantene commercial. Her thigh-high stiletto boots were studded with LED lights down each side, the colors changing in random fashion, adding to her already double-take height.

Then she turned with her drink in the same hand as Lysandra and leaned back against the bar, mimicking Lysandra's posture. Eyes casually perusing the crowds, the woman swirled the contents of the glass in gentle circles but did not drink from it. "There can be no cause without an effect." She stated to no one in particular.

That was a code phrase if ever Lysandra had heard one. Using a passcode helped to weed out posers and narcs. It was a way of legitimizing the chain of communication. Who could be trusted and who couldn't. Unfortunately for Lysandra, there had been no hint of a passcode from the contacts at the other clubs. Had Esben kept something from her? If she did not respond soon, the woman would move on.

She had to try something. "An effective cause is worth dying for." Lysandra cringed. It had been a shot in the dark. When she had been an active merc, the wrong response would have gotten her killed.

The woman turned her head and cocked it to one side. The sharp-edged, violet irises of her gaze peered at Lysandra. "Let's go." She abandoned the side car to the bar and started walking. Lysandra left her drink as well and fell into step behind the Amazon.

Lysandra jostled partygoers to keep up. She lost sight of the bar and began scanning the crowd around her. Deviating from the plan was a bad idea when she had no way of communicating with her partner. There were hundreds of people here, and if she was going to disappear into a back room behind a false wall, Esben's chances of finding her were also disappearing.

It had been months since she had been in such a precarious situation. Old instincts told her to be ready for the worst. The two of them passed what had once been an industrial kitchen, darkened with disuse, and into a dank service hallway. It was a short distance to the door at the end. Lysandra was led inside into an impromptu storage room, dimly lit and crammed full of cases of varied liquor and kegs of beer. A stubby man perched on a silver keg like a medieval gargoyle, watching them as they entered. The Amazon closed the door behind them.

The insistent thumping bass from a makeshift sound system shook the walls and rattled the bottles to the same rhythm of the garbled nonsense passing for music. The gargoyle leaned forward on his knees with his thick forearms. The raised muscles in his neck twisted and pulled as he cracked his neck. "What's your stake in the cause?" He spat at the floor.

The test. She had been unprepared for an interview. Hyperaware that the Amazon was directly behind her, Lysandra scrambled. "My sister." She swallowed hard and took a shaky breath for effect. "She had been—"

"Where's the rest of your team?" His eyes shifted behind her for a split second.

Rude. Wouldn't even let her finish lying before calling her bluff. Lysandra shifted her weight and crossed her arms. "I came alone."

The brute's frown deepened. Again his eyes looked past her for a second. Obviously Amazon was signaling something to him. "We watched you. You converse with many people. How many did Drake send with you? What do you really want?"

"Drake?" Lysandra shook her head. "I don't know what you're talking about."

Brute looked behind her again.

Amazon handed Lysandra a long-distance photo of herself with Nolin. "We know you work for Drake." The sight of the photo made Lysandra catch her breath. The photo was several months old and had been taken when she had first become a regular in Edward's group. It was a time in her life that had been fabricated. A jumble of memories of it crashed in on her. While she lived in ignorant bliss with Edward's group, he had her brother running around the globe collecting Elbie. The sudden feeling of loss for her brother left a dull ache in her chest.

"Explain," Brute grunted as he bounced on his haunches.

Lysandra blinked at the photo. She thought she might start to cry, the grief on the edge of her thoughts.

Knocking erupted on the door behind them. Insistent and urgent. Amazon opened the door. A large bouncer type man came into the room dragging a raver kid by the shirt.

"It wasn't me," the kid proclaimed immediately. His arms flailing, black emo hair covered half his face. "I swear."

The bouncer shoved the kid forward. "Robin, we found this kid making Molotov cocktails in one of the make-out rooms."

The kid got up from the floor, shoved his bangs away from his face. "I don't know what happened." He looked first to the Amazon and then at Lysandra. "Ah!" His eyes widened with panic as he pointed at Lysandra. "She's one of them!" He ran past everyone and threw himself at the door. "Let me out of here!" He struggled with the handle.

Relieved for the distraction, Lysandra shook her head. "Druggy loser, am I right?" She looked around the room for confirmation.

"Quiet." Amazon kicked Lysandra in the back of the knees.

Lysandra dropped unexpectedly. Just to one knee, but it was enough to make her cheeks burn. Amazon snapped her fingers and jerked her thumb over her shoulder.

Brute jumped off the keg and circled around Lysandra. Bouncer brought the kid back to the center of the room, the soles of his shoes sweeping the floor. His mascara and eyeliner ran down each side of his face as he cried. "I didn't want to do it. They made me do it." He shrank from Lysandra, pressing himself into the bouncer. "You gotta believe me."

Brute passed Amazon as they traded places. Brute shoved Lysandra. "What is he talking about?"

Lysandra made sure her movements were controlled as she stood up again. "Obviously, he's on something."

"Liar!" The kid screeched. "I'm straight edge. I was possessed. Something—"

"First time for everything, eh kid?" Lysandra shrugged.

"She's the leader." He looked at Amazon as she sat back on the edge of a keg. "They're everywhere."

Sitting with her back as straight as an iron rod, Amazon rested her hands in her lap and set her gaze squarely on Lysandra. "If Drake thinks that he can bribe his way out of our crosshairs, he is wasting his time and ours."

"Those photos are almost two years old." An exaggeration. "And out of context, I might add." Would telling them she was a hostage at that point would help or hinder the situation?

"Ow!" The bouncer dropped the kid and nursed his wrist.

The kid scurried for the door and succeeded this time. He bolted into the hallway. "They won't get me!" he shouted as he went.

The bouncer took up the chase.

Lysandra checked her watch. They were running out of time. She set her gaze on the woman. "I take it you're Robin Hood."

The woman drummed her fingers on her knee, looking at Lysandra like a disappointed schoolteacher.

Lysandra could feel her fuse running short. "You need to abandon your campaign against Edward Drake and his company."

"Absurd." Amazon flicked her head in a way that made her ponytail swish like a fish's tail.

Brute, shorter than Lysandra, cocked his fist and, with a small hop, punched down onto the top of her shoulder.

Lysandra held her ground with a suppressed groan. It took all her willpower not to punch the man back in retaliation.

Robin clenched her fists. "I intend to expose Alpha Cortex's corruption. They win every patent and successfully block all other companies bidding for similar patents."

Lysandra massaged her soon-to-be bruised arm. "It's called the free market."

The ponytail swished. The floor creaked as Brute moved in for another attack. Lysandra rolled her shoulder forward, causing the brute's blow to graze the back of her arm. He grunted in frustration, his left fist making contact with her rib cage.

Lysandra bent over with the impact. She took a deep breath, both to ease the pain and to calm her growing rage at the small man. Leaning against her knee as the pain subsided, she glared at Robin Hood. "Lady, if you've done your homework, you'd know they've never lost a human test subject." Lysandra had never been interested in what Alpha Cortex did, but she did know they had never been in the news for accidental deaths.

"Exactly the problem. They have a one hundred percent success rate in all their drug trials. No scientific endeavor is without failures. It's impossible." She hammered her clenched fist on her thighs.

Lysandra didn't know anything about patents, but she did know that just as the DPA used Elbie to help advance neuroscience research, so did Edward. But unlike the DPA, Alpha Cortex's work with Elbie was not public knowledge. "How did Mozart know how to play the piano at four? It's an unexplainable gift."

The woman eyed her suspiciously. "What aren't you telling us?"

Lysandra stood up, staring back at the woman. "You've got nothing on Drake or his organization, so I'm telling you to back off."

"Or what?" Robin raised her eyebrows.

Out of the corner of Lysandra's eye, Brute moved forward for another blow. Planting her feet, she grabbed a handful of his shirt as he came at her, dodged his fist, and threw him with telekinetic force into a pyramid of beer kegs. Robin Hood skirted out of the way of the falling kegs with an indignant yelp of surprise.

The pulsing thump of electronic music stopped. The rattling of the bottles silenced. An air horn blasted several times, and a muffled voice replaced the music. The door flew open, and the security guard that had gone after the kid stood breathless in the doorway. "Fire." He pointed behind him. "Have to go." He swallowed hard. "Now."

That would be Esben. The whole night had been shot to hell. Criticize later, escape now. She pivoted and rushed at the security guard. He blocked the doorway, feet spread apart, ready for her. She barreled into him with a telekinetic push, tossing him to the ground.

With a leap over him, she sprinted down the hallway and into the main room. She had missed the initial stampede for the doors. People were still fighting to get out the exits, but the center of the room was cleared out. The acrid smell of smoke gathered above the dance floor. The air horn cut mid-blast as the DJ folded up his computers and ran with one under each arm.

Flames climbed up several of the support beams across the room.

"Help!" A distant call.

Lysandra's eyes started to burn and water. She ran to the "bar" to see if there was anything that could retard the fumes. A clawfoot tub of melting ice took up a good portion of space behind the improvised counter. No towels or cloth of any kind. She took off her jacket and plunged it into the icy depths.

"Help us!" The call came again.

Peering through the thickening haze, a lone figure stood on the makeshift stage, lobbing flaming bottles into the air. In the garish orange light, Lysandra could now see that it was the door check guy. He glanced at her as she ran up, lighting another bottle with a lighter.

"Esben!"

The man paused in mid-throw. Fragments of fire plummeted to the ground from the cloth stuck in the top of the bottle. His arm dropped as he looked around. "Lysandra?" He tossed the bottle aside.

"Let us go!" Someone screamed from close by.

Her heart stopped at the sight of five heads sticking up from the side of the stage. What were those idiots waiting for? Holding the wet jacket over her mouth and nose, she jumped up on the stage and ran to the other side. Five young adults in club attire were tied to the supports underneath. One of them she recognized from an earlier club—the one who had told her to come here.

She looked up at Esben. "Did you do this?"

Wood creaked and groaned from somewhere above the smoke.

Esben jumped down and took her arm. "We've got to go."

She yanked her arm from him. "We can't leave these people here. Help me with them."

"They're with the activists," he protested.

Lysandra got on her stomach, crawled under the edge of the stage, and started to pull on the cloth restraining their hands. These kids were innocent recruits.

One set of hands. The person leaped up and disappeared.

They did not pull the trigger that had almost ended Edward's life. If anyone was responsible, it was Robin Hood. She would have been the person who contracted the hitman. Paid the fee. Not these gullible kids.

Second pair of hands set free.

The growing flames sounded like a rushing wind now.

The stage shook suddenly. Stomping and shuffling moved back and forth above her.

Third person set free.

Hands grabbed her ankles and pulled her across the floor. Lysandra caught the support leg and she jerked to a stop. With a twist, she rolled onto her back to see Robin Hood gripping her legs, eyes squeezed shut and teeth gritted as she tried to dislodge Lysandra. "Are you crazy? Get out of here." She pulled her legs in, dragging the woman to the floor.

Robin crashed down next to her. Lysandra threw her weight on top of the woman's back and started to untie the fourth person. She looked into the eyes of a terrified raver girl with pink straw hair. "You need to help your friend out." Lysandra's eyes went to the last victim secured to the stage. The girl nodded her agreement as Robin kicked and screamed under her. "Then you run," she told the girl as Lysandra pulled Robin up by the waist.

Her lungs began to burn as she stood up. The ceiling of smoke sunk lower, the blistering heat suffocating her as sweat soaked through all her clothes.

Robin got her feet on the ground and clawed Lysandra's hands off her and groped for her neck. "Murderers!"

Robin leaned into Lysandra, pinning her legs against the edge of the stage. Lysandra fell onto her back. Sounds of grunting and punching were out of her line of sight. Craning her head back, she could see Esben wrestling with Brute, the two of them rolling and punching each other across the shuddering stage.

"Esben!" Lysandra held Robin's hands away from her face. "This is the one you want." Lysandra sucker-punched her attacker in the ribs. Robin gasped and lost all strength as she collapsed into Lysandra. Lysandra shoved her off and got to her feet. Between racking coughs and blurred vision, Lysandra staggered toward the two men.

The two men had rolled so that Brute was on top. Lysandra grabbed the back of his shirt and pulled up. In the heat and smoke, she could barely concentrate on anything other than breathing. With some telekinetic help, she heaved Brute a couple of yards away. Coughing, she pulled Door Check Guy to his feet. "Go get her." She pointed at Robin Hood on the edge of the stage, struggling to get up.

Door Check Guy wheeled away from her with wild eyes. He glanced behind her at Brute before leaping off the stage and disappearing into the smoke. Lysandra turned around. Brute shook himself as he stood up, a tearful scowl set on Lysandra. Brute put his hands on Robin and she dropped to the floor unconscious. Esben had switched to Brute.

Pieces of the ceiling crashed to the floor off to one side. A howl sounded above the din of the fire behind her. A wrenching crack reverberated above the smoke. "Help me." Lysandra pointed back at Robin.

Without waiting for a response, Lysandra knelt beside Robin, ready to put her over her shoulders, when Esben-Brute came up on the other side and took Robin's arm around his non-existent neck. Together, the two of them trudged through the chemical-laced smoke and flaming debris.

They crashed through a side door and into the alleyway between warehouses. Black smoke poured out behind them. Lysandra stumbled and dropped to one knee, rolling Robin off her shoulder and onto the dirty pavement. With a cry of alarm, Brute dropped Robin and took off running.

Lysandra fell back a few steps, gasping the semi-fresh air. "What the hell, Esben?" She caught one last glimpse of Brute before he disappeared into the night. Leaning down, Lysandra put her hand on Robin's neck. "Esben, you in there?" Robin didn't move. Lysandra's hand warmed, and heat started to move quickly up her arm. Lysandra lost all sense of her body.

Robin Hood sputtered and coughed as she pushed herself off the dirty pavement and looked around in confusion, no doubt wondering how she had gotten outside.

Esben-Lysandra reached down and pulled Robin off the ground by both shoulders and held her within a few inches of her face. "Believe me when I say we know absolutely everything there is to know about you, Elizabeth Carter." Esben-Lysandra's voice was a low growl. "You will abandon your agenda against Edward Drake and Alpha Cortex Solutions, or you will regret it. Do we have an understanding, Ellie?"

Black rivulets of makeup streaked Robin's face. "What are you?"

Esben-Lysandra let her go, dropping the woman to the ground, and then stood up to leave.

The woman scowled at her as she backed away from Lysandra. "This is not over."

The sirens of emergency vehicles were too close now. Esben did not want Lysandra seen by any authorities. They had no doubt Robin Hood meant what she said, but it would have to wait. Esben-Lysandra pulled the collar of her shirt up over her nose and ran back through the exit into the billowing black smoke.

"Wait!" She heard Robin Hood call after her.

Esben-Lysandra's eyes burned immediately. The most important thing right now was to flee the area before being seen by anyone else. Pushing further into the collapsing structure, she made sure to be out of sight of the door. She fumbled with the buttons on the side of the watch. The bright white light of the portal opening cut through the smoke and heat. She threw herself through the tear and tumbled onto the plush carpet of her room. Feeling for her watch so closed the portal.

With a crash, she was suddenly looking down on a faded floral carpet. The two of them were back in the little theater. She picked herself up from the floor and rubbed her hands where she had landed on them.

"What the hell was that about?" Esben stood over her as Edward, his face darkened with rage.

"Me! You're the one who went nuts in there. You could have killed hundreds of people. We had one target."

"And you let her go."

Lysandra opened her mouth to argue, but he was right. Robin Hood was a fanatic. She believed Edward Drake and his corporation were a threat to humanity. Their troubles with Robin and her group were not over. "You had your chance. You could have rendered her brain dead, but you didn't. Why?"

Esben's whole body relaxed and the anger in his eyes disappeared as he looked away from her.

"Answer the question, Esben."

"I realized that killing her would only make her a martyr. It would encourage the others to press even harder. A direct attack is the wrong strategy."

He was probably right. Robin was the kind of leader who was synonymous with the organization. Killing her would have only added fuel to the fire.

"Lysandra!" Edward's voice crackled from the speaker on the wall.

They both looked at the speaker and then at each other. The mental image of Edward dispersed into light.

She felt herself yanked up suddenly. She braced for the imaginary impact against the imaginary ceiling.

A burning in her chest crawled up her esophagus as she coughed. The thick carpet under her, the bed against her back as remnants of smoke churned in the air above her. The first light of dawn seeped through the break in the curtains above the bed. They had made it back to her room in Edward's house.

Edward stood in the frame of the bathroom door, the light behind his head obscuring his face. "Lysandra?"

"Hey." She waved at him, getting a forced smile out before a fit of coughing.

"Are you alright?" He knelt next to her and took her arm. He pulled his hand back. "Esben."

Lysandra-Esben nodded, trying to suppress an upcoming cough but failed. He quickly brought her a glass of water from the bathroom, a grim look on his face. He held the glass out to her. Lysandra-Esben gratefully gulped down the liquid. As she did so, she put her hand on Edward's neck.

A wave of relief washed over her as Esben flowed from her hand into Edward.

Lysandra left the empty glass on the floor and threw her arms around Edward's neck. A sudden sense of longing filled her. "I missed you so much."

11

DRAKE ESTATE

0800 hours PST

After a long shower to wash out the stench of chemical fire and soot from her hair, Lysandra threw her clothes in the trash. She never wanted to see those again. The window in her room had been opened all the while, and it still reeked of the torched nightclub as she dressed in fresh clothes.

Under normal circumstances, she would have just gone to bed. It had been a long night, and she had not slept at all, but being that it was a weekday, Edward was getting ready for work, so this was her chance to spend a little more time with him. She could nap once she returned to the DPA.

Lysandra made her way into the already occupied dining room. Nolin was eating his breakfast with zeal as L'heilh turned the pages of a fashion magazine. Nolin nodded at Lysandra between bites, while L'heilh simply raised her eyebrows as Lysandra sat down. It was now the second night in a row she had stayed at the house. Lysandra's presence was also the second time in their short history together that she was a part of their social group. Nolin and L'heilh accepted her readily.

As she savored her coffee, she watched Nolin directly across from her. The thing about being a host was that you got residual memories from the previous host. Even while Esben had been separated from Edward, the lifeform had still thought like him, and any memories he had come with were now imprinted on her own synapses. The transferred memories tended to be fuzzy or incoherent in a dream kind of way, but Edward's thoughts on the scrawny kid from London were humorous. When Edward and Nolin had met, Nolin had already been a host. Elbie changed the course of Nolin's life, and L'heilh's, to be sure. Edward Drake would be in the same position as he was right now, Elbie or no Elbie.

Nolin finally looked up from his plate. "What?"

Lysandra sat up. "Sorry. I was spaced out. Didn't mean to stare." She set the cup down and served some food to her plate.

Edward stopped in the doorway of the dining room, dressed in a pressed dark suit with a brilliant turquoise shirt. He stopped suddenly and looked at Lysandra. He knew, of course, what she had done only a few hours previously. She and Esben, that is. The memory of it would have been carried with Esben back to Edward. It had occurred to her that Esben could possibly hide the events in some way, but maybe he didn't want to keep secrets from Edward.

Still, the look on Edward's face was hard to interpret. Not anger or disappointment—those two she was familiar with all too well, from other people. It had to be sadness.

He closed his eyes momentarily and breathed deeply. She couldn't tell if it was Edward or Esben in control, if control was even a question between them. The fleeting emotions playing in Edward's face made Lysandra think Edward was the dominant personality this morning. Edward tugged on the cuffs of his jacket and walked into the room. He sat stiffly in his seat at the head of the table and unfolded his napkin.

Lysandra's spot was to his right, Nolin to his left, and L'heilh next to him, with their backs to the French doors and wide balcony. A servant hustled into the room, poured coffee for Edward-Esben, and set the morning paper on the table by his arm. Both Edward-Esben and Lysandra looked at the paper. The headline emblazoned in bold black letters announced the financial collapse of some European institutions.

Lysandra sat frozen in her seat. Distance between them had always been her choice. Now that she was on the receiving end of it, she did not like it.

"Edward." She put her hand on his wrist. "I'm sorry about what happened."

Nolin stopped eating. "Okay. We"—he indicated L'heilh and himself with a frantic hand motion—"don't need to hear about what you two did last night. All right?"

"It was stupid. We were in over our heads."

Edward nodded. "Agreed," he said quietly.

"What are you two on about?" Nolin sat up, his English accent thickening with each syllable.

L'heilh put her hand on his arm. "Nolin, sweetie, can't you see he's upset?"

Lysandra rubbed his wrist, hoping for a response of some kind. Anything. She needed something back from him.

Edward sat back and looked at her. She was uncomfortable with his scrutiny. His opinion of her meant too much. The thought of disappointing him stung her, but she wasn't sure that was what he was feeling.

She pulled her hand away. "No one was hurt."

"You think that's what I am upset about?"

"I don't know. Just say it already."

He glanced at Nolin and L'heilh, who were watching the two of them intently.

Nolin reached across the table and took more bacon for his plate. "What's 'appened?"

Edward took a sip of his coffee. "Lysandra and Esben played vigilante last night, tracked down the people who tried to kill me."

"Esben?" L'heilh glanced at Nolin. "You mean he..." She put her hand over her mouth, as if some unspeakable horror had crossed her mind.

"I..." Edward shook his head and focused on his empty plate

Nolin whistled. "That. Now that is ballsy, Lysandra."

"It wasn't my idea. I mean, those people needed to be brought down a notch, but the partnering up thing, that wasn't me."

"Partner?" L'heilh clicked her tongue.

Nolin pointed his fork at her. "I'm confused. I thought you were the one who said you never wanted to see another Elbie again as long as you lived. And yet, here you are living in a house with 'em, and now you're borrowing them. You lot—"

"You're mad at me? We… I was trying to help you guys out by taking those guys down. I did it for you guys."

"Let me guess." L'heilh stood up from the table. "Esben made you do it." She closed her magazine shut with a sharp snap and walked out. Nolin scooped the last of the eggs onto his plate and followed her out of the room.

Lysandra twisted in her seat to follow their retreat. "Two nights in a row is not me living here. Technically."

Edward stared at his plate, knife, and fork frozen in mid-action, gripping them so hard his knuckles were white. Something was going on inside his head. Not knowing what else to do, she ate her breakfast. She had gotten over her aversion of Elbie to help the greater good, and people were mad at her for it. Was there no winning? Maybe nice guys really do finish last.

"I can't tell if Nolin and L'heilh are loyal to you, the person, or you, the Elbie."

"I'm not angry," Edward said finally, setting the silverware down and turning to her. "It was just unexpected. Esben has never done that before, and I'm surprised that you went along with it."

"I don't know why it's surprising. It's something I'd wanted for you. Ask Nolin. Ask Matt. I've been working on exposing that organization ever since the protests started. And I thought that since Esben was so keen that it was what you wanted."

Edward nodded slowly. "Maybe I did on a subconscious level. They attempted to kill me, after all. But it was not an active desire. Justice, certainly, but not revenge. What happens if the fire gets linked back to you? How will Eriksson and Draegg have to respond if there is any kind of public outcry?"

"I took out bad people. Who's going to get upset about that? Honestly, I don't understand why this is so wrong?"

"Besides that, you could've been killed. You shouldn't be so careless with your life."

"Careless?"

"Yes. Careless. You can't just throw your life away. Especially on something so trivial."

"They shot you. I don't call that trivial."

"Lysandra, you're so afraid of having anything for yourself that the tiniest piece of happiness will be ripped away from you at any moment. And then you just waltz into a den of vipers for some hand-to-hand combat."

To have her greatest fear laid out so succinctly made her feel naked. She sat straight as a board in her seat, staring at him. Embarrassment and regret churned in her stomach. Edward understood too much. Esben had found the root of her fear and brought it back with him. Deliberately or accidentally, she had no idea.

Lysandra would never let herself be happy, because she believed at the core of her being that once she did, it would be taken away from her. This was the biggest problem of sharing Elbie: there truly would be no hiding anything from the other person. Memory and psyche of anyone who shared an Elbie would blur indefinitely.

"More than anything, I feel betrayed." Pain crossed his face. "If I can't trust Esben, and I can't trust you, what does that leave me with?"

That hurt. She understood that feeling. Being able to truly trust someone was a rare commodity. In her line of work, she had never let herself trust anyone. Trust was a new thing for her; keeping it was her most important priority.

"You're right." Lysandra got up from her chair and took his hand. "I didn't think about it like that. I had mistaken Esben's intentions for your own."

Edward nodded and pressed his lips together. "I understand." He massaged his temple.

She touched his cheek and waited for his eyes to meet hers. His eyes sparkled with their usual vivid green, but now the downward curve of his eyebrows gave them a touch of sadness. "I'm so sorry."

Edward nodded. "I believe you." He wound his arms around her waist and pulled her into his lap.

Her arms encircled his neck and held him tightly as she buried her face in the crook of his neck. How much could he recall of the events of the previous night? It was hard to say. Transferring memories from one brain to another was not an exact science. Acutely aware of the heat of his skin against hers, the weight of his arms around her, she never wanted to feel that distance between them again. After a few minutes, she looked him in the eyes again. "Forgive me?"

Edward smiled, his arms still tight around her. "Yes, of course. I forgive you."

"Thank you." She pulled him close again. Xander may have been a threat to their relationship before. But this had been so much worse than she could have imagined. She did not want to feel this way again.

He smiled at her, but it was not a genuine smile. "Will you need a ride to work?"

"If I could be dropped off a few blocks from HQ, that would be great."

"Do I embarrass you?"

"Not at all." She brushed the hair at his temples with her fingernails. "I'd rather not publicize our relationship to my co-workers."

"I see. Do you mean Eriksson or Matt?"

"Both."

"Of course." He patted her leg. "We should get going."

Lysandra got up. A sense of unease grew in her stomach. Edward was troubled. He said he forgave her, but she did not feel the relief that should have come with forgiveness. Riding in the car with the three of them would be the most uncomfortable forty minutes of her life.

12

DRAKE ESTATE

0800 hours PST

t's not her fault.

The words echoed in Edward's mind. He sat up. The other side of the bed was empty. He shivered, a chill clinging to his skin. He pounded the mattress with his fist. Esben had taken Lysandra again. But to what end? The answer had to be in his head, but Esben had hidden it well.

It was even hard to recall the past twenty-four hours. After what had happened at the nightclub with Esben and Lysandra, it had been a difficult day for Edward. He and Esben did not argue, but a divide had widened between them, where previously there had been no separation.

Lysandra had come over for dinner at his request. Tension between them made their interactions stilted and awkward. Nolin, who did not like confrontation, insisted that they all watch a movie. Lysandra had fallen asleep in Edward's arms shortly after the movie had started.

"It's not her fault," ran through his head again. Esben wanted it made clear that Lysandra was not to blame for his absence. Edward reached over to the phone on the nightstand. He dialed zero to call the security suite.

"Yes, Mr. Drake?"

"When did Miss Carlisle leave this morning?"

"She has not left, Mr. Drake."

"You mean she did not exit out any of the doors."

"Correct, sir."

"Thank you. Send Nolin to my room immediately."

"Yes sir."

Edward hung up the phone as he opened the drawer to his nightstand. The drawer was used for one purpose alone. His heart sank to see the empty interior. She… They had taken all of the portal cards. Seven of the portal cards, one for each of the Alpha Cortex offices and Edward's second house in the Caribbean.

He closed the drawer and sat on the edge of the bed, trying to figure out where Esben and Lysandra would be going.

It's not her fault. The phrase continued to whisper in his head on a continuous loop, in his own voice. Esben had intended for the thought to pardon Lysandra from any wrongdoing in whatever was happening, but it was also a distraction or cover-up for what Esben was hiding from Edward.

Esben did have an objective in mind. However, to control a host who did not want you required an immense amount of work. So while Esben was using Lysandra for his own ends, he must be accomplishing something she wanted as well. Edward massaged his temples; a headache was coming on. A protective measure Esben probably put in place to keep him from digging too deeply.

His thoughts turned to Lysandra. After what happened with the activist leader, it was easy to accept that she had an equal part in all of this. It certainly would make Esben's life easier to have her as an ally and not simply a vehicle to his next destination. Edward couldn't help thinking that history was repeating itself. Brendan had been in the same position as she was now, with the same Elbie. The correlation was too strong. Maybe that was the key.

A knock sounded on the door. "You decent?" Nolin called from behind the door.

"Come in." Edward stood up from the bed.

Nolin walked in with one hand over his eyes and the other out in front of him, groping the air. "Everyone properly clothed, yeah?"

"Nolin!" Edward said sharply. Too much. Edward clenched his fist in frustration. Nolin froze and dropped his hands. "I'm alone."

Nolin looked at him. Really looked at him. And his shoulders dropped. "Where are they?"

Edward went into the closet and put on his robe. "I don't know. Security has no record of her leaving."

"She must have gone on foot over the fence." Nolin took out his phone, switching into security mode.

"All my portal cards are gone. We need to account for all of them and then find out if anyone at the portal locations has seen her."

"Got it. I'll get back to you in a few minutes. Where are you going to be?"

"In my office. I have a few phone calls to make."

Edward called downstairs to make sure his car was ready. He requested any video footage they could find of Lysandra. He was pulling on a jacket when Nolin came into the room.

"She got 'em all. All of them!" He paced around in an agitated state. "That woman of yours snuck into my room and took the portal cards right out from under my nose." He stopped as suddenly as he had started. "She's good."

"Yes, be that as it may, why don't you call the Seattle, Raleigh, and San Francisco offices and put them on alert. Of those options, only a few are useful to her."

"Do you know what she's up to?"

"Esben," he emphasized, not wanting Nolin or L'heilh to blame Lysandra for anything, "has an objective, but he's hidden that from me. Every time I try to figure it out, I get a headache."

"Qur'ag can suss it out. I'll make sure he's ready for you."

"Thank you, Nolin." Edward went into his closet to get dressed as Nolin rushed out. Edward had confronted Lysandra about breaking his trust, but it never occurred to him to do the same to Esben. Hopefully, Lysandra would not pay the price for that oversight.

13

DOWNTOWN LOS ANGELES

0800 hours PST

Lysandra's cheek itched from the rough surface under her. A slight swaying motion made her feel queasy.

"Goddamn it!" She pounded the floor with her fist and pushed herself off the ground. The viewing pane of the small theater displayed the interior of a grubby taxicab as it weaved in and out of traffic.

She walked up to the pane. "Esben!" She punched the center of the screen. Pain stabbed behind her eyes. Electricity crackled and snaked around the screen. She crashed to the ground as the whole place shifted. She waited for the pain to subside. "What did I say last time?"

No response.

She stood and walked over to one of the curtained walls. "I told you." She kicked the wall. Pain exploded in her left temple. "If I am locked up"—she rammed it with her shoulder, piercing pain radiated through her rib cage—"in this goddamn theater"—another kick, pain sliced through the top of her foot—"with no control"— she moved along the wall and punched as she went, pulses of pain moving through the jaw—"we would both regret it." She faced the wall and started speed punching it with both hands. The waves of pain dropped her to the floor on the verge of puking.

Edward appeared next to her. "I had to do it. I'm sorry." He reached down to help her.

Esben appearing as Edward was an insult. Lysandra slapped his hand away. "No, you're not." She leapt at him. They crashed to the ground. Straddling the top of him, she punched down at his face. The image of Edward dissolved and her hand hit the floor, sending a shock of pain into her hip.

"Are you okay, lady?" a strange voice said through the speakers on the wall. On the screen, the taxi driver was looking back at her, one arm over the top of the seat.

"I'm fine. Just a really bad migraine," she heard herself say.

The driver didn't seem fully convinced, but he turned back to the road and started driving again.

"I truly am sorry." Edward's voice reverberated around the room. "I'm desperate. I am begging you for help."

Lysandra stared down at the worn carpeting, waiting to catch her breath. Esben was telling the truth. He felt bad taking her hostage, and he really did feel like he needed her. She was not ready to forgive him, but she would hear him out. "Why?" She grabbed the back of the theater seat and pulled herself up. "What's so fucking important that you would break Edward's trust? You know how he feels about the last time."

Edward reappeared. All of this was, in the most literal sense, in her head. Esben could take any form he wanted and he picked the one person she could not bear to see right now. "Wrong."

Edward's form morphed into Matt.

She responded with an exasperated sigh. "Pick someone I don't know."

The image of Matt thought about this for a moment in exactly the way Matt would, with one finger tapping his chin as he looked up, searching his thoughts.

Matt shifted into another male, this one much older. His bald head took on the yellow hue of the light above. A faded, unbuttoned Hawaiian shirt parted down the middle revealed a plain gray shirt underneath. His sharp, intelligent gaze met her eyes. Lysandra recognized him but couldn't place from where. That could be worked out later. She clenched her fists and focused on the issue at hand. "That will do, Esben. Explain."

He put his hands in the pockets of his khaki trousers. "It has been for some time that we've felt restricted, trapped. Being tethered to the human mind limits us."

"How can you feel trapped? You've never known anything else."

"True, not by experience, but knowledge is a curse. Possibility can lead to dissatisfaction if it goes unfulfilled."

Being a host meant a loss of privacy. She could feel what he was going to say before he did. She suddenly had that dread in the pit of her stomach that came anytime Matt dragged her in his weekly call. "The conversations with Derek."

"It is not the first time that computers or the internet have occurred to us as an option worth exploring, but no one in our immediate circle works with those things. At first, we thought a new host would be enough, but Derek's conversations about quantum computers and ubiquitous computing have real promise."

"Why not explain all this to Edward? He'd understand."

"He is ambivalent about the possibility of not being a host. He could come around to the idea eventually, but we cannot wait any longer. The more time that passes, the more suffocated we feel. The rift with Edward will grow, and we don't want to watch that happen. Besides, Edward cannot be associated with anything that happens."

"But I can? Glad to know you think I'm expendable."

"Don't be so dramatic. You have the connections we need."

Now his line of thinking was obvious. Like the idea of it all had been sitting just outside her line of sight and had now been moved into the crosshairs. Esben intended to contact the hackers she had worked with before her life at the DPA. He was leading her back to her previous employer.

"You know our intentions are to protect you."

Lysandra could feel his sincerity in her bones, but it had only been twenty-four hours since she had told Edward he could trust her. "I'm sorry, but we have to go back."

"Please try to see it our way. There is only one place where we can be fully ourselves without losing what we have gained from our time with people. The internet is a limitless space for our kind. We could go anywhere it goes. Be anywhere in a matter of seconds."

"That's insane. Why would I agree to something so completely bonkers?"

"Because you, more than many people, understand what it means to be free of your past. Draegg erased your crimes, paving the way for new opportunities for you. All we want is the same opportunity. We don't know if it will work. The long-term implications are completely unknown, of course, but we have to try."

"Can't you all live in a plasma globe, one big happy ball of energy?"

"That was Varoth's vision. We have been changed by our contact with people. He had the right idea but the wrong execution."

Lysandra winced, and Esben knew immediately why. Brendan had lost his life because of Varoth's ill-fated plan to reunite all the Elbie from their cluster. "You want to bring other Elbie with you?"

Esben nodded. "That's why we need all the portal anchors we can find."

"Edward trusts us." She shook her head and walked away from him. "I can't betray that again. If his trust hasn't already been broken beyond repair."

He nodded. "For me it has, but not you. We left him a message. Told him you have nothing to do with our choices."

Lysandra quietly exhaled, feeling like a tremendous weight had been lifted from her shoulders. A sense of relief from Esben rippled through her thoughts.

"We will protect you. We promise. Help us with this, and you can go back to your life with Edward and the DPA. Once you help us make contact with your crew, your part is done. We are asking you to put yourself in our position. What would you want?" He held his hand out to her in a plea. "We could even wipe out the memory if you want."

Tampering with her memory was a notion she did not like, and there had only been one Elbie that ever messed with her in that way. "Hold on. You keep saying *we*."

A sudden wave of disgust washed over her, as did unbearable shame. She glanced around the theater for someplace to hide, as if every horrible thing she had done or thought was being telegraphed publicly. With all her willpower, she remained standing tall. "Hate you too, Qur'ag." She looked about the room, not sure where in her body he had parked himself. She half hoped he would project himself into the theater so she could throttle him. She looked at Esben. "You know how I feel about him. I can't believe you didn't talk to me first about this."

He shrugged. "He was not looking forward to it either, but there was no time. We had to move quickly."

Lysandra watched the screen as her hands opened the duffel bag and reached inside, pulling out a glass cylinder. A containment unit. "When we get the chance, Qur'ag will gladly transfer to this," Esben assured her.

A sigh escaped her as the memory of going to the DPA earlier this morning flooded back to her. Lysandra herself had not been consciously aware at the time, but it was something her body had done, and her brain had recorded it; hence there was a memory for her to access. This would make her second betrayal to the DPA. To Matt. To Draegg. To Eriksson.

"My betrayal, not yours," he said. "I was in complete control at the time, and you are free from the guilt of that."

"Yeah, well, I doubt Eriksson will see it that way."

"Eriksson, more than most people, understands what it means to be in your position. Edward will vouch for you."

"You assume."

"I know."

Lysandra looked down at the containment unit again. That did help, knowing Qur'ag would be removed quickly. Then there was the old gang. Some days, in the mundane routine of security shifts and report writing, she would daydream about her time as a freelance merc, but now, with the prospect of seeing those people again, the nostalgia quickly became apprehension. It was not a world many could escape alive, and now she was waltzing into the heart of it.

"There are plenty of other hackers in the world. We don't need to go back to my old crew."

"We don't have the time to vet possible candidates. Edward and Nolin are probably already searching for us. We need to collect the other portal anchors before they can alert any security. The more we can get done in the next hour, the better. Your crew has the skills. We know where to find them, and they will talk to you. No need to establish trust."

"You don't know Gregory."

"Exactly. You know them. With your experience, we can anticipate any potential betrayals." Esben put his hand on her shoulder. "We've got the advantage. They won't take us by surprise."

"Yeah, well, best laid plans of mice and men."

"True, but we can discuss that more when time is on our side."

Lysandra massaged her temples. A headache was coming on. Manipulation or pure physiology of having Esben and Qur'ag taking up space in her brain? Helping Esben was a big risk on every level, professionally and personally.

"I know." Esben's hand dropped from her shoulder. "We don't have anyone else to go to. We need your help. Like how you helped those people at the mall."

"I helped those people because I know what it's like to be treated like trash."

"They were trapped in a no-win situation, like you when you were younger. For us it's no different. To be forever chained to the mind of another is a life sentence."

"So find a new host."

"I could, but eventually, I would need to find another and another after that. There are Elbie who jump from person to person in that way. Do those people deserve to be hijacked because of my restlessness?"

"You've gone from the exploited to the exploiter."

"Taking the need for a human host out of the equation is a benefit for people and Elbie."

Lysandra crossed her arms. "Let's say it works and you can transition to living electronically on the net. That's just a bigger box. You're still dependent on the system."

"We would be no more trapped than a whale that roves from ocean to ocean. The internet is an open system. With the right code, we can make sure there are always open doors."

She could feel his desperation as he waited for her answer. Maybe Elbie didn't start with emotions of their own, but they sure understood how they worked. "Alright. But remember our agreement."

"Shared control." Esben clasped his hands together with a big smile. "Absolutely."

"One thing." Lysandra grabbed the collar of his Hawaiian shirt.

He paused and put his hands up. "Do what you must."

"Thank you." She twisted up the fabric for a stronger hold and balled her right hand. Her fist collided with his jaw. A satisfying crack echoed in the room.

His head whipped to the side with the impact. Cracking his neck, he straightened himself. "Feel better?"

There was no pain for her, and obviously none for him, since his body was imaginary, but that didn't matter. "Tremendously."

"I'm glad to hear it."

"That'll be twenty-three fifty," the cab driver announced.

Esben disappeared. Lysandra took a seat in the one chair in the private theater. They were about to be on the move, and that always made her feel a little sick.

Esben-Lysandra gave the driver forty bucks. "Keep the change." She grabbed the duffel bag of classified government equipment. The

DPA logo had been ripped off the bag to avoid any unwanted attention. The presence of the DPA had an effect on people, and that was the last thing they wanted.

They stepped onto the sidewalk and started walking. Lysandra tried to see street signs or landmarks within the view provided by the screen. She didn't recognize this part of L.A. They stopped at a crosswalk. Lysandra looked up, and her eyes focused on the building straight across, Bank of the West.

Of course. "Please tell me that Edward uses the same bank as I do." But she knew immediately from Esben that was not the case. Even if she wanted to use the card Edward had given her, she wouldn't use it and give away their location. They had to leave as little of a paper trail as possible.

"Did you have plans for the money?" Esben asked.

She did not. For the first time in her adult life, she had a bank account, and she had accumulated a significant chunk of change. Living at the DPA meant she had practically no expenses and a steady paycheck. She hadn't been trying to save money; she simply did not have anything to spend it on. "It's not enough. You need at least eighty K."

"It's a start," he said as they crossed the street.

"Why should I foot the bill for your freedom?" She closed her eyes, trying to calm her stomach.

"We don't have any resources of our own. Besides, you'll get your money back."

"How? One cent at a time from every credit card transaction in the world?"

"You realize that would take us less than a day."

Her skin pimpled. She opened her eyes to see they were now inside the bank. "My point is, I'm the last person who should be paying."

"We understand. We will pay it back. With interest."

Lysandra slouched down in the cushioned seat. She really didn't care about the money. It was his assumption that pissed her off. "You better."

They went to the nearest teller window.

"Good morning. How can I help you today?" The teller smiled at them.

"I need to make a large withdrawal from my account."

"Of course. How much would you like?"

Esben-Lysandra leaned close to the glass. "Sixty thousand. In cash. Large bills will be fine."

The teller gave her a double take. "No problem. For transactions of that size, I need to have my manager assist you."

"Understandable. Thank you."

Lysandra watched as the teller talked to the manager. If Edward hadn't told the DPA yet, this would do it for sure. Going AWOL on the DPA and betraying Edward's trust all so Esben could self-actualize may not have been the best decision, but it wasn't the worst. She hoped.

14

DOWNTOWN LOS ANGELES

0845 hours PST

espite the two-inch glass and cavernous space, Esben-Lysandra could hear the whispers of the bank personnel as they passed through the lobby toward the exit. The employees were being incredibly discreet; it was simply a matter of the enhanced hearing of being a host. None of the other patrons of the bank seemed to have any idea of an unusual transaction that had just happened. The head bank manager walked beside her. For someone in charge of so much money, she expected more composure.

"I really rather you wait inside for a taxi or one of your friends to retrieve you." His eyes glanced at the backpack she held over one shoulder.

"I appreciate your concern, Mr. Simmons. I assure you, I'll be fine. Thank you so much." She smiled warmly and took his hand. Esben had been ready for the contact. Lysandra held the bank manager's hand long enough for Esben to send a few signals to the man's brain. Mr. Simmon's visibly relaxed, though his eyebrows still betrayed his angst.

The security guard opened the door for her, and she stepped out onto the sidewalk in downtown Los Angeles with several thousands of dollars of cash in the bag tucked under her arm. In her other hand was a duffel bag of classified government equipment.

Now to find a quiet place to portal in private. Moving into the brisk flow of foot traffic on the sidewalk, it was as expected for a weekday morning. A quick scan of the area yielded a bustling coffee shop. It was too close to the bank, but too much time had passed already. Most likely, Drake and Nolin had already realized what had happened and would be looking for them.

The interior of the coffee chain was filled with morning drinkers. She bypassed the line and headed straight for the bathroom. A combination code box controlled who could use it. She banged on the door. No response. She put both hands over the keypad and pushed an electrical charge into it. The fried device failed and unlatched. She ducked inside and locked the door.

She went straight to the mirror, looking into their reflection for mutual assurance. This was phase one: get all the portal cards. They laid out the anchors left to retrieve: San Francisco, Seattle, the Caribbean house, Raleigh, and NYC. San Francisco would be first.

It was the next closest location to the DPA, so it was possible they could have officers or at least affiliates onsite. San Francisco and Seattle would need to be more deliberate because, unlike the other locations, they would need to return to the two West Coast cities.

Because Drake was a creature of habit, it would be easy to find the portal anchors in each location. He kept them all in basically the same place. At the Caribbean house, the other half of the anchor would be in the nightstand next to Edward's bed. All the others were in the CEO's office, top right drawer of the desk.

One last check; anchor cards, gun, cash, capture equipment. Upon pressing the activation button of the SF card, a large disk of light expanded into the middle of the tiny bathroom, shimmering. Gripping both bags, they stepped through the opening in time and space.

On the other side, San Francisco.

She closed the portal and listened. The office was just opening. Morning sun slanted through the windows overlooking the FiDi district. As expected, the anchor was in the top right drawer. However, instead of taking it with them, she needed to make it look like it had been taken.

Under the couch. Lysandra suggested. Esben let her think it was her idea.

The brilliant part about the way the portals worked was that no matter where they were opened, they temporarily canceled out any matter in the way. As long as it opened into a space the traveler could exit from, there was very little risk.

He mentally thanked her for the suggestion as he found the tape.

Attaching the anchor to the bottom of the couch, they made sure a casual observer could not see it. Satisfied, they portaled to the Seattle office next.

Here, the offices looked out over Puget Sound on one side and Highway 5 on the other. Again, the other half of the portal card was only moved to an inconspicuous place in the room so they could return to the city quickly when they were ready to implement the plan. This time, they attached the anchor to the bottom of the desk chair.

They had already collected the portal cards from the Caribbean house and Raleigh office without incident.

With one step, Esben-Lysandra appeared in Drake's posh office in New York City. The humid air was a notable difference from the other locations. The spire of the Chrysler Building gleamed in the afternoon sunlight. Edward's New York City office was arranged in the same layout as his L.A. office; only the furniture here took a modern turn. Straight lines and bold colors. Even the wet bar followed the form of the other pieces in lime-green and white.

Esben-Lysandra checked the time on the row of clocks above the couch, lunchtime local time. Drake would be awake by now for sure and realized that the anchors were gone. What action he would take next, they were not sure. Unlike everywhere else they had visited, here they would need to actually exit the building. There were no more anchors to collect, and they needed to get out into the city.

She sat behind the desk and opened the top drawer on the right. Underneath the Cross pens in their foam casing was the other half of the portal anchor. She glanced up at the door that led out into the lobby. It was the only way out of the room. The nearest fire exit was down the hallway. It was lunchtime here; hopefully that meant less people around. This would be the best time to make her escape from the building. They had to assume that Nolin had put people on alert for them.

No point in waiting any longer. She walked up to the door with her hand on the lock and pressed an ear to the door. If any sound came through it was too muffled to be of use. The quicker they got this over with, the better. She tightened the straps of the backpack in case she would have to make a run for it. Checking that everything was secure, including her gun, she closed her eyes and took a few deep breaths.

It's a trap, Lysandra shouted in her head. She may have agreed to this arrangement, but she was not making it easy on him. Her constant mental pacing and muttering were distracting.

Reflexively she reached for her gun under her right arm and unsnapped the strap on the holster. Harming anyone, most of all staff of ACS or DPA for that matter, was the last thing they would want to do. But the gun was there if needed.

Her hand started to turn the doorknob.

Don't do it, Lysandra warned. She mentally tensed up, causing a ripple effect into her whole body.

It's the only way out. Esben quietly opened the door enough to see out. Voices came from further away, but the immediate area remained quiet. Esben tried to recall the layout of the office, where the nearest stairwell or elevator could be. They visited this office so rarely since meetings were conducted virtually now, the need to travel to each location had become obsolete.

Evasive maneuvers!

She peered between the doorjamb and the door. *Shut up,* he thought at her.

Now!

"Now!" Esben-Lysandra blurted out involuntarily.

The door flung from her grasp as a large man elbowed it open and grabbed her coat. Unbelievably monstrous in size, he towered over her. "Stop right there."

Esben-Lysandra grabbed his wrist. Electricity burned his skin. Esben-Lysandra dropped to the floor. Letting go of the bags, she ducked his clumsy grasp and maneuvered behind him.

Springing to her feet, ready to run, she felt an arm shoving her back into the doorjamb. Another man blocked her from the hallway. They both wore the dark-blue uniforms of ACS security staff. How much had the staff been told?

Now that she was completely in the lobby, she could see two other guards blocking the hallways, preventing anyone else from coming into the area while a fifth, the only bald one of the group, kept the receptionist at a safe distance. Nolin or Edward had told them enough to bring decent numbers, at least.

Hands grabbed her from behind, pinning her arms to her sides. The giant man forced her forward.

"We've got this." The bald guard with the receptionist looked back at Lysandra. "Let Mr. Drake and Mr. Nolin know we found her."

The woman made a hasty retreat from the room. The second guard who had blocked her path took one arm while the large guard held the other. The man who had been shielding the receptionist stood in front of her. Esben recognized the bald guard as the head of security for this location but could not remember the man's name.

Bald Guard reached under Lysandra's jacket and pulled out her gun. "Seems unfair, five of us to one of you."

Esben-Lysandra cocked her head to one side. "That's quite alright. Edward and Nolin know who they're dealing with. You do not."

The two men holding her suddenly released her and started looking at the hands and arms wildly.

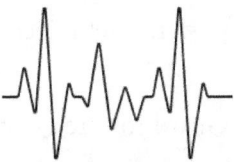

Lysandra recovered her sense of space as Esben and Qur'ag migrated down her arms. The small theater dissolved, and she found herself looking through her own eyes again. The shift back to full control disoriented her for a second.

She set her gaze on Bald Guard in front of her. He still had her gun, taunting her like he knew it was her most valuable possession. She visualized his trajectory and gave him a telekinetic push. A startled yelp escaped him as he fell back. The gun dropped to the floor. Snapping it up, she flipped the safety off and fired two shots into the ground.

Everyone covered their ears. Too late. Her goal: keep any other employees from entering the area. It might bring more security, but at least it would keep everyone else out of their way if they thought it was an active shooter situation. The Esben and Qur'ag controlled guards went after the other two guards.

Lysandra went to the reception desk to see if there was any kind of map to the floor. "How do we get out of here?"

"Look out!" The big guy, Esben-Guard, ran toward her suddenly.

Bald Guard pounced toward her. The two of them crashed to the floor. A sharp pinch bit into her arm. "Ah!" She kicked him, the extra telekinetic force sending him up into the air and across the room. She gasped as he crashed to the floor unmoving. She had not meant to use that much power. A jet injector dropped from his limp hand.

"Lysandra." Esben-Guard towered over her. "Are you alright?" He helped to her feet.

She could feel the drug taking its effect already. The room began to wobble. She grasped his arm for support. "Can you stop it?" She looked at him. Focusing her eyes was getting harder by the second. She fell against the guard.

Esben-Guard knelt with her as she lost the ability to hold herself up. "Depends on which drug they used. We'll try." He glanced at Qur'ag, "Get the bags."

"We've got you." Esben-Guard squeezed her hand as awareness of her surroundings faded.

Lysandra slipped into unconsciousness in Esben's arms. A decent attempt on Nolin's part to stop them, but not good enough. He lifted her from the floor, cradled in his arms. "Let's go."

Qur'ag-Guard put her gun in the backpack with the money and they headed for the elevators. No employees could be seen. They were probably hiding because of the gunfire. The doors opened to the lobby and a group of ACS guards ready for the fight.

"Stand down," Esben-Guard told them. "We've apprehended the intruder. Mr. Drake is sending the authorities now."

They got out of the elevator. Qur'ag-Guard held the door. "Anyone with EMT experience that can assist the guards on eighteenth should go now."

A few broke away from the group and went into the elevator.

Esben-Guard shifted Lysandra in his arms. "The rest of you, check all the exits, find out how she got in."

The remaining security staff scattered in all directions, doing what they were told. Esben and Qur'ag went outside. Thankfully the ACS office was downtown, and this was New York City. Qur'ag hailed a cab. For now, they needed to find a place for Lysandra to sleep off the drug and work on getting transportation for the next phase of the plan.

15

DPA HEADQUARTERS

0900 hours PST

Commander Eriksson sat at his desk, reviewing the shift roster for the upcoming month. An alert chimed on his phone. It was a classified message. Since he was at his desk, he logged onto his computer and into his government intranet email. The message had been sent to him and to Draegg, of course. Since they were co-leaders of the Department of Planetary Affairs, equal in authority, any messages to do with the Department went to them both.

It was an email string that started as an automated message from a local bank to the Internal Revenue Service. That message had then gone to the office of Homeland Security, and finally to the DPA.

Lysandra Carlisle had walked into the Los Angeles branch of her bank and emptied her account. Over $60,000 in cash.

Eriksson picked up the phone and called the security center. "I need a location on Officer Carlisle."

After a few seconds, the person on the other end responded. "The log shows that she checked out this morning just before seven-thirty."

"This morning? The last time I checked, she had left last night. What was her check-in prior to seven-thirty?"

The officer on the other end clicked his tongue as he searched. "Six forty-three, sir."

"She was back for less than an hour." He tapped his fingers on his desk. "Send me the logs of her activity and send me all the video footage for the time she was here this morning."

"Yes sir."

Eriksson ended the call and started to dial Commander Draegg. They would need to work with the City of Los Angeles to get any public video footage of Lysandra. And he would need to call the bank.

Another alert chimed, telling him someone was at the door. "Enter." As soon as the door opened, he set the phone down.

Commander Draegg walked in with Edward Drake.

Until Lysandra had come on the scene, Edward was a rogue host whom the DPA kept a watchful eye on. Now it felt like he made a regular appearance there. And every time he did, he became more of an ally.

"Alex." Drake shook his hand. "I have a feeling that you know why I'm here."

Eriksson nodded. "I do." He looked at Commander Draegg. "I just got a report that Lysandra emptied her bank account this morning. Over sixty thousand dollars in cash."

Draegg pressed his lips together in thought. "Where was that at?"

"Here. Downtown Los Angeles."

"Let's sit." Commander Draegg offered a seat to Edward. "Tell him what happened."

Edward sat down. Leaning forward on his knees, he pressed the tips of his fingers together. It was a gesture of habit with him and one that emphasized the now missing pinky finger on his left hand. One of several consequences from the events in India.

With a sharp intake of breath, Edward looked up at them. "Esben has taken Lysandra. To what end, I don't know." He sat up and rubbed his hands on his thighs. "I believe that the information has been hidden from me and his purpose could be revealed if someone"—he glanced at Commander Draegg—"would go in there and see if they can find the information."

Commander Draegg cleared his throat. "Why not have Qur'ag do it?"

Edward grimaced. "Esben took Qur'ag as well."

"Are Nolin and L'heilh still with you?" Draegg asked.

Edward nodded. "I could ask them, but being as close as we are, having one of them in my head could potentially strain our relationship. I thought it would be best to collaborate with the DPA directly. Nolin is working on trying to track her down, but again, I think working together will be to our advantage."

Eriksson opened several windows on his monitor. "We know she was in Los Angeles this morning. I am requesting video footage from the bank. I also want to see if any cameras in the area will give us any idea of where she went next. You're sure you have no idea what this is about?"

Edward sat back in his chair. "I'm sure you're aware that Lysandra's been with me the last few nights."

"I am." Eriksson frowned. Members of the Department were allowed to have personal lives. There were few policies that governed officers' activities outside of work hours. As government employees, they were all held to a higher standard. Lysandra fraternizing with a notable person on the DPA watch list was not ideal.

Edward suppressed a smile. "Well, on at least two occasions, Esben switched to Lysandra."

Both Draegg and Eriksson shifted in their chairs.

Eriksson sat back in his seat. "Any ideas as to why?"

Edward shook his head. "When Xander had extracted Esben, it was the first time we had ever been separated. While separated, I struggled with keeping my emotions in check. Self-control was nearly impossible." He looked at Draegg. "How did Justin fair when you were removed?"

Draegg shook his head. "No way to know. I was replaced with an Elbie loyal to Varoth, so Justin hasn't had to go through that."

"Yes, of course." Edward shook his head. "How could I forget?" Edward and Esben had been there. He had helped orchestrate the whole thing.

Draegg leaned on the arm of his chair. "You found being Elbie-free difficult?"

"I did." Edward looked down. "It has only been a few hours right now, but I am not looking forward to the next twenty-four hours."

"So you think that initial separation by Xander is what prompted this?" Eriksson rocked in his chair.

Edward shook his head. "To be honest, I don't know. I didn't think he was unhappy, if I can even use those terms. If anything, the probable cause is boredom. Being with the same mind for years at a time. I have this idea that he is looking for a challenge."

Draegg stood up from his chair and began to pace. "If that is the case, Esben could have jumped into any human in your organization. Why choose Lysandra?"

"Proximity." Eriksson sat forward and leaned on his desk with his elbows.

"Possible." Edward turned to him. "Despite my extreme dissatisfaction with him for having done such a thing, I believe that he continued to visit Lysandra while we slept. I remember dreaming, so I know he was gone. The first time it happened, I asked him not to do it again, but he did it anyway." Edward leaned back into his seat. "What I'm about to tell you has to be held in the strictest confidence."

"Of course." Draegg glanced at Eriksson.

"Agreed." Eriksson shut off his computer.

"Esben and Lysandra colluded in the takedown of the people who tried to kill me."

"They were working together?" Draegg asked, taken back. "Are you sure?"

"I am. I questioned Lysandra about it the next day. She told me she had been researching the organization for weeks before they had shot me and that pushed her over the edge."

Draegg sat on the edge of Eriksson's desk. "It's true. We know she's been obsessing over what's been happening with Alpha Cortex."

"Obsessing?" Edward raised an eyebrow. "In any case, I told her she shouldn't jeopardize her life nor her relationship with the Department. She told me she wouldn't do it again, which is why I think that this is a kidnapping or hostage situation."

Eriksson drummed his finger on the desk. "There must be a specific reason to pick Lysandra."

Draegg stood. "Perhaps with Kwin's help, we can figure that out."

Eriksson turned his computer on again. "I'll work on getting the footage while you do that. Let's reconvene after you're done in the med center."

Edward stood to follow Draegg out.

Eriksson looked up the bank information. No matter what happened, the most important question he needed answered was: Who was in control? Esben or Lysandra?

Commander Draegg waited for Edward by the door, and the two of them walked out into the hallway, leaving Eriksson to his tasks.

Draegg never had the animosity toward Edward Drake that Eriksson had at one point, but that was probably because of their Elbie connection. He glanced over at Edward, who appeared to be lost in thought. There was something in his demeanor that seemed to be missing, but he couldn't pinpoint what it was exactly. If he didn't know Edward was Elbie-free, he wasn't sure if he would know the difference. "Edward."

"Hmm." Edward looked over at Draegg as they walked.

"When Xander separated you and Esben, did it change your connection?"

"I was so relieved to get him back." Edward looked down at his feet, his hands pulled behind his back. "I didn't realize until there had been a change. This thing with Lysandra makes me very uncomfortable. I'm sure she is cooperating with him on some level; otherwise, it would make things difficult for him. I can only conclude that either she wants the same thing he does, or he had planted the idea in her head so that she thinks it's her own desire."

"Once we discover what he's after, maybe you'll have your answer."

"I hope so."

They walked into the medical center. The staff of the medical division had a full schedule, and everyone's attention was on the patients. Commander Draegg escorted Edward straight back to one of the private rooms.

A robot appeared at the door. "How may I be of service, Commander?" The robot had yellow eyes at the moment. He turned to Edward. "Mr. Drake."

"Kwin." Draegg waved him in and closed the door behind the robot. "What do you see?"

Kwin turned his body square to Edward and froze. The yellow drained from his optic photo sensors and filled with a luminescent green. This robot shell housed three Elbie, each represented by a different color for the sake of the humans it interacted with. Kwin was yellow and the most interactive. Khullus was blue and seen less often than Kwin. Finally, green for Nevik, his direct observations tended to make humans uncomfortable.

"Mr. Drake is Elbie-free. From what I can read of his vitals, it has only been a few hours. Are you alright, sir?"

"I'm fine, physically. I am concerned for Lysandra."

"May I?" The robot held up his hand.

"Of course."

Nevik softly pressed his hand against Edward's collarbone. "Your cortisol levels are elevated. May I suggest meditation?"

Draegg stepped forward. "Thank you, Nevik, but that is not why he has come here."

"I see." The robot stepped back and continued to stare at Edward. Since it did not have eyelids or pupils, staring was the only way it could look at someone.

"Esben has switched to another host, but Edward doesn't know why. It's our suspicion that Esben has buried the information, and we need an Elbie to help dig it up. Who would you recommend?"

"Tampering with memories is always a dangerous activity. We do not recommend this course of action. It would be best for the memories to surface naturally."

"A very safe answer, Nevik."

"Safety is one of our highest values. Here at the Department of—"

Draegg put a hand on the robot's shoulder. "Yes, I understand that, but we don't have the time."

"I see. In that case, the best choice would be you."

Draegg's hand dropped to his side. "Me? Why is that?"

"You are the paired designation to the Esben designation and therefore could make the most progress with the least amount of damage."

"Damage?" Edward said.

"Damage is always a possibility when tampering with a person's mind."

Edward looked down.

Commander Draegg cleared his throat. "You make a good point, but I have no experience with this kind of thing. You work with humans all the time. You helped to rehabilitate Brendan. I won't know what to look for or how to get past any mental blocks Esben may have set up."

All motion from the robot stopped. "They're discussing it," Draegg explained, his eyes flicked at Edward momentarily and then back to Nevik. Draegg forced his shoulders to relax. What Nevik suggested made perfect sense. The Draegg-Esben designations were paired in their natural state. Though structurally similar, every mind had to be approached individually. Draegg had not been in another person's mind for many years. Draegg had never altered the memories of any of his hosts.

The robot's arm jerked, and the eyes had bled back to yellow and turned to Commander Draegg. "Nevik will go with you."

That was a relief. Nevik was probably the most experienced of all of them present. Draegg turned to Edward. "You still want to do this?"

"It's our best chance of finding them." Edward looked at the robot. "If what you say is true about the damage thing."

"It's settled then." Commander Draegg nodded to Kwin. "The sooner, the better."

"We do not recommend speed for these sorts of things."

"Just a figure of speech. I trust Nevik will exercise extreme caution."

"Thank you, Commander." The robot went to the wall of machines. "Mr. Drake, it has been our experience that it is best for the patient to be in a relaxed state."

"You mean asleep?"

"Not necessarily. No human is the same. Since you have been a host for years, you know what state you are most relaxed in?"

"I'm not myself today. It's probably best I be asleep."

"Very well."

"What do you need from me?" Draegg shifted to his other foot. It was going to be a strange experience being separated from Justin. Even stranger to be in the mind that Esben has inhabited for years.

Kwin turned to Draegg. "Would you prefer to transfer to us first or go directly to Edward?"

"Let's keep the transfers to a minimum."

"Very well." Kwin moved around the room, working the machines. "Nevik will go first, and then once Mr. Drake is under, you will transfer."

"Agreed." A little nervous, Commander Draegg unzipped his uniform jacket. "Is there anything you need before we proceed?"

Edward sighed. "I'll be fine. Nolin and L'heilh know where I am. Should I give you my phone in case something goes wrong?"

Draegg shook out his hands. "It won't be needed."

"Very well." Edward sat up on the exam table and lay back.

Kwin attached wireless electrodes to both of them. Brain wave activity and readings on all their vitals brought the machines around them to life.

Edward pressed his hands flat against the padding next to him, taking deep breaths as he stared at the ceiling. Perhaps he was nervous too.

Kwin moved to stand at the top of Edward's head. "Are you ready, Mr. Drake?"

"Yes."

Draegg stood nearby as Kwin placed his hands on each side of Edward's head and went still. Edward kept his breathing steady. His eyes fluttered shut, and all the tension in his body drained out.

Kwin stepped back. "We'll give Nevik a few minutes to get oriented."

Draegg nodded, trying to control his breathing. Justin was just as uneasy about the separation as he was.

"Your turn." Kwin stepped aside for him.

Draegg stood at the head of the table, looking down on Edward's face. "Should I put my hands in the same place?"

"Yes." Kwin moved his fingers to the ideal locations. "Okay, Commander Draegg, whenever you're ready."

Draegg nodded and took a deep breath. Draegg had been with Justin for years. Before him was Miranda Grant, and before that, Matt Holloway. Before that, nothing but the vacuum of space.

Draegg unmoored from Justin's mind completely and entered into his nervous system, flowing like a river down the spinal cord and into the arms. There was a moment of darkness as he made the leap from Justin Meyer into Edward Drake.

Justin Meyer stumbled back. Kwin held his arm to steady him. Once the room came back into his senses, he cautiously sat back into a chair. He watched the monitors. Lights bounced and numbers vacillated.

"Kwin." He looked around the room. "Do you know what happens next?"

Kwin had picked up a report tablet as he monitored the machines. "It's hard to tell. Most of it will depend on what protective measures Esben has put in place to prevent the information from being found out."

"I meant with me." He rubbed his hands together. A chill ran from the back of his neck and down into his arms.

"Oh." The robot stopped short. "You will not be Elbie-free long enough to feel any effects. It usually takes several hours for your body to start feeling the effects. Since your relationship with the

Draegg designation is a partnership, you would not experience anything of significance."

"So anything I think I may be experiencing right now is all in my head?"

"Yes." The robot tapped on the screen a few times. "All your vitals are functioning within normal parameters."

"Okay. I believe you." Justin grabbed his jacket and put it back on.

The two of them sat in silence. As Kwin recorded all the results from the machines, Justin thought about what Esben could be planning. They had all reached a sort of status quo, the DPA and those they monitored. Whatever had motivated Esben to action had nothing in common with Edward; otherwise, Esben wouldn't need Lysandra.

"May I ask, sir, is Esben's current host Lysandra?"

"Yes." Justin rubbed the back of his neck.

"Since Brendan was Esben's original primary host, I wonder how that will affect him and her."

"Why should it have any effect at all?" Justin cracked his knuckles. "They are two different minds."

"Yes, but relatives often have neurological similarities."

"Is Lysandra in danger?"

"When is Lysandra not in danger? She has a habit of finding trouble. So yes, but she is no worse off than she would have been otherwise."

Justin chuckled. "You're absolutely right."

Edward's body jerked suddenly. A machine beeped.

"I'll be right back." Kwin put his hands on Edward's head and his optics went dark.

Justin sat forward, watching Edward's face for any indication of what was happening.

Kwin's eyes started to glow again. "It's done."

Kwin stepped away from Edward. Justin came around and put his hand on the top of Edward's head. The heat came back into Justin's palm and moved up his arm. He swayed on his feet. Kwin took his arm and guided him to a chair. Justin-Draegg sank into the cushioned seat, his mind flooded by Edward's thoughts.

16

DPA HEADQUARTERS

1030 hours PST

Edward felt himself falling through open space, into a black void with no beginning or end. Like this had been the only way he had ever existed, tumbling head over heels into deep nothing. His eyes snapped open to fluorescent lights overhead. A machine beeped rapidly somewhere behind his head. A robot appeared at his side. "You are safe, Mr. Drake."

It took a moment for Edward to realize that it was Kwin and that he was in the DPA medical center. The terrible lighting and ionized air reminded him of his recent hospital stay. He nodded at the robot and let himself relax into the pillows, taking several deep breaths to calm himself. His head pounded something awful. He had not had a headache since the last time he was Elbie-free. That was one huge advantage of being a host: automated pain management.

Draegg stirred in the chair next to the bed. He shook himself and sat up. "Can we bring the lights down a little bit?"

Kwin went over to the wall controls and dimmed the lights. "Would you like some pain relief, Mr. Drake?"

Edward nodded. If he squinted hard enough, he could pretend it was Qur'ag, their design was so similar. "And some water, please."

The robot left the room to fulfill the request.

"Edward." Commander Draegg got up from his seat and stood at the side of the bed. A warm smile spread across his face. "How are you feeling?"

Edward sat up with a wince as he straightened his back. "What's that smile for?"

Commander Draegg clapped him on the back. "Congratulations are in order, I believe."

Heat rose in Edward's cheeks. Draegg would have had access to every thought and memory Edward ever had, and the ones about Lysandra would have been at the forefront. "You mean my lamentable proposal?"

Draegg chuckled. "Probably should have waited until after breakfast to ask."

Edward pinched the bridge of his nose, thinking about the horrified look on Lysandra's face. At least Draegg could be trusted to keep anything he learned between them. "If you know that, then you know her answer."

"I do. But I also know her. She's the kind of person that has to think it's her idea."

Edward laughed. "You're absolutely right. That's where I went wrong." She was stubborn like that. Maybe too stubborn. "Am I being a fool, Justin?"

"It's never foolish to hope for the best. Believe the best. She'll come around."

Edward dropped his gaze to the floor. "As long as Esben doesn't do something too drastic to her in the meantime."

Draegg gave him a reassuring squeeze on the shoulder. Kwin entered again, handing each of them cups of water and Edward some painkillers.

Commander Eriksson came into the room, a data pad in his hand. "We found them." He held up the screen to show them the security photos. Edward sat forward, recognizing the location. "Nolin said that she showed up at the New York office. Security tried to detain her, but she was assisted by two guards who turned on the rest of the group."

"Esben and Qur'ag probably." Edward reached for his jacket and pulled out his phone. Sure enough, several missed calls from both Nolin and the New York office. He checked the texts, many of which were shots from the building's security system. "They've taken all the portal cards possible. Looks like New York was the last place they hit."

Eriksson crossed his arms. "How many portal cards did you not turn in when the DHS asked?"

Edward wondered when that would come up. Like many things, he would have to deal with the consequences of that later. "With the one that she had in her watch, seven in total."

Eriksson shook his head. "What use would it be to have them all in the same place? That limits her mobility."

"Esben's," Edward corrected as he massaged his temples. "Lysandra is not making these choices."

Eriksson glanced over at Draegg, who seemed lost in thought. "Won't he need her cooperation if he wants to succeed at whatever it is he's up to?"

"It will certainly help, but there is also Qur'ag. The two of them together could subdue a stubborn personality; they know her brain very well."

Draegg rubbed his chin in thought. "Do you really believe that Esben and Qur'ag would do that to her?"

Edward shook his head. "I don't want to believe either scenario. Neither her willing cooperation with them nor their outright betrayal to me. Whatever Esben is after, it's an act of urgency, perhaps desperation."

Eriksson turned to Draegg. "You've been in his head. Did you find anything out?"

Draegg glanced at Edward but quickly went back to Eriksson. "Unfortunately, not much. Images of Seattle were very strong."

"But no idea why?"

Draegg shook his head. Edward did the same. "I'm in that office about once a quarter. Any significant connections are related to business matters."

"We need to send a team there immediately then." Eriksson got out his phone. "Any chance it could have something to do with her brother?"

"No," Edward answered. He focused on the Seattle thoughts. There was nothing there about family, only a strong emphasis on the geographical location. "I feel like there is something there he needs, but it has nothing to do with her family."

"Two teams then." Eriksson started typing into his phone. "I'll take a team to New York. Draegg, you take Seattle. Good?"

"Of course."

"We leave in an hour for the airport." Eriksson turned to leave.

"Wait." Edward kicked his legs over the side of the bed and stood. "I'm coming with you."

Eriksson shook his head. "We cannot have a civilian on a government mission like this."

"If anyone can get through to Esben or Lysandra, it's me."

"Goddammit." Eriksson paced in a circle. "You're right. I hope it's true." He looked Edward in the eye. "Fine." He looked at Draegg again. "Make sure Matt's on your team. That way, we both have someone she's close to."

Draegg nodded. "Will do. One hour."

Eriksson exchanged glances with both of them. "Let's keep the information loop open, send any new information between the three of us." Draegg and Edward nodded their consent, and Eriksson exited the room.

"I have to assemble my team." Draegg went to the door. "You alright here?"

"I'll be fine." Edward put his jacket on. "Good luck."

"You too." Draegg hurried out.

Edward sat back on the edge of the exam table. He texted his driver to drop off his overnight bag immediately; he always had one ready. Until then, he would have to wait. He reviewed Nolin's texts. The last of which was a video following Lysandra and the two guards as they worked their way out of the building. The last few minutes were of Lysandra being carried outside, the three of them climbing into a taxi, and the taxi disappearing into traffic. "Esben, old friend, what are you after?"

17

HIGHWAY 80

1500 hours EST

Lysandra woke to the white noise of tires on the road. She opened her eyes to the ceiling of a car, streaked with orange sunlight. Before she could even ask the question, Qur'ag responded. *We're en route to Chicago.*

"How long have I been out?" She sat up, reaching down the side of the seat to pop the seat back upright. To defend herself against the late afternoon sunlight, she dropped her sunglasses over her eyes.

"Almost five hours." The driver responded.

She looked over at the person driving them toward their destination at a harrowing ninety miles an hour. He still had the rounded cheeks of a college student. The blue-and-yellow polo shirt he wore looked like a school uniform except for the Best Buy logo emblazoned on the shoulder.

"Got you coffee." He tapped a cup in the middle console between them.

"Thank you." She picked it up and took a sip; the smell alone helped to clear the fog still lingering in her head. She had to hand it to Nolin and Edward. They knew having enough people to confront her might not do the trick. Drugging her had been a move neither she nor Esben had expected.

"You're welcome." He smiled at her. For a moment, she saw Edward. Maybe it was the effect of his voice inflection. No matter what host Esben inhabited, the way the person spoke came out sounding Edward-like.

Shaking herself, she took another rejuvenating sip. "We'll need to make contact with the guys before we can meet them."

"I picked something up for that." He pointed to the back seat.

Lysandra turned in her seat. On top of the DPA duffel bag was a cell phone encased in plastic. She reached back and grabbed it.

"I took care of the watch too." He handed her a FedEx receipt. "It will get there by eight-thirty a.m., no signature needed."

Lysandra checked the address. Once they had the hackers, they would need to set up a base of operations. Since all the action would be on the West Coast, it made sense to send the watch back there. She crammed the receipt into her pocket. "We should find a place to ditch your host soon. It will be a challenge for him to get back to the city."

"At the next rest stop."

Lysandra nodded in agreement as she stretched her legs, wishing for a toothbrush. That would be easily remedied next time they got gas. "Who is this guy anyways?" She opened the glove box and searched for the registration. Stapled to the car manual, she read the name out. "Brian Matthews."

Her heart skipped a beat at the sight of the name Matthew. Would Matt approve of her actions? Even as she formed the question, Qur'ag's thoughts berated her for even caring what others thought. She had never cared about the approval of the crowd, just a select few. But this was Matt. When she was too busy learning protocol or radio code, Matt had become one of those few.

Such sniveling sentimentality.

"That's it." She shoved the registration back into the glove box and slammed it shut. "First things first." Leaning over into the backseat, she unzipped the duffel bag. The containment unit sat on top. She grabbed the glass cylinder and settled into her seat again. She pressed the power switch on and put both hands on the glass. Heat moved through her left hand and into the glass. A pinpoint of bright light gathered at the center of the glass and hovered there. Qur'ag was as satisfied with this new arrangement as she was. With a sigh, she relaxed into the seat. "That feels so much better."

"Problems?" Esben laughed.

"He's such an asshole." Lysandra dug in her pockets until she found her pocketknife. She extended the blade and started cutting into the packaging around the cell phone. "At the next stop, let's drop Brian off somewhere safe, and you can plant some memories to make him think he had some crazy adventure. No killing him."

"Of course not. Why would you say that?" Esben nodded solemnly.

Lysandra stabbed at the plastic, trying to find the widest opening for the damn phone. "I don't know, just trying to be clear. Since we have to communicate with words for the moment."

"Fair enough."

She ripped the plastic apart and finally freed the phone. "We should leave him some money for the car."

"Agreed." His focus sharpened and a smile grew on his face.

The tone of his voice sounded exactly like Edward. Lysandra looked over at him. The glint in his eye totally reminded her of Edward. "Stop doing that."

"I'm not doing anything." His smile widened.

Somehow the Elbie could mimic Edward in another person's body. She shook her head. "You are totally doing an Edward imitation thing."

"Not on purpose. It's just what I'm used to." His demeanor changed back to a twenty-something, starving student.

"God, you're an ass sometimes." She popped the SIM card into the slot along the side of the phone.

"Is this why I'm here? Violating the Department code of conduct so you can berate me?"

This made her laugh. "You've never followed the code, not once." She held down the power button on the phone until it came to life. "And no. We're here to emancipate you or whatever."

"Are you mad at me for that? What is going on with you?"

Lysandra sighed and dropped her head against the headrest. Maybe it was a side effect of the drug. She looked down at the phone in her hands. In a few short hours, she would be face to face with her old teammates. Back in her old stomping grounds. All of it a life she had left behind. "Probably too much in my head about being back in Chicago and seeing everyone."

"I see. It's only for this one thing. And once we make contact, you can get out. I'll take over one of the others, and then you yourself can be free."

"Yeah. I know. I'm worrying over nothing. Didn't mean to take it out on you."

"We really appreciate your help."

"We?"

"Qur'ag would never admit it, but he appreciates it too."

"I doubt it, but I'll accept it." She didn't feel much better about the whole situation, but there was no point in stalling any longer. Once they dropped off Brian, she would need to drive and would be unable to make the call. Hopefully, the only phone number she had committed to memory would not fail her. With a tinge of dread, she dialed the number. She didn't really want to see these people again, but it was the fastest way to get what Esben needed.

The line picked up after two rings.

"The dog barks in the meadow," Lysandra said in a flat tone.

There was a moment of someone breathing into the receiver from the other end. "Who's this?"

Lysandra thought it could be one of the hackers, but she wasn't sure, sure. "Put Nicholas on."

"Nicholas? Nobody's allowed to call him that."

Definitely a noob and someone she had never met before. "That's right, except for me. Now get him on the phone!"

"Lady, how do I know—"

"I gave you the passcode already, so what's the problem?" *Punk.*

"It's an old one."

"Listen very carefully. I've been doing deep undercover work. If Nicholas Miller is not on the phone in the next minute, when I meet you, I will present your head on a pike to Gregory. How's that sound?" She hated to get vicious, but if it worked, it worked.

After a couple of heartbeats, the voice said, "Hang on."

There was a tumbling sound as the phone receiver was put down. Nick's name was yelled repeatedly, fading into the distance. After some muffled sounds, a familiar voice came onto the line.

"Well, well, well," Nick answered. She could always tell if he was smiling or frowning just by the tone of his voice. At the moment, he was definitely smiling. "Undercover, is it? Funny word for what I would call defection."

"I'm in need of your services."

"Mine?"

"Actually, not you in the least," she said with great delight. Nick was an infiltrator like her, a very skilled thief and master manipulator. "Some of the hackers."

Nick clicked his tongue. "We don't have discounts for traitors."

"I've got cash. Lots of it."

"You invoked the name of Gregory."

"Well, the guy was being stubborn. I thought it would scare him into cooperating."

"Oh, it did, but it means you'll have to pay the penance."

"If Gregory wants to see me, what do I care?"

"Hubris."

Lysandra didn't know what Nick meant by that, but having dealt with the megalomaniac Xander, Gregory was tame by comparison. "If he wants to get the band back together, I'm not interested."

"Thought you should know what's expected."

"Yeah, I got it. I'll see you when I get there." She started to hang up.

"Not so fast, Sandra Dee."

"What now?" An edge of irritation crept into her voice.

"You're not one of us anymore. You can't come and go as you please."

Lysandra restrained herself from an agitated sigh. "Go on."

"Be at the gate at eleven a.m. sharp. If you're ten seconds early or late, your appointment will be canceled."

"That's ridiculous. This is a time sensitive operation."

"We've got other clients, sweetheart. Besides, getting the gamers out of bed any earlier will put them in a bad mood." She could hear the smile in his voice again. He was really enjoying this little power trip of his.

She took a deep calming breath and glanced over at Esben. She would not let Nick get under her skin. He might think he had the advantage over her, but he was in for a surprise. "Fine. See you at eleven, Nicolas." Lysandra hung up the phone.

Esben kept his eyes on the road. "I take it we're in?"

Lysandra deleted the number from the call log and took the battery out again. "Yes, but they're making us come in the morning. We should have surprised them instead."

"When the time comes, let me handle it."

Lysandra nodded. Esben had had dealings with criminals before, but only with the contacts two or three times removed from the top tiers of power. Now they would be walking right into the viper's nest with no one to back them up. Maybe the money would be enough to buy some forgiveness.

18

NEW YORK CITY

0144 hours EST

E riksson closed his laptop. The neon lights of Times Square, visible from the hotel room, did not help his burning eyes. He looked over at the alarm clock between the two queen beds. In California, he would be in bed by now. The predictable routine of the DPA had gotten him out of the habit of fieldwork. Ian had a collection of surveillance photos strewn around the room, constructing a timeline of their target's activities in Manhattan.

The five-hour flight from LAX to JFK was not wasted. Eriksson had put Special Agent Ian Reynolds in charge of the investigation. Before his run-in with Elbie, Ian had been one of the best analysts he had ever seen. Having an Elbie only sharpened this innate talent. By the time the plane touched down in New York, they had a few photos with time stamps of Lysandra and the two Alpha Cortex Solution guards. NYPD had already arrested one of the ACS that had been seen with Lysandra. While Agent Ian and the rest of the team checked into the hotel and got set up, Eriksson and Drake went down to the precinct to question him.

The police had picked up the guard for public endangerment—typical post host behavior. The interview was short. Before waking up in the holding cell the ACS guard remembered confronting a woman outside of Mr. Drake's office. Edward paid for the man's bail and a taxi home. The employee promised he would contact them if he remembered anything.

Eriksson glanced over at Ian, who sat on the couch continuing to scan through thousands of images provided by various city agencies, traffic lights, ATMs, store security feeds. So far, they had tracked down the taxi driver who had dropped the trio off at a Catholic church where they had taken refuge for a few hours. Several cameras in and around Grand Central Station had recorded one of the guards on a series of errands. Once he returned to the church, he had been left there while Lysandra and the other guard disappeared into the downtown crowds.

Eriksson started a fresh pot of coffee. "Anything new?"

Ian kept flipping through images. "I think we have a complete list of businesses the guard visited in the station. I'm still waiting on receipts and statements from all the businesses there. Without more information, there is no discernable connection between the establishments."

Eriksson nodded. "But we're sure that based on the information from Nolin, this was the last city they portaled to?"

"It's a best guess." Ian looked up from his laptop. "Once they knew Esben had taken the anchors, they were able to check all possible locations within a few minutes of each other. It's not one hundred percent, but it's close."

"As close as we can get without confirmation."

"Correct." Ian went back to searching.

They had next to nothing. Without a motive, they were shooting arrows into the dark. A polite knock at the door disrupted Eriksson's train of thought. Rubbing his eyes, Eriksson went to the door and peered through the peephole. Edward.

Eriksson opened the door. Edward looked as exhausted as he felt. Eriksson stepped back to let Edward in. "Morning. What brings you here?"

Edward's eyes were drawn to the gurgling coffee pot. "I've remembered something. I think."

"That's great." Eriksson grabbed his computer to take notes. "What've you got?"

Edward settled in one of the armchairs. "I was asleep, but I'm positive these are memories. One was Lysandra being shot in the gut. The image is from her perspective, so I don't see her. She's facing a man, they're in a half-lit hallway, very industrial, when he pulls a gun on her and fires."

Ian had been the first on the scene when Lysandra's team leader had turned on her. Eriksson knew the location of the confrontation from the incident report; the hallway they had been in was very plain. "What did he look like? To verify if it's a memory."

"Dark hair, brown eyes, kind of weathered looking. I had originally met with him and Lysandra when making arrangements for the break-in, so I already had his image in my head, but he was in one of your uniforms."

Eriksson poured a cup of coffee for both of them. "So the question is, why that memory. Any other details?"

Edward gladly accepted the hot drink. "There is. A theater. I was never a big dreamer before I was host, but even when I did dream, they were scattered. This was like a walk-through. The place was totally falling apart, few lights, debris everywhere. It had to be condemned. The feeling I get from it is familiarity. Almost the comfort of home, but I can't imagine such a place being comforting. The amount of detail is far beyond my imagination."

"Ian." Eriksson's mind was spinning. Was it possible the two images were related? If so, how? "How far is Chicago from here?"

A few quick clicks on his keyboard. "About eight hundred miles."

Eriksson took a deep breath. "How likely would you say it is that Esben and Lysandra are headed there now?"

After a few minutes of thought, Edward nodded. "The more I think about it. Crime was definitely on Esben's mind."

"Agent Reynolds, your opinion."

Ian's fingers flashed as he typed with lightning speed. "I'll start the request for any stolen car reports and camera images from all possible routes."

Edward set his cup aside. "It's still a gamble."

Eriksson knew all too well what a risk it was to leave the last confirmed location based on a hunch, but a lot of this job depended on instinct. "What does your gut tell you?"

"She's got to spend that cash somewhere. Whatever Esben wants, it's expensive."

"I'll leave a few team members here in case they reappear, but the rest of us will head to Chicago." Energized by this new direction, Eriksson was sure they were on the right trail.

19

CHICAGO, IL

1100 hours CST

Somehow the light in the alley was always the same, perpetual dusk. One could suppose it was perpetual dawn, but that would be too optimistic. Lysandra-Esben stood in the alley of a burned-out theater on the east side of the city. The outside had been boarded up so long ago the wood was warped and gray. Even the glued movie posters and music ads were years old, tattered, and graffitied. Burned-out drug addicts and homeless vets lined the outside of the building. The police were never seen in the area. Ever. With no visible way inside, a person needed to know how to gain entry.

After kicking debris from the hinges, Lysandra-Esben stomped on the flat of two rusted sheets of metal with the heel of her boot. The rhythm of her stomping was actually Morse code. The password changed often, but the current code had been sent to her in a text. She stamped the code a second time just in case whoever guarded the door missed the beginning. Soon after, a loud bang reverberated through the metal below her feet. Her code had been accepted.

She moved off the cover and waited. At the moment, she had her thoughts all to herself without Esben eavesdropping or interrupting. It had been a request of hers to let her be in full control of her thoughts and actions when dealing with Gregory and the others. Instead, he was circulating in her nervous system. This resulted in a heightened sense of exhilaration. The environment around her crackled with possibility. She tried to think of a time in her life when she had experienced this much freedom. And confidence. She felt like a goddamn superhero. Invincible. It was intoxicating and probably addictive. Now she understood why some people sought out Elbie to partner with.

The screeching of metal echoed off the brick walls. A few of the slumbering inhabitants stirred. If they had been here long enough, they knew that some sort of criminal organization operated out of here, but if they knew that much, then they also knew the man behind it. One run-in with him would be enough to banish the thought of reporting this place to the authorities of any kind. She had seen Gregory make an example of snitches and spies, and the results were burned into her memory. The gruesome sights were meant to make an impression on anyone who saw them.

The two halves of the metal cover split open and lifted up as a platform ascended from below. The acrid smell of smoke plumed out of the opening. A red-hot pinpoint of light from below was the first thing she saw. Lysandra's first instinct was to draw her gun. Since she had come in peace, she held up her hands, palms open, near her face so that it was clear she was not a threat.

Nick had come alone. As his body emerged slowly from the ground, she took a step back. The only thing in his hand was his cigarette. The last two times they had seen each other, he had attacked her. A little revenge for both affronts had crossed her mind, and she did not doubt that he would expect exactly that.

"Sandi, Sandi, Sandi." He shook his head. "You are the last person I expected to see on my doorstep." He took a drag off of his cigarette.

"Oh Nick, you were always so ambitious. Don't let Gregory catch you claiming the place as your own."

The platform stopped, and he stepped to one side. "You coming or not?"

"I didn't drive all this way for nothing." She stepped onto the platform next to him.

"Gregory is looking forward to talking to you."

"I'm sure he is," Lysandra-Esben said coolly, grateful for Esben and the way he imbued confidence in anyone he inhabited. At this moment, she was glad to have him with her.

The ancient motor that powered the elevator churned with ear piercing squeals and the faint scent of smoke as the two of them descended below the pavement. The door covers closed in above them by the force of gravity until they clanged shut on top of them. Nick held a flashlight in one hand and the cigarette in the other. A beam of light shot through the musty darkness. She should have remembered to bring a flashlight. That was the only redeeming feature of this location: low lighting.

Nick turned to her. "You know the drill."

Lysandra-Esben set her duffel bag of stolen DPA equipment and the backpack of cash on the ground with exaggerated precaution to indicate it was fragile. Reaching behind her back, she pulled out her gun, popped the clip, and held them out to him. Nick smiled at her. He knew what the gun meant to her; he had held it hostage on many occasions to get her cooperation. He checked the chamber for a bullet and dumped the bullet on the ground.

He put the gun under his belt, the clip in his pocket, and flicked his head at her. Lysandra-Esben raised her hands in the air. With the flashlight under his arm and the cigarette in his mouth, Nick slipped his hands under her jacket and slid them down the full length of her back and all the way around her rib cage and stomach with more pressure than necessary.

Smoke from his cigarette floated in her face. "Hope you're having a good time there."

"Don't you worry about me, darlin'." He chuckled. "I'm having a fine time." He smiled at her before his hands went down the side of her hips and thighs. His fingers dug into the top of her boots, where, on occasion, she had been known to carry knives and extra ammo.

He stood up again and did a quick pat down of her arms. "I'm disappointed. Only one weapon. That day job of yours is making you soft." He pulled the gun from his belt and held it out to her with an open palm. The clip remained in his pocket. "Something's different about you."

"Maybe it's you who's changed." She took the gun and put it in her holster.

He looked her over again. "It's you." He picked up the backpack and slung it over his shoulder. "Let's go."

She grabbed the duffel bag, and they started walking in the direction she would have expected, with only his flashlight to lead the way. Right now, they were in the service hallway, where back in the day, the oversized stage sets would be loaded in. Wide and high ceilings made it possible to bring in the larger set pieces. As they went, other people passed them in the hall. Voices could be heard from the rooms they walked by. Gregory had several dozen people he employed, and a big location like this was perfect for housing all of them.

Nick and Lysandra-Esben climbed a staircase that she knew moved around the outside of the theater until they appeared out in the lobby. High stained-glass windows above the boarded entry doors allowed more natural light in here than in anywhere else in the building. The once elegant staircase in the lobby climbed up the center of the room and split in each direction to take patrons to the balconies. Below were double doors onto the main seating level.

Nick opened the doors with a flourish and led her through into the orchestra level of the theater. In here were the remnants of electric light. Sconces along the walls washed the room in a garish yellow tint. What remained of the red velvet seats were torn and gutted cushions and tarnished brass.

Still hanging from the center of the ornate and rotting ceiling, Lysandra recognized the chandelier immediately, and it made her head spin. The frosted glass panels and pewter mosaic flowers of the art nouveau era were the same as the theater in her head. The mental prison that had been created by her original Elbie captor the first time she had been made a host. That place had been fashioned after this theater. The seats were exactly the same as the one in her mental images and in her dreams.

"What's the hold-up?" Nick shined the flashlight on her face.

Lysandra shook herself. "Nothing. I forgot how big this place is, that's all." Not to mention the smell of mold growing unchecked for years. Pieces of the beveled ceiling hung precariously above the seats. Parts of the catwalk and light rigging collapsed onto the theater boxes on either side. Chunks of wood and plaster littered everything. Rotted paper gathered in corners. There was a time when she called this place home. This had been her reality once upon a time.

The pathway before them led downward toward the front. Roman colonnades framed the stage on both sides, holding up the sagging ceiling. Faded frescos could still be made out at the bottom of each column. At center stage, a mahogany desk sat alone. This one place had actually been swept recently. Starting at the steps and going from the edge of the stage to the orchestra pit opening and all the way back to the painted backdrop of Roman ruins against an idyllic countryside. The desk and the backdrop in stark contrast to everything else in the space.

A high-back chair with purple velvet cushions. The same dark-stained wood and over the top wood worked craftsmanship as the desk, but nothing else occupied the stage except these two things. Nick waited at the bottom of the stairs, and with a sweep of his hand, indicated ladies first. She stepped up onto the stage. She looked back at Nick who had not moved from the bottom of the steps. She was in the lion's den now. Point of no return, so she walked up to the desk and waited.

"Do my eyes deceive me?" a voice echoed through the room. Footlights flickered on behind her, illuminating the stage and casting her shadow across the desk.

Gregory had gotten more theatrical since she had worked for him. He always had a flair for the dramatic in an understated way, but this was reaching epic proportions.

A steady beat of footfalls on the wood planks reverberated in the air. Gregory strutted from the shadow of the wings. Hands hidden in his jacket pockets, he approached with slow, deliberate strides, as if he waited for the sound of each step to end before making the next. No interrupting.

As per usual, his black hair had been slicked back with a comb. The light-blue sports jacket was a familiar sight. How he had an endless supply of those she did not know, but it was the only one he ever wore, like he had stepped out of an eighties cartoon. A toothpick protruded from between his thin lips, cracks visible and peeling as he smiled at her. She could not flinch. Any show of fear at this moment could be detrimental.

He stopped on the other side of the desk, examining her. "So the prodigal returns." He sucked on the toothpick. "Did you come to your senses?"

Lysandra-Esben stood as tall as she could, shoulders back, meeting his gaze at all times as he began to circle her. "Leaving your employ had been coming to my senses. However, that being said, I'm in need of your services."

"In need of our services?" His tone mocking. "You've come a long way from the sniveling drug addict I found on my doorstep."

"If you're inferring that I somehow owe you something for getting me clean, Gregory, I think ten years under your tutelage was penance enough." She kept her eyes on him as he circled around. He had always been bigger than her in height and width, but now she perceived him as smaller, less of a threat. Still dangerous, but the playing field has been leveled now.

"Infer?" Gregory looked at Nick. "Tutelage?" He clicked his tongue and shook his head. "When Nick left you for dead in that place, I never imagined you would join their cause."

Lysandra-Esben tilted her head and set a steely gaze on him. "Disappointed, are you?"

Gregory smiled. "Not at all. I think you've learned your lessons well." He leaned closer to her.

Lysandra-Esben did not move; the smell of stale whisky and cigarette smoke wafted off of his clothes and permeated his skin. "I did indeed." Her hands shot up, and she grabbed his coat lapels. With raw force, she lifted him onto the tips of his toes. The toothpick dropped from between his lips. The sudden and wild look in his eyes was gratifying.

Using the swell of adrenaline and power Esben provided, she dragged Gregory backward and slammed him hard onto the desk. With her forearm across his collarbone, she pinned him there. "Having made such a good disciple of me, I suggest you tread lightly, or I will see to it I repay you in full for the years of pain."

The metal click of a gun hammer rang in her ear. The cold barrel pressed against the back of her neck. "I suggest," Nick rasped, "you exercise a little self-control, young lady."

Lysandra-Esben turned her head slightly and looked at him sidelong. He had already shot her once. She doubted he had the guts to actually kill her.

A chuckle rumbled from Gregory's chest. Lysandra-Esben looked back at Gregory. The triumphant smile across his face made her want to smash his stained teeth in.

"Agreed." She opened her hand and held them up. Nick took a step back so she could give Gregory room. Though she could not see him, she knew he still had the gun trained on her.

Gregory continued to laugh from his hollow chest. He sat up, remaining on the desk. He dug into his jacket pocket and pulled out a box of cigarettes. "I like her. Lysandra Two-Point-Oh is a drastic improvement over the whelp from the gutter." He flipped open a silver lighter and lit the cigarette, not taking his eyes off her the whole time. After a long drag, he flicked his eyes at Nick behind her. The hammer of the gun released, and Nick appeared at her periphery.

Gregory breathed out the smoke. "I'm always willing to help out an old friend, but there is a price."

"As expected." Lysandra-Esben smiled. "I need two to three elite coders and this list of hardware." She took a piece of paper out of the front pocket of the backpack and handed it to Gregory.

After an evaluating look at her, he took the list from her, his eyes moving down it quickly. "Why return to me?" Gregory's dark eyes glittered from the footlights that illuminated his face.

"Short time frame. Has to get done quickly, and I didn't have time to find new contacts. I knew you would have the resources I need."

"And do you have the resources you need to solicit my assistance?"

"Here's her bag." Nick set the backpack on the desk.

"Come bearing gifts, did you?" He sneered and pulled open the main compartment. A pure white light beamed out of the recesses of the bag. "Well…" He reached in and pulled out the containment cylinder. The Elbie, Qur'ag, burned brightly at the center of the device.

Gregory's eyes were riveted to its blinding light. It was how most people reacted. Elbie make for very pretty things, and it was hard to imagine that something so small had created so much chaos. A whole new government agency, laws of the land passed unanimously, and activist organizations that protested their existence. It was just light, after all.

"Such a little thing and yet..." He stared unblinking at the captured light. Forcing himself to look away, he searched in the bag again. She had hastily tossed bundles of cash into the bottom of it. "This all of it?"

"Of course not. I know who I'm dealing with."

"How much do you have to offer?"

"I know what the going rate is for a couple of hackers. I've brought plenty to cover your costs, convenience fees and all. That is only a down payment. I'll bring the rest when I have what I want."

"Cybercrimes are in high demand these days. High demand leads to high prices."

"Yes, well, that little token there." She indicated the Elbie in his hand. "That is worth more than your entire network. So I would say it's covered."

Gregory turned the cylinder in his hand. Secretly she hoped he would accidentally hit the power switch. Qur'ag would have nowhere to go except into that especially demented mind. She wasn't sure who would suffer more: Gregory or Qur'ag. She shivered involuntarily at the possibility of them being a perfectly matched pair. Thankfully Qur'ag found humans thoroughly disgusting, no matter who they were.

Gregory set the cylinder on the desk next to him. Folding his hands, he leaned on his knee. "What's the objective? What is it you're after, officer?"

"Infiltrate three separate tech companies. Plant new code into the servers and the hardware on that list."

"So it's really three jobs?"

"One job, three parts. They all have to be successful or the whole thing is a waste of time."

"What's the ultimate objective of this three-part job?"

"That's no concern of yours. Not very professional of you to ask either."

He looked at the list again and then at the Elbie on the desk. Finally, he stood up. He put the containment unit back in the backpack, zipped it up, and handed it to her. "Nick, take our client back to the green room while I get a couple of candidates for her."

Nick led her across to the stage's right wing. In the dark backstage, he used the flashlight again. She knew where the green room was; this building had been their central hub for years. Once upon a time, she could have found her way around the entire building in the dark.

They went into the hallway behind the stage. Nick walked right into the first room with an open doorway. The door had been torn off years ago.

"Make yourself at home."

The decent-sized room was smaller than she remembered, but the teetering piles of trash probably had something to do with that. Some smart ass, long before Gregory had taken over management, had painted the walls an actual green. A reclaimed lamp in the corner with a torn and browned shade gave off a garish orange glow.

A coffee table between two torn-up couches had been rendered useless by the stacks of pizza boxes stacked so tall Lysandra-Esben could rest her arm on it standing. Touching anything in the room made her stomach lurch. The place had always been a pigsty; time had only intensified the smell.

"I can't believe I lived in this filth." She had been with the Agency for the better part of ten years, living like a vagrant in this pit of a home base.

Nick turned on her. "Aren't you high and mighty now with your government-provided housing."

Anger flaring in her gut, she balled her hands in place of a smart remark. A slight smile crossed his lips when he saw her tense. "I don't recall you complaining before. Sounds to me like your brother and his government buddies have really brainwashed you."

She looked at him, smirking. Nick thought he had delivered a real zinger. He had no idea how things had turned out after leaving her to bleed out on the floor of the DPA. The team had gone in there for a database, and Brendan, and had left with the database and one less team member: her. Nick had no idea her brother was dead now, and the mention of brainwashing stopped her cold.

"*Tardé una hora en conocerte y solo un día en enamorarme. Pero me llevará toda una vida lograr olvidarte,*" a warm dulcet voice crooned behind her.

The world disappeared as she was snapped back in time to the worst years of her life.

Between run-ins with the cops, experimenting with drugs, and living in fear from her father's constant abuse, she had been befriended by one boy at school. They shared a similar dislike of school, and he excelled at distracting her from the daily boredom. They became inseparable after a few months. It took only a couple of dinners with his family for her to feel like she belonged there. They had brought Lysandra in and loved her like family. It was the only time in her life she had known what it was like to have parents, grandparents, and siblings. Through those dark and terrible years, this immigrant family from Puerto Rico had been the one bright spot in her miserable existence.

Heart thrumming in her throat, Lysandra took a deep breath and let it out slowly. Bracing herself, she turned around to face him. "Raul."

20

CRIME DEN

1130 hours CST

"*Dios mio*, I'd recognize that ass anywhere." Raul whistled. He leaned against the doorjamb, arms and legs crossed, his eyes sparkling with amusement. His dark hair was cut short, professionally, within the last few days by the clean lines. Uncharacteristically dressed in a button-down shirt and dark slacks, totally out of place on him. Even his brown shoes reflected the dingy light of the room. A far cry from his Latino gangster phase. Had their paths crossed on the street, she would have walked right past him.

He had been Lysandra's first genuine friend and probably only true boyfriend. He had been there when she discovered her telekinetics. Raul had been her comfort and refuge when her father had been cruel. A safe space and happy place rolled into one. They had helped each other through the worst years of their lives.

After his family had been deported, they only had each other. For years they stayed together through several criminal networks. They finally broke up when he wanted to work for an up-and-coming crime boss who she thought too cruel and unpredictable. That was ten years ago. She had not seen or heard from him since. "What the hell are you doing here?"

"Gregory called me last night and said to come in today. Didn't say why. You know how it is with him, *corazón*."

Every time he said something in Spanish, it sent a tingle down the back of her neck. This is why she should have waited to call ahead of their arrival. Gregory clearly knew Raul would throw her off balance. Bastard. "When did you start working for Gregory?"

Raul shrugged. "Almost a year now."

Shock streaked through her. If she had never done the DPA job, she could have been working with him again. Her eyes flicked in his direction as she realized this. He gave her a knowing smile. Had he come to Gregory looking for her? "Have you been stalking me, Mr. Reyes?"

"Don't flatter yourself, Miss Stephens." A smile hinted at the corner of his mouth.

"That's not my name anymore."

"It is to me." Raul swaggered over to where she stood. "It doesn't take long for word to travel that a woman has walked into the building."

"Yes, well, Gregory always has made it a bit of a boys club."

"Somehow, I knew it was you." He regarded her with hooded eyes.

"And how is that?" She crossed her arms and squared her shoulders.

"Well, the security feed mostly." He smiled at his own cleverness.

Nick forced his way between them with his elbow first and then his whole body. With a hand on Raul's shoulder, he looked at her. "Raul, here, had nowhere else to go." Nick pushed the two apart and shot a look at Raul. "Why don't you tell our client what brought you to the Agency."

"Nah. It's not nearly as exciting as Lysandra's life as a government agent." He gave his classic I-told-you-so smile. A smile that got under her skin, and he knew it too. He knew she hated government as a general rule, and to now be an employee of one was laughable. It had been years since the last time she had seen Raul, worked side by side with him, and even now, that look made her want to do violent things to him.

Lysandra-Esben turned aside, nonchalantly pretending to be interested in the peeling paint. "At least you can put all that stalking practice to good use."

"Is that why Gregory wants to see us in the control booth?" Raul looked between the two of them.

Nick frowned. "Is that why you came down here?"

"He said I was needed for a job and to go bring Nick and 'our guest' up."

Nick growled and flicked Raul on the shoulder. "Don't keep Gregory waiting. Let's go."

Lysandra-Esben bent down to grab the duffel bag and backpack. As she gripped the handle of the duffel bag, Raul leaned close to her and put his hand over hers. "Not on my watch, *mi cielo*." He pulled the bag from her grasp and slung it over his shoulder.

Heat flushed into her cheeks and neck. It had been years since she had heard that word and never from anyone else other than him. She clutched the backpack tightly and refused to look at him as she brushed past him and out of the green room.

Esben paced around the miniature theater. Watching that man flirt with Lysandra irked him. It was hard to tell which event was more agitating, being locked in the mental prison or watching her reconnect with the street thug. Keeping her in check had been tentative at best. He had been prepared for the likes of Gregory, but Raul had taken Esben by surprise. Lysandra had so thoroughly banished Raul from her mind that Esben had no idea that he existed. Raul's voice alone had been enough to dredge up all her old memories of him, and in an instant, Esben found himself confined to the mental theater.

So far, this trash heap of a secret hideout and every person encountered were so emotionally charged for her. Esben had never encountered anything like it before. Esben was in awe of her ability to keep her emotions under wraps. Since he had no emotional connection to any of this, it would be better for him to be in control. Wresting control from her when she least expected it could result in severe damage to her neural pathways. For now, he would have to wait for a window of opportunity. He wasn't even sure she remembered why she was here at all.

The room shifted and they were on the move. Esben took a seat in the lone chair so he could focus.

Nick barreled down the corridors, the light from the flashlight jumping erratically as he went. Raul and Lysandra stayed close behind him. Because she had spent years at this location before landing at the DPA, Esben understood that Nick was leading them to the control booth at the top of the nosebleed section, which required a lot of stairs to get to. Even though Lysandra was looking at her feet as she walked most of the time, it was easy for Esben to see Raul in her periphery, stealing glances at her every couple of steps. She knew when Raul was watching her, a few times for her own satisfaction, Lysandra intentionally looked over to catch him in the act. Each time she did, the reward center of her brain released a burst of endorphins.

She stole a few glances at Raul herself, and every time, it set off a chain reaction across several areas in her brain and totally hijacked her amygdala. As they ascended the steps, memories from her teens and twenties popped up at random, causing fireworks of brain activity. Having their first kiss, laughing with his family at the dinner table, confronting her father. Nostalgia was threatening everything Esben hoped to accomplish. Now that those memories were out in the open, Esben knew Raul was a top-rate hacker and could prove to be a valuable asset.

They finally came to the booth door. The enclosed interior of the booth was lit solely by a wall of monitors that lined up along what would have been the lighting and sound boards in a working theater. Billy and Devin were both staring at the screens and tapping away on keyboards in their laps when Nick, Lysandra, and Raul came in. Even seeing Billy and Devin together again jolted her. The last encounter with her old teammates had left her several injuries, though most of those were dealt by Nick. Her animosity toward him grew every time the two of them talked.

Gregory came into the booth from the door on the opposite side. He tapped Devin and Billy on their shoulders and stood between them, facing the group. Nick, Lysandra, and Raul all leaned against the cushioned back wall facing them, the cavern of the theater as the backdrop behind Gregory and the hackers.

"Since we're all old friends here, this will be the team." Gregory looked at Lysandra. "That is, if her highness here approves."

Lysandra looked over at Billy and Devin. She was confident of their abilities, and it helped that she intimidated them. Then she glanced at Nick. "Be on your way, Miller. I'll be overseeing this operation."

"Hardly, darlin'." He pulled out a cigarette and his engraved Zippo lighter. "I run the op, or you get none of us."

Lysandra stood up straight. "Don't you trust your colleagues?"

"It's got nothing to do with them." He lowered his gaze at her and lit the cigarette.

Gregory cleared his throat. "Nick will be the point person. Now lay out your master plan, so everyone knows what they will be doing."

Lysandra's cortisol levels surged. "Fine." She cracked her knuckles "Phase one, writing a self-replicating code. Phase two, embedding the code in as many places as possible, but I do have a few specific targets to hit. Third, I need some hardware built and installed at one or more of the targets."

Raul rolled along the wall to face her. "To what end, *Cariño?*"

Lysandra cracked the knuckles in her other hand. "The end result is none of your business, Mr. Reyes."

Raul clicked his tongue. "We can't write code if we don't know what it's for."

Lysandra turned her back to Raul to face Nick. "For the sake of deniability, I think each part should be explained only to those directly involved in each specific piece. Besides, each person is going to have to act independently with little to no communication."

Nick took a drag of his cigarette. "And how will we get into each of these places?"

Lysandra pulled a portal anchor card from her pocket and pushed the activation button. An iridescent disc materialized a few feet in front of her. The brilliant white light made everyone in the room block their eyes.

"Oh god," Billy cried in exasperation. "Not this again." He put his head down on the edge of the monitor bank.

Gregory approached as close as he could to the two-dimensional anomaly. "This will get us into anywhere?"

Lysandra shrugged. "There are a few rules to how they have to work but nothing we can't get around with a little planning."

Gregory tore his gaze from the light to look at Lysandra. "You are full of surprises today."

Lysandra closed the portal and turned squarely to Gregory. "Do we have a deal?"

He smiled, his eyes wandering to the backpack of money at her feet. "Nick, go prep the gear while the techies are briefed."

"You've got to be fucking kidding me." He threw his cigarette on the carpet and smothered it with the heel of his boot. Nick looked past her to Gregory. "Do not trust this one, Gregory. You'll regret it." Gregory waved him out of the booth, Nick grumbling as he went.

Nick's absence had an immediate effect. Lysandra's blood pressure dropped and her muscles relaxed the most they had all morning. Since she started talking about the details of the job, her adrenaline had tapered off too.

The dark velvet walls of the theater shimmered with iridescent light. That was new. Esben went to the edge of the room and pulled the curtain back in a few places. Still no door. He pushed against the wall. The surface gave way, stretching as he applied more force. Also, a new development.

He leaned against the mental construct with his full weight. The chandelier above flickered. Rays of white light burst between his fingers and his hands disappeared into the wall as he fell forward.

The room shifted abruptly under Lysandra's feet, and she stumbled backward. She reached out for the wall to steady herself and missed.

"*Mi celio.*" Raul caught her arm and pulled her toward him. Her head narrowly missed the edge of the monitor station as she crashed into him.

That word again. It sent another shockwave across both spheres of Lysandra's brain and straight into her amygdala. Exactly the opening Esben needed. He was very aware of the heat from Raul's body. Esben looked up into Raul's face as Lysandra now.

"Are you alright?" Raul's face etched with concern.

"Get away from me, hombre." Esben-Lysandra pushed him viciously.

Raul's cheeks burned red as he stood up and started mumbling in Spanish. Lysandra was still disoriented from the switch back to the mental theater to translate his rant. When she said nothing, Raul moved to the far end of the room and leaned against the wall, arms crossed.

The booth had gone quiet. Esben-Lysandra realized that Gregory was observing her with a gleam in his eyes and a smirk on his face. He was most dangerous when he was silent. He had to know something was different with her for sure. She stood up and dusted herself off. "It's all the black mold in here. How you all aren't dead yet from it is a mystery."

Gregory took out a pack of cigarettes. He offered the pack to her. Esben tried not to react, but he saw it on Gregory's face. She must have frowned. Edward had never smoked, and Lysandra had quit months ago. If she didn't take one, Gregory would be even more suspicious. She took one anyway. He lit hers and then his.

"It feels weird smoking inside again. Can't do that anywhere in California." She took a drag off of the vile thing. The visceral effect made Esben's head spin. It had been a while for Lysandra and he could feel her relaxing already.

Gregory did not take his eyes off her as he smoked his. "How would you assess the level of difficulty for the installation phase, Miss Government Agent?"

Esben-Lysandra ignored his taunt. "For that phase, we will break up into teams to hit multiple targets at once using the portal technology."

"We?" Gregory cocked a smile. "I told you, you're the client. You pay us to get our hands dirty while you drink cocktails from a safe distance."

Esben-Lysandra kept her posture casual. Control in front of a lunatic like Gregory was paramount. "Wrong."

That would not go over well. Gregory was not used to people dismissing him. That ended in a world of hurt for most people. The micro muscles in his face twitched as he kept himself in check.

She continued, "I will be overseeing the execution of each part. I can't be seen at any of the target sites, but I will be calling the shots."

Raul raised his hand. "With so many pieces, chances are one of them will fail."

"Redundancy and proliferation are built into the plan. If one part fails, that is not ideal but not the end of the world. Since I don't know enough about computers, I am relying on you guys to come up with creative ways to spread the code. We're going to include some of the most used software, but it can't stop there."

Billy raised his hand. "But what is the code for?"

Esben-Lysandra smiled. "I'm glad you asked." She reached for her backpack.

The lights in the booth flickered and went out. Even the stage lights way down at the front of the house were gone too, leaving them in absolute darkness. All of them could hear muffled banging and clanking echo from afar. A cell phone in front of Devin lit up. One word: raid.

Gregory held up his cell phone flash to illuminate the dense darkness of the booth. "Scrub this place, now."

Raul, Devin, and Billy scrambled into action. Devin pulled a stack of empty backpacks from under the control consul and threw them in the middle of the floor. Raul and Billy grabbed a few and immediately started shoving computers and equipment into them.

Devin started typing away. "I'll start the Cole Protocol."

"What's a Cole Protocol?" Esben-Lysandra asked as she watched Devin.

"We can't take everything. What's left behind has to be wiped out." He closed the computer and stuffed it into a bag. He quickly grabbed a spray bottle from underneath and tossed it to her. "Spray anything that might have fingerprints."

Esben-Lysandra threw on her backpack and spritzed the whole console in front of her. This had to be a coincidence. Even if the DPA had guessed where she was going, there was no way they could have tracked her here. They would need to double-check all the gear she had stolen later for trackers.

Gregory opened the window that looked out over the seats. Now the horde of footsteps could be easily heard. He unhooked his holster and pulled out his gun as several beams of light spilled out into the stage.

The beam of a flashlight came up the stairs toward them. "PD," Nick shouted as he leaped up the stairs in great bounds. "We can't go back that way."

He crashed into the booth and shut the door behind him, dropping a metal crossbar across the center of the door. "Let's go, people." He dashed to the other side of the booth and yanked open the door. "Move."

Gregory went first, gun drawn, followed by Devin, Billy, and then Raul, all weighed down with equipment. Esben-Lysandra grabbed the duffel bag and slung it over her shoulder. It was cumbersome, but they absolutely needed everything in it to complete their plan.

"You too, sweetheart." Nick pushed her out the door.

He closed the door behind them as banging erupted from the other side of the booth. Hooks for a crossbar were on this side of the door as well. Nick grabbed a piece of metal pipe that had been behind the door and dropped it into the braces.

As he turned to run down the steps, Esben-Lysandra pushed him up against the door and pinned him there with her forearm. "You have something I need." She reached into his pocket and fished out the clip for her gun.

Now that she had her ammo, she pulled out her gun from the holster and loaded the clip.

Nick tried to push her off, but Esben-Lysandra made sure to press into his chest enough to restrict his breathing. She flipped the safety off. "Eye for an eye."

"You are one cold-hearted bitch," he sneered.

Esben-Lysandra fired a single bullet into Nick's gut, about where he had shot her.

Several flashlights from the seats below swung in her direction. Nick cried in agony, as she let him drop to the ground, clutching his side, and she ran down the steps after the others. Gunshots rang out in other parts of the theater as Gregory's other minions evacuated. All those nameless members of Gregory's network would be a great distraction for their escape.

She crashed into a door at the bottom of the steps and pressed the push bar. She fell into a dimly lit hallway. Gregory's hand pulled her forward by the throat and slammed her into the wall.

"Did you bring them? Whose side are you on, officer?"

Esben-Lysandra planted her hands at the center of Gregory's chest. His mocking sneer told her he was unimpressed. In a flash, Esben moved into Lysandra's hands and pushed an electrical charge into Gregory's chest. His eyes widened as the heat from her hands burned into him. Gregory fell backward and rolled onto the carpet in spasms.

Lysandra half-collapsed, suddenly aware of the stale air suffocating her. The jumble of sounds was coming from several directions: people shouting, random gunfire, pounding of all kinds. She was in control again. A low-grade burning boiled under the skin of her hands, causing a string of involuntary obscenities to come out of her. She could feel Esben energizing her whole body.

More shots were fired from the direction of the control booth. An agonized cry made both her and Gregory look back.

"Hey, *vamanos.*" Raul appeared from a hallway. "What the hell?" Raul glared at the two of them in disbelief.

Gregory struggled to his feet. He set his bloodshot stare on Lysandra-Esben, ready to murder her, no doubt. She wasn't going to take any chances. She sprang forward, burying her shoulder in the same spot Esben had burned. Gregory flew back into the wall.

"Freeze!" Two police officers burst through the door they had escaped from. Raul broke into a sprint with Lysandra-Esben right behind him. Gregory roared in anger.

Lysandra-Esben focused hard on the steps as she raced down more stairs with only a few footlights to help her from tripping. She could have passed Raul, but she was armed, making her the cover for their escape.

"Come on!" Billy shouted from a dark recess at the bottom.

"Freeze." The command came from behind them on the stairs. A fired shot pinged above her head, sparking off a wall sconce.

Billy pulled them through the entry and slammed the door shut behind them, barricading it like the booth door. Now they were out in one of the side hallways. Devin held open a backstage door, a faded sign telling people "Cast Only."

"Where are we going?" Lysandra-Esben tried to keep an eye on their six.

"The exit," Billy said like an exasperated teenager.

"I have our exit with me." Lysandra-Esben did another rearguard check.

Billy pulled back a heavy black curtain, turned around, and started going down into a dark hole backward. "Well, let's go then!" And he disappeared.

A barrage of bangs thundered against the last door.

Devin descended down into the dark room below.

Bullets penetrated the wood frame.

"Do your mind thing." Raul turned around, stepping down onto the first rung of the ladder below.

"Mind thing?"

"You know, moving stuff around."

Raul knew her secret, of course. He knew more of her secrets than anyone except for Esben, probably. "There's no time. Go!" She started down into the dark and dropped the heavy black curtain over their exit.

Plunged once again into total darkness, she could hear footsteps ahead of her but also above her. Officers shouted at each other.

"Stop!" she whispered loudly. "We don't need to go anywhere."

"What are you talking about, woman?" Raul's voice was closer than she expected.

Someone grabbed her arm. Lysandra-Esben pulled her arm free. "Give me a light, damn it."

Raul grunted in frustration. After some rustling and a metallic scrape, a small orange flame appeared.

She searched her pockets. "Where are the other two?"

Raul swung the lighter around, casting the wavering light behind him. The faintest outline of Devin and Billy's faces could be made out at the back. Raul waved them forward.

"Lysandra." Edward's voice echoed from somewhere above; he had to be on the stage. She froze. A pang of guilt stabbed in her chest. What was he doing here? He should have stayed out of it.

"Hey, what's the plan here?" Raul shook her.

"Esben," Edward called, his voice nearer.

"Sorry." Lysandra-Esben shook her head. "This." She held up the anchor card she had used up in the booth and pressed the activation button. The disc of iridescent light bloomed once again in the middle of the room, blinding them all. Its dancing colors shed light on the underside of the stage with all gears and pulleys used once upon a time for creating stage illusions, now in shambles from years of disuse.

Lysandra-Esben pulled on the straps over her shoulders. The bags were getting heavier by the second. "Time to go, boys."

"Ladies first." Raul stayed back from it.

"I have the anchor; I have to go last." She tried to push Billy through it, but he rolled off her hands and back into the dark.

"Esben," Edward called again, only this time his voice hit the floorboards directly overhead.

Lysandra-Esben grabbed Raul by the shirt. "You have to walk into it." She pushed him into the light "Go!" she whispered harshly at Devin and Billy.

A few feet from her side, a sharp clicking sound a few feet away followed, but the scrape of old hinges pierced her ears. New sources of light shot down onto her as part of the floor opened.

"Officer Carlisle," Eriksson barked from above.

Lysandra-Esben squinted up at the shadowed figures of Commander Eriksson and Edward side by side. She waved her cohorts forward, grabbing at their clothing and pushing them along as they argued with each other in tense whispers.

"Lysandra, thank god." Edward knelt and lowered his hand to her.

Another pang of guilt spiked in her chest. They had both betrayed Edward's trust. Again. Esben could try to take the blame all he wanted, but she certainly deserved some of it.

"Lysandra." Edward leaned as far forward as he could. His green eyes pleaded with her, urging her to come with him. Pain gave way to a flush of heat. To be with Edward was truly the one thing in the world she wanted. Had helping Esben jeopardized that? A renewed wave of guilt hit her. She lost all sense of her surroundings.

Esben-Lysandra backed away from him. Commander Eriksson left, his footsteps banging across the stage at a fast clip and fading into the distance.

Edward glanced at the portal. "Esben, whatever it is you're trying to accomplish, let me help you."

She took another step back. The energy of the portal tingled on the back of her neck. "I'm not sure you would."

"All you had to do was ask." Edward pulled his hand back. "You don't have to go through any of this."

"You don't have the resources to get me what I want. She does."

"What makes you think I would have stopped you? When have I ever gotten in your way?"

"Don't make me choose. The more you interfere, the more it will force my hand. So don't."

Flashlight beams came from the back of the room. "Carlisle, don't move," Commander Eriksson ordered in a military tone.

Arms reached through the portal and pulled her backward through the wall of light by the waist. Edward's face burned from sight as the world flashed white for a second.

"Lysandra!" Edward's voice traveled through the breach. The world spun for a second as she crashed to the ground with someone under her. The prism colors of the portal disappeared, and everything went dark again.

21

ARCADIA, CA

0930 hours PST

Amid the flailing of limbs, Esben-Lysandra fumbled for the portal card and pressed the button to close the doorway linking Chicago and Arcadia. There was a jumble of exclamations, but Esben was still too disoriented to know what exactly was happening.

The thirty-second encounter with Edward had disrupted Lysandra enough that Esben had been able to wrest control back of her body. Until Lysandra could regulate her reactions to Raul, Esben would need to steer the ship. He had no doubt she would let him know her displeasure at this arrangement, but he could handle it.

As Esben-Lysandra's eyes adjusted to the low interior light, the shapes and smell of a living room came into focus. The smell of the house, the arrangement of the furniture had not been changed since the last time Esben had been here. Everything about this auxiliary home felt completely right to both of them.

"Aye, *mi cariño*," Raul said from under her. Raul's hands gripped her waist. With her elbow, she pushed him back and rolled onto the floor.

"Why you mad at me? I ain't the one on top of other people." Raul pushed the duffel bag off his lap.

"Grow up." Esben-Lysandra lifted the duffel bag strap over her head and left the bag on the floor as she stood.

Smoothing her clothes, she took in their new surroundings. As they reoriented, Esben shared Lysandra's sense of familiarity and fondness for the space. Esben had intended to use the house from the start; that was why they mailed the watch here. What he had not expected was for the house to have such a profound effect on her. This was not her childhood home, nor Brendan's. It was an empty vacation rental her mother owned and yet something about the house had completely arrested her.

When the Elbie first arrived, this place had been their retreat. It had been one of the first places Esben was acquainted with when Brendan was his host. This was not the first time she had the feeling of things being both familiar and new. The last time it had been her memories that had been tampered with. This time it was all tied to what Esben recalled as Brendan. Now that they were here, the strange familiarity gave them a sense of peace. Stability.

"Where are we? Where are we?" Billy walked around the room in long strides past bookshelves, the fireplace, the couch, as he alternately ran his hands through his hair and chewed his nails.

Dusting himself off as he stood, Raul went over to the front door to a puffy envelope on the floor below the mail slot. Turning it over, he read the address. "Arcadia. Who's Susan Carlisle?"

Billy pulled on his hair as he circled the room. "Where's Arcadia?"

"California." Raul set the envelope on the end table and slowly surveyed his surroundings. "Let me guess, your childhood home?" He wiped a layer of dust off the TV as he walked by it.

She glared at him. She and Raul had grown up together. "You know it's not. This is where my brothers grew up, sort of. More importantly, it is the last place on earth anyone will look for us. We will be setting up our base of operations."

Raul blew the dust off some books. "Is this anywhere near the targets we are after?"

Esben-Lysandra walked over to the end table and picked up the puffy envelope. "As you have just experienced, distance is relative."

"Hang on a minute." Devin set the gear down on the coffee table. "What happened to Nick and Gregory?"

Raul sat on the couch and stretched his arms along the back of it. "Go ahead, Lysandra. Tell them what you did." He stretched his legs out and dropped his feet on the coffee table with a smile.

"Nick will not be joining us." She ripped open the envelope and pulled out her watch. "Gregory does not have any of the skills we need. He would only be a distraction."

Raul put his hands behind his head. "If either of them are captured, they will be questioned, and this whole party could be over before it gets good."

Esben-Lysandra shrugged. "All they know is that I needed hackers. Thanks to the DPA's brilliant timing, they don't know why or what the targets are."

"Nick will never forgive you for it." Devin went into the kitchen and opened the fridge.

"Then we're even."

Raul clicked his tongue. "Gregory will seek retribution for ditching him."

"Spilt milk. Moving on." Esben-Lysandra put on the watch. "Which leads me to our next step. Devin. Billy." She waved them over to the couch. "We are going to pick up where we left off." She took off her backpack and set it on the coffee table. Devin came into the room and sat on the couch with Raul. Billy settled next to Devin.

Esben-Lysandra dug the containment unit out from the backpack and placed it on the coffee table in front of them. Qur'ag floated in blissful isolation within the glass confinement. She had no idea if any of them had ever encountered Elbie before. Chances were they had not. They most certainly would have heard of Elbie, but their opinions about Elbie were another matter.

"Okay." With her hand still on the top of the device, she leveled her gaze at them. "We have three objectives. The first is writing some code. Then we have to infiltrate the targets—Google, Microsoft, and Apple—as quickly as possible to plant the code into each of their systems in such a way that the code is then sent out to their users in the next software update. Lastly, install the hardware that Raul and I will be building."

"Hardware for what? And where is it being installed?" Billy pushed himself into the back of the couch.

"Do you know what this little thing is?" Esben-Lysandra patted the top of the container.

Devin and Billy looked at each other for the answer, but neither blurted a response. When it was clear they had no idea, Devin leaned forward. "Can I touch it?"

"Sure." Esben-Lysandra removed her hand.

Devin touched the curve of the glass with the back of his hand. The glass would be slightly warm to the touch, but nothing more. Immediately he picked it up, closely examining the mechanics of it. The angle or position of the glass tube did not affect the light inside. The artificial gravity well would keep in the precise center, no matter how he held the device.

Meanwhile, Billy had moved away from Devin. "If that came from your bag of tricks from the DPA, then I don't want to have anything to do with it." He perched on the arm of the couch, ready to bolt.

"Is it?" Devin glanced up at her for a second but went back to turning the glass in several directions. "What are they called again? Lightning bugs?"

Clearly, Devin would be easier to convince than Billy.

"Yes. That is what they are called by some people." Esben-Lysandra turned to Billy. "You are already in deep on this one, I'm afraid. Since you're already on the DPA's wanted list for the break-in last year.

You know, where you all ditched me."

"That's not how Nick tells it." Raul glanced at the light in the glass before smirking at her.

"*Escucha.*" Esben-Lysandra snapped at Raul. "Write the code, build the devices, infiltrate the targets. Everyone goes their merry way."

"You really think that, *mi celio?*" Raul sat forward, scowling at her. "Do you honestly believe that your commanding officer will welcome you back into the ranks after all of this?"

"That's none of your concern."

Raul put his hands in the air in surrender, shaking his head, mumbling under his breath.

Esben-Lysandra followed Billy as he started to circle the room in his agitated state. "Needless to say, this second infraction of helping me out now will move you and Devin up their most-wanted list for sure."

Billy's eyes started darting between all the doors and windows in the room. "How come Raul is exempt from their list?"

"Raul hasn't been seen by them; he isn't on their radar at all."

"That's hardly fair."

"You're a black hat. I'm not sure *fair* is something you can complain about. Would you relax?" Esben-Lysandra moved toward Billy. "Sit!"

Billy sat heavily on a loveseat against the stairs going up to the second floor. Esben-Lysandra moved back so that she could see all three of them. "Here's the deal. Once we're ready for the infiltration phase, each of you will need to carry an Elbie with you to plant the code."

Devin finally set the containment unit down and rested his chin on his knees, staring at the point of light. "You have more of these glass things?"

"No." She shook her head. "You will be the carrier. The Elbie will be in your body. No incriminating or bulky devices needed."

Billy began to shake his head and crack his knuckles.

"Look, I know it's intimidating. But it's perfectly safe." She tapped her temple. "I'm telling you, asking for your cooperation, because if you can work with the Elbie, things will go a lot smoother."

Billy hung his head with an agonized sigh, hands on each side.

Raul laughed. Anger or annoyance must have flashed across her face because he started to laugh harder. Esben sent a signal to Lysandra's brain to pump out oxytocin to keep her calm. "Something wrong, Raul?"

Wiping tears from his eyes, he stood. "Yeah. You."

Esben-Lysandra crossed her arms. "What are you talking about?"

Raul mimicked her stance. "You're such a hypocrite."

She sighed. Esben had no idea what Raul was talking about. Lysandra was in a state of disbelief.

Raul rolled his eyes. "You left because you didn't want to work for a human trafficker. That was the one line you wouldn't cross, and here you are, ten years later, doing it to us."

"Firstly, Raul, you all volunteered for this job. A job you're getting paid for. Secondly, no one is being forced to do anything here."

"Billy doesn't want one of those things." Raul pointed at the containment unit.

"When the time comes, if Billy still doesn't want one, that's fine—a person can carry multiple Elbie."

"Fine. Whatever you say, *chica*." Raul sat back down and stretched his arms across the back of the couch. "What does our code have to do with those things?"

"That code will cover up any record of an Elbie intrusion so that they can travel anywhere they want across the internet without being detected. If needed, removing security and firewall protocols from each type of OS and as many programs as possible would be good too."

"Oh, is that all?" Raul shook his head.

"Beautiful." Devin shifted the containment unit.

"What!?" Billy popped his head up. "You want to release those things onto the net?"

Esben-Lysandra turned with him, and he went along. "If Elbie could be in people or computers, which would you choose?"

Billy shook his head. "I don't want that kind of responsibility. No way." He looked at the containment unit in horror.

"Alright, Billy." Esben-Lysandra pushed an ottoman toward him and sat down. "Let's get this all on the table. What have you heard?"

Wringing his hands, he swallowed hard. "Okay. Sure. They delete your memories and you become a kind of zombie."

"Well, first, memories can't be erased. Sometimes Elbie might bury memories so that the host doesn't know what has happened, but usually, it's for the protection of the host. A kind of built-in plausible deniability."

He nodded slowly. "Okay. What about the zombie part?"

"If you treat it like a partnership, that's what it will be. Some people choose to take a passenger role, but if you want to be the driver at any time, you can start driving again."

"Zombie optional?"

"I feel like *zombie* means you have no input, and that is not possible. You are present with the Elbie the entire time. Did you know that with an Elbie you can think better? You'll be stronger too."

Billy shook his head.

"See." Esben-Lysandra slapped her knee. "You've only heard all the bad stuff. With an Elbie, you can't get hurt. You sleep less but better. More energy and hours for all-night gaming."

"Are you sure?" Billy looked to Raul and Devin for confirmation. Raul looked away while Devin shrugged his shoulders. "That doesn't sound too bad."

"I know, right?" Esben-Lysandra smiled. "It can be kind of fun. I'm not gonna lie, it feels pretty good too."

"Like how?"

Esben-Lysandra thought about it. "It's like that moment when you've completed a legendary level campaign with your online comrades and you take that first sip of icy cold Mountain Dew. Only that feeling is there all the time."

Billy stopped himself from smiling. "I'm not sure. How do I know you're not lying to me?"

"Billy. It's me… Lysandra. You've put your career in the hands of men like Gregory and Nick, two of the most wretched people you can know, but you're gonna question me?" Esben-Lysandra looked down at her hands. "I thought we were friends."

Raul laughed.

Esben-Lysandra gave him an angry glare, shutting him up immediately.

"Besides." Esben-Lysandra put a hand on Billy's shoulder. "It's temporary. I bet you'll be bummed when it's gone."

Billy cracked his knuckles again. "I'll think about it."

"Excellent. You don't need one while writing code anyhow; you have time to get used to the idea."

Raul sat forward on the edge of the couch with his eyes riveted to her. "Who's Ezban?"

"Where'd you hear that name?" Esben-Lysandra narrowed her eyes at him.

"At the theater, some guy called it out when you didn't answer."

Esben-Lysandra stared Raul down. He seemed like he genuinely wanted to know, and there was no reason to hide the information. "Esben is the name of the Elbie I'm carrying."

Billy shrugged her hand off his shoulder and moved away. "Carrying, right now?"

"I knew it!" Raul jumped up again, mumbling to himself in Spanish. "I knew there was something wrong with you. Is that why you're being such a bitch?"

Esben-Lysandra cocked her head. "It's your total lack of unprofessionalism that I find to be most irksome. Wouldn't you agree, *Lindo*? I mean, that is what you were going for. Was it not annoying?"

"I was going for charming."

"You failed." Esben-Lysandra's pronouncement did nothing to diminish Raul's self-satisfied grin.

Devin picked up the containment unit. "I get one of these?"

Esben-Lysandra nodded.

Not taking his eyes from the luminous orb, a smile spread across his face, "Let's get started."

22

CHICAGO GENERAL HOSPITAL

1200 hours CST

Chicago PD stationed a guard outside the room. Eriksson didn't think anyone would come for his suspect, but making sure the suspect stayed in custody was valuable. Nick Miller was their only link to Lysandra at the moment. Time was running out. Eriksson stood over the patient's bed and waved smelling salts under the man's nose.

Nick jumped awake, rattling the restraints on his wrists and ankles. His eyes widened as he saw Eriksson and looked around the room for some hint of where he was.

Eriksson capped the bottle on the salts and moved to the foot of the bed where he could have the best eye contact. "Do you know who I am, Mr. Miller?"

Nick's eyes searched him. Since Eriksson was in civilian clothing, there were no blatant indicators of who he was, but since Nick had already cased the DPA once, Eriksson figured he should know him.

"Ex-military, by the way you stand."

"I'm the co-commander of the DPA. I believe you've heard of us."

Nick paused for a moment. "You're Lysandra's boss." A slight smile on his lips.

"Her new boss, yes."

"Lucky man." Nick relaxed into the pillows with a wince.

"Why did she shoot you?"

"How do you know it wasn't someone from your raiding party?"

"The bullet they pulled out of your gut is one of hers. That and the commonly known fact that the DPA does not use bullets. All of our weapons are energy based and most likely will not kill a person."

Nick nodded. "Then I would say poor judgment on her part." He shrugged. "I would have done the same thing if the tables were turned, so who am I to judge?"

"Why would she risk having you fall into custody?"

"Vendetta."

"You think Lysandra would jeopardize her plans just to get back at you?"

"I think you have the answer to that question already." Nick chuckled to himself. "The woman has a temper."

Eriksson stared at him. He was entirely too comfortable with all of this. Being in the custody of the DPA meant federal charges as severe as treason. "What do you know about her plans?"

A smile broke out on Nick's face. "Tsk, tsk, commander. Not without my attorney present."

"Mr. Miller, the DPA is a federal organization, and as such, we can invoke special privileges that do not apply in the usual criminal circumstances you would be accustomed to."

Nick's smile faded. "I still get a goddamn attorney."

Ignoring him, Eriksson went to the door and opened it. Edward Drake and Agent Ian Reynolds walked in. "I believe you know who these men are." A moment of recognition passed over Nick's features, but he recovered quickly. Eriksson took out his phone and pulled up a picture of an Elbie. "Both of them carry one of these." He held the phone up for Nick to see. "You've seen something like these before?"

Nick shut his gaping mouth. "I don't have to say nothin' until my attorney's present." He looked over at Edward. "You been one of them this whole time?"

Edward nodded gravely. He didn't have an Elbie at the moment, but Nick had no way of knowing that. Eriksson leaned on the footboard with both hands. "All it takes is one. They go straight into your brain, rummage around that trash heap until they find the memories—"

"It wouldn't be admissible evidence."

"I'm not interested in putting you on trial, Mr. Miller. I need to know what Lysandra is up to so I can find her." Nick stared at Edward and Ian and swallowed hard. Eriksson hoped that all the sensational stories about Elbie that got played up in the media were filling Nick's head. "You can tell me what you know, or they can go in and get it. Cooperation can only help you."

Nick turned from them and stared at Eriksson with smoldering anger. This was child's play for Eriksson; he could stare the man down all day, but it would not be needed.

"Does it change you?" Nick asked, his voice unexpectedly quiet.

Eriksson blinked, his shoulders relaxing slightly. "Change you?"

"Yeah. Lysandra, she was different."

Eriksson frowned. He did not like the sound of that. "Is it possible she was not in control of herself?"

Edward moved toward the bed. "How was she different?"

Nick looked out the window for a few seconds and shook his head. "Harder. More calculating." His eyes flicked to Edward for a second. "Cold."

Eriksson and Edward exchanged looks. Her change in demeanor was strong evidence that Esben was acting on his own as the instigator of it all, but again, he would not get far without her cooperation. Eriksson thought about all the hosts he did know. Draegg and Rewlos had become so integrated with their people it was impossible to tell who was in control. It didn't really matter either when it got to that level. That was how it had been for Edward and Esben, but something had changed with Esben.

Eriksson turned his attention back to the suspect. "Mr. Miller, why did Lysandra come to you guys?"

Nick rested his head on the pillow.

"Agent Reynolds." Erikson waved Ian forward. "Please proceed."

"Yes sir." Ian took off his jacket. As he uncuffed his sleeves and rolled them up, he stared menacingly at Nick. Ian clapped his hands together and gave them a quick rub, all the while keeping his eyes on Nick. After a deep breath, Ian moved toward the bed with his palms facing outward. Eriksson had instructed him to make a show of it.

Nick sat up and moved away from the agent as much as he could with the restraints on. "I want my phone call."

"You won't even remember this happening." Eriksson gave Nick a tight smile.

The restraints rattled as Nick attempted to pull his hands free. In vain.

Ian leaned over the railing and reached for Nick's head. "Please hold still." Ian touched the top of Nick's head.

"Code!" Nick blurted out, pushing himself into the pillows as much as possible. "She needed someone to write some self-replicating code."

Eriksson put his hand on Ian's shoulder, pulling him back only slightly. "For what?"

Nick shook his head, eyes on Ian's hands, which hovered an inch from his face.

"Anything else?"

"She wanted the code to be shared, like a virus, sent to as many places as possible. She had some specific targets in mind, but—"

"Did she say which ones?"

"She wouldn't tell us. She was only giving a piece of the plan to each person."

Eriksson walked away, pacing in thought. There had to be thousands of possible targets. If only he could figure out Esben's goal, then maybe they could narrow down the options for their next move.

"Call him off."

"Agent Reynolds, stand down." Eriksson came back to the foot of the bed. "Congratulations, Mr. Miller, you will not be charged with treason at this time. You are still under arrest for resisting arrest and whatever else the Chicago PD has on you. If you remember anything more, have the officer outside call me."

Eriksson nodded to Edward and Ian. They walked out of the room. Out in the corridor, Eriksson gave the officer his card. Eriksson, Edward, and Ian started down the hallway.

"Does any of that mean anything to you?" Eriksson asked Ian.

Ian shook his head. "There's still not enough information to go on. A team of us can go onto the dark web and look for anything new, but it would be like looking for a needle in a haystack. Viruses are a dime a dozen there for anyone to pick up."

Eriksson sighed and rubbed his face. They had been so close. "What about the portal? Do we have any way of tracking those?"

"Sorry, sir. Elbie energy can only be detected within close proximity unless it is a high concentration. Since the portals only use a single Elbie, we would have to be pretty close to the end point."

Edward spoke up. "Is it safe to say that wherever they went, it has to be the West Coast? That's where most of the big tech companies are."

"Yes!" Ian said. "They would have to go to Silicon Valley."

Eriksson mulled over the idea of Elbie and tech. The idea of Elbie crossing over with the medical industry had been a natural and immediate idea. Besides Edward's innovation to use Elbie for instantaneous travel, any tech that had been developed was focused on how to control Elbie. Even Brendan's nanotech had been a result of extracting Elbie that refused to leave his body. There was one person who had experience with Elbie and technology. "Do you think Jared Moore would be able to lead us in the right direction?"

Ian stopped walking. "Perhaps," he said after a moment. "But no one has seen or heard from him for years."

The DPA had kept an eye on Jared Moore, as it did with all prior hosts. On the rare occasion he communicated with the outside world, it was through the members of his activist organization. Even so, Jared Moore was probably their best resource, considering his knowledge of computers and history as a host.

"I'll let Draegg know we're headed back to California." Eriksson took out his phone.

The three of them started walking again.

"Sir," Ian said. "Were you really going to make me use my powers on the detainee? And you implied Mr. Drake also had powers."

"Powers?" Edward raised an eyebrow.

Few people understood that Ian lived in a literal fantasy world. His Elbie had created a narrative for Ian, and everything that happened to him was interpreted through the filter of Special Agent Ian Reynolds, the FBI's only superpowered agent. Being unable to fully restore Ian to his former self was one of Eriksson's and

Miranda's biggest regrets. At the time of his injury, creating the fantasy had been the only thing that had gotten a response from an otherwise vegetative Ian. "No, Agent Reynolds, that would have been against our code of conduct. I was counting on the detainee being more afraid of you than his boss."

"I'm relieved the lie worked."

"Me too, Ian. Me too."

23

RENTAL HOUSE

1300 hours PST

Lysandra-Esben had kept a constant appraisal of the street activity all morning. Since she had nothing to do while the others set up their systems, she settled for securing the perimeter. After hijacking several of the neighborhood Wi-Fi networks, Devin and Billy got started on writing the basics of the code. Devin looked up at her, but kept typing as he talked. "I checked the darknet message board, and Gregory would like you to call him."

Lysandra-Esben remembered something about the online communication protocol they had from her days as a member of the group. Since she almost never touched a computer, she always resorted to the rendezvous point or calling into HQ. Like their phone protocol, the message board used coded messages. If an operation went sideways, she could check it, but it was always a pain in the ass. It was a good way to stay in contact without being traced. "Can he tell if you picked up the message?"

"He can't, no."

"Good. Leave it that way. Do not contact him. In fact, let's get rid of our phones. We don't know if he's in custody or not. I don't want the DPA tracing anything."

None of them had eaten for a few hours, and their stomachs were all on East Coast time. They were in desperate need of tools and material to build the device needed to transfer Elbie to the internet. The rental house had almost zero provisions. Time for a raid on the childhood home of her brothers.

It was a quiet neighborhood. Not much happened here, and it was the middle of the day. Two strangers walking around could make some of the neighbors nervous. Lysandra-Esben stood in front of the two hackers. "I will need to borrow a hat and a shirt from you guys."

Both Devin and Billy indicated the pile of gear next to the stairs. All their backpacks and equipment were stacked in a neat pile. When out in the field, it was a good habit to always be ready to move. No unpacking or settling ever. Lysandra-Esben dug into the bags and pulled out one of their baseball hats and a couple of flannel shirts. "Thanks, boys. We should be back in about thirty."

Both were back to typing as Lysandra and Raul had left the room. Out in the living room, Lysandra-Esben wound her hair up and put it under the hat. She put on both flannel shirts to hide her figure.

"Where are we going?" Raul followed her into the kitchen.

"This is the second house my mom owns." She started opening drawers, bending over to look under them. Once upon a time, they kept a spare key at this house as backup. "The first one, where my brothers lived back in the day, is a couple blocks up the street. People are living in that house now, so I am guessing that they will have tools and hopefully some food."

"A good old-fashioned breaking and entering?" Raul perked up.

The two of them had spent their adolescence breaking and entering into all kinds of places. She nodded. "Sort of." After the fifth drawer, she found the spare key taped to the underside of the drawer.

Raul looked crestfallen. "I was hoping to pick the lock."

"You got your tools?"

Raul nodded.

"If they've changed the locks and this secret key no longer works, you're up." She put the key in her pocket. "Let's go." She started for the back sliding glass door that led out into a yard full of dirt, scattered with patches of dead grass. From the periphery of her eye, the shining white door of the fridge arrested her. For a split second, she saw a word written across the front of it, but she did a double-take. There was no writing.

"What's the matter?" Raul flipped the lock on the back door.

"Nothing." She walked around the center island and opened a drawer next to the fridge. A set of colored dry erase markers were lined up inside. "We should bring some bags with us."

"Good thinking." They both searched until they found some old folded-up paper bags and left out the back door.

Donning baseball caps, Esben-Lysandra and Raul exited out the backdoor and made their way up to the main street leading to the Carlisle home. Since it was a sunny day, it would not be totally suspect, and the hats shaded their faces. There weren't a whole lot of people around anyways. An occasional car would pass by, but the drivers never glanced at them.

After walking for a few minutes in silence, Raul finally spoke up. "Do you know where you're going?"

Lysandra-Esben looked up the street. From their approach, she could see Matt's old house. They would have to walk by it to get to the main Carlisle house. Matt's parents still lived there. She could knock on the door right now and meet them. In many ways, Matt's parents had been surrogate parents to Brendan. While Brendan had thought that growing up with only his big brother watching over him was a dream come true, he did love eating dinner at the Holloway's table with Matt and Kristy on either side of him, especially around the holidays. Lysandra could practically taste the baked honey yams now.

"Hey." Raul snapped his fingers in her ear. "Why'd we stop?"

Lysandra-Esben shook herself. So entrenched by the flood of flashbacks, she had stopped walking and was staring at the Holloway house, dead center of the driveway. "Sorry. I thought this was it." She continued walking.

The Carlisle house was only a couple hundred feet away now. Its two stories looked out over the pine trees that surrounded it on three sides. The trees were several feet bigger than in Esben's recollection. As they approached, flashes of images blipped in her mind's eye. As fast as an eye blinking. One second, four kids were racing past them on dirt bikes, and the next, nothing but a quiet neighborhood street. Since none of the memories were her own, she had no emotional ties to anything she saw except to recognize Brendan, Kristy, Matt, and Derek at much younger ages. If she had been around to live life with them, she was not entirely convinced she would have been part of their group.

"Hey." Raul snapped his fingers again. "What is going on with you?"

Lysandra-Esben was looking back down the street where they had come from, just staring at the empty road. "Sorry. I'm really distracted right now."

"Yeah, no kidding." He put his arm around her shoulders and started walking her along. "So we're just gonna walk in?" Raul scanned the street.

"That's the idea." She stared up at the darkened second-story windows where the roof came out underneath. Brendan's favorite stargazing spot. "Act natural." She stood frozen at the end of the driveway.

"There is nothing natural about this." Raul took the key from her hand and guided her toward the house.

They walked up the few steps to the front door like Brendan had done a million times. Raul slipped the key in the lock, unlocked the door with ease, and waltzed into the living room with her in tow.

Raul closed the door behind them. "Knock, knock," he called loudly. "Anybody home? We come in peace."

A hundred-gallon aquarium gurgled as it churned water. No other response.

"Fish tank?" Lysandra-Esben frowned. "Don't like that."

"Should we start in the garage?" Raul opened a door, revealing a coat closet.

She locked the front door. "Try the kitchen first. Stay alert, I'll be right back."

"Where are you going?" He watched her as she sat on the couch.

"Give me a couple of minutes." Lysandra-Esben slumped into the cushions. To Raul, it would look like she was asleep since he had no context for how Elbie interacted with people. Raul would probably freak out if she stayed in this state too long.

Instead of the door-less theater, Lysandra found herself standing in the living room of the Carlisle house as her brothers knew it, the round dining room table covered in glue and cardboard for Halloween costumes. Blanket forts that dominated the living room during movie marathons. As she walked down the hallway, she could examine the photo collages and school photos that lined each side.

Every room of the house had bits of fossils and artifacts, items their mom had sent back from her fieldwork. Not valuable, of course—she was too much of an archeologist to do that—but small tokens mailed home to show that she was thinking about her boys.

Upstairs in Brendan's bedroom, a much younger Brendan and Kristy had holed up for hours with textbooks and notebooks as they prepared for tests or wrote papers. This was a common practice for them, and they had done it for hours all through middle and high school. Each room held some token for Lysandra. Brendan spent his whole life here until he left for college. When college had been sabotaged by their first contact fame, all of them went to live at the DPA.

Esben-Lysandra came back to the real-world living room of the Carlisle house. Lysandra was still absorbing all the scattered memories and residual feelings.

"What just happened?" Raul was leaning against the round dining room table, paper bags filled with groceries next to him.

"How long was I out?" She brushed the hair out of her face and sat up.

"Long enough to raid the kitchen for all the good stuff." Raul looked at his watch. "Fifteen minutes."

"Come on. Tools are this way." She stood up from the couch and headed for the hallway.

Raul followed her down the unadorned hallway. "It all makes sense now."

Esben-Lysandra checked the hall closet as they passed by it. "Be direct. Being passive-aggressive is such a bore."

"Oh my god!" He forced the door closed on her. "Who the hell are you? Because you sure as hell aren't the Lysandra I know."

Esben-Lysandra turned to him.

"That bullshit you fed Billy down there will not work on me, so you better start getting honest with me, or I'm out."

Esben-Lysandra crossed her arms. "I can do honest. If that's what you really want."

Raul's features softened and he narrowed his eyes. "I will not be intimidated by whatever you are."

She smiled. "Good. That would've been disappointing." She stepped closer so that they were only a few inches apart. She could see his muscles twitching as he resisted the urge not to move away from her. "What I told Billy was no sales gimmick. Those things are true." She latched onto his head with both hands.

"What are you doing?" He pulled on her wrists, trying to free himself. His eyes glazed over, and his legs gave out from under him.

Esben-Lysandra held onto his jacket to make sure he didn't fall too fast. "How do you feel now?"

Half sitting, half lying on the ground, Raul blinked into the imagined horizon beyond the walls. "I feel good." A grin grew on his face as the artificial high she had induced unfolded. "Is this what it's like all the time?"

"No." Esben-Lysandra continued toward the garage. The high would last only a few minutes. Meanwhile, she would see what supplies the garage could offer.

Esben-Lysandra opened the door, and the dusty, paint-tainted air of the garage hit her in the face. It smelled as it had when Brendan was growing up. Brendan's workbench had been left exactly as she saw it in the past. Except for the layer of brown dust that covered his gloves, protective apron, and goggles, the workbench appeared like Brendan had just cleaned up after a project. C clamps, pliers of varying kinds and sizes, welding wands, and tongs.

Esben-Lysandra's throat tightened and the room shifted around her. Susan Carlisle may have been an absentee mother, but to leave Brendan's prized possession, his welding workbench, intact and untouched, spoke to a longing and grief that even Esben recognized.

Raul crashed clumsily into the doorjamb, eyes still unfocused. With a lot of effort, he managed to look in her direction. "How did you do that?"

"Elbie can manipulate and control all the chemicals in the human body. Pain relief, sound sleep, runner's high, love, fear."

"What else?" He stumbled down the steps toward her.

She opened up the standing storage cabinets. "Can we use any of this?"

Raul came up behind her, took her by the waist, and pulled her to him. With a still glassy look in his eye, he leaned forward for a kiss.

Esben-Lysandra immediately sucker-punched him in the rib cage. His hands dropped from her as he doubled over, grunting. She stepped away from him. "Do that again and you will wish it was you bleeding out on that rotten theater floor and not Nick."

Raul forced himself to stand, wincing as he did so but smiling. "*Ahí está mi corazón.*"

Esben-Lysandra frowned. "I'm asking for the last time. Stop calling me that."

"*Si, senorita,*" Raul said in a mocking tone, forcing himself to stand straight.

In the strained silence that followed, Raul started to rummage through the high-end toolbox. "What were you doing back there, on the couch? More importantly, will it happen to me?"

She shook her head. "It was a sort of memory download. I had to reconstruct the layout of the house from her brother's memories."

"That's not weird or creepy at all." Raul set aside items for them to take back.

"It comes in handy from time to time." She continued opening boxes and drawers. The whole experience was becoming more emotional for Lysandra than anticipated.

"Sweet." Raul rushed over to a pair of computer towers on the floor. A thick layer of dust covered each of them. "These should give us most of the components we need." He took a Leatherman tool from his pocket and started to pry open the outer casing.

After breaking the computers down into essential pieces, Raul scoured the garage for anything else that could be useful. Neither Lysandra nor Esben had any experience in building hardware, so she gathered all the items Raul designated into bags. They went back into the house to get the groceries.

Leaving the Carlisle house behind, the two of them headed up the street, back to the rental house. Raul clutched the bags to his chest, somewhat obscuring his face. "Hope this neighborhood isn't full of paranoid types."

Esben-Lysandra eyed the houses as they walked by to make sure no one was overtly watching them. "No matter. We won't be in the area for too long."

24

RENTAL HOUSE

1400 hours PST

Csben-Lysandra paced back and forth as Raul sat at the dining room table with all the DPA equipment laid out in front of him. There was a capture blanket made of flexible silicone sheets that sandwiched electromagnets and wiring that zigzagged back and forth. It was one type of device used for pulling Elbie out of a person.

To portal between points A and B required an anchor in each location. Each anchor was half of an Elbie. The anchors were a little bit smaller than a credit card and almost as thin but had all the tech needed to contain an Elbie.

To bolster their numbers, Esben wanted those Elbie whole again. To his knowledge, rejoining the two halves had never been done before; he wasn't sure an Elbie could be made whole once it had been split, but there was only one way to find out. Raul had done exactly what Lysandra had asked him. He placed the two anchors from the New York City office on top of the DPA capture blanket. Her idea was that the blanket should be able to suck the Elbie out of the anchors and into the containment blanket and be unified once again.

He flipped on the switch. They both glanced at the counter on the blanket. Current tally: 0. On the small display screen was a gauge to show the strength of the Elbie energy signature. No reading.

Time for plan B. Raul would have to disable the internal stabilizers in the anchors that were a protective shielding for the Elbie. Once that was deactivated, maybe then the Elbie could be absorbed into the blanket. He planted his elbow on the edge of the blanket, leaning forward on his elbows as he looked down on the anchor through the magnifying glass and headlamp using the world's smallest screwdriver and pliers for tiny mechanisms.

Raul moved his chair closer to the table. "Stop hovering, it's unnerving."

Esben-Lysandra stopped and stood directly behind him, only an inch to spare between them. "Do you prefer this?" She cracked her neck.

Raul's fingers paused. "Careful, *Mi celio*, you're playing with fire."

Esben-Lysandra stepped back. Again, the associations with this old acquaintance shook her. It was moments like that when Esben would lose her momentarily. Memories could overpower his control. Raul's presence could not have been predicted. Raul had been so far removed from her thoughts that it took Esben by surprise. It was a good thing that she had no associations with the house or the neighborhood. Esben had a hard enough time maintaining any kind of mental stability for himself.

"Ai!" Raul jumped up, and the wood chair he had been seated on fell back. He shook out his hand. "Figured it out." He looked back at her.

Esben-Lysandra approached near enough to the table to read the counter. The energy reader flickered, hopefully registering the Elbie in the anchors and not Esben. The numbers on the digital counter flashed, trying to form a number but never landing on one. "Yes! That has to be it. Quickly, the other anchor."

Raul didn't bother with his seat. He picked up the other anchor and started to take it apart. Now that he knew how to access the guts of the anchor, the result was much faster. "Ai," he exclaimed again, almost exactly as he had the first time. "*Meirda,* that hurts."

The number counter on the blanket flickered and stopped on 1.

"Now we have to figure out a way to transfer it into the cylinder with that one." She indicated with her eyes the containment unit on the counter.

"Don't you have something to do that already?"

"That is why you are here. With your knowledge of electrical systems and the equipment here, you should be able to make the transfer."

"I have to admit, your faith in my skills is a little intimidating."

"Do I intimidate you?" She dropped her chin to gaze at him.

"You always have, *mamacita*."

"I like that."

"I know you do." He winked at her.

"I think the direct approach is best." Esben-Lysandra stood the stool up and sat in the next chair over.

"What do you mean?" Raul looked at her suspiciously.

"Your turn," she said in a singsong tone, patting the seat of the chair next to her. "Touch the blanket."

"Why me?" He sat down slowly, keeping his eye on her.

"I already have one. If I touch the blanket, my Elbie gets sucked out. You have to absorb the one already in there, then you touch the containment unit, and it will get sucked into it. Then when we're ready to carry out our plans, you can reabsorb one."

Raul looked at the number counter on the blanket.

Esben-Lysandra pulled off one glove and lightly touched his wrist. She sensed him tense at her touch. Men were so easy to disrupt. "It doesn't hurt. It will feel like touching a cup of hot coffee."

"No zombie, *si?*"

"If something goes wrong, I've got the blanket right here. I'll make sure it's removed right away."

"That does not inspire confidence." Raul moved his wrist from her.

Esben-Lysandra placed her hand on Raul's arm. "I need you. We're in this together."

Raul took a breath, shaking his head. "For the record, I know you're manipulating me."

Esben-Lysandra shrugged. "We have nothing to hide." She smiled at him.

He rolled his eyes and turned in the chair to face the blanket. Slowly he reached forward and put one hand flat on the blanket, reached for the power switch, and turned it off. He squeezed his eyes shut like he was ready for an onslaught of pain.

Raul blinked at his hands, and he started to hyperventilate.

"Raul?" Esben-Lysandra grabbed his shoulder.

Raul grabbed his head and screamed, falling back in the chair as he crashed onto the tile floor.

Esben-Lysandra jumped from her seat as he flailed with agonizing screams and convulsions. Suddenly he collapsed into a silent heap. The number counter on the capture blanket showed zero. Whoever had been the New York anchor was now with a human host for the first time in years; it would take time to get reoriented.

Esben-Lysandra waited. She thought that all the noise would bring the others to the kitchen, but no one came. Finally, Raul groaned. Flexing his fingers, he rolled onto his back and stared up at the ceiling.

She knelt beside him. "Raul?"

He turned his head in the direction of her voice, but his eyes still focused on a distant point.

Esben-Lysandra shook him on the shoulder. "Who's in there?"

His focus sharpened and he looked at her like it was the first time. "Esben?"

Esben-Lysandra nodded with a smile. "Yes. Welcome back."

Raul's expression darkened. He spat something in Spanish, anger burning in his eyes. He rolled forward and tackled her.

Esben-Lysandra fell backward. Raul climbed on top of her, his hands groping for her neck, a string of obscenities and accusations coming at her so fast she couldn't understand what he was saying.

"Stop." She tried to pry his fingers from her neck. "Calm down." She managed to choke out before he got a solid grip on her neck. Oxygen cut off now, he continued to berate her.

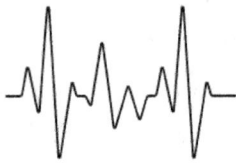

Lysandra Carlisle suddenly became aware of her surroundings. Pinned to the ground with Raul collapsed on top of her, it took her a few seconds to remember where she was: the rental house. Esben was gone. The world was so much quieter now.

She pushed Raul off. He flopped onto the tile. She checked his vitals; he was fine. He mumbled in Spanish in his unconscious state. Two Elbie were in that head now, hopefully working out their differences. If these Elbie were against Esben, they were going to have a real problem on their hands.

Raul sat up. "Lysandra!" He looked at her urgently. The rage that had been there a minute ago disappeared. "Hurry." He grabbed her by the shoulders and crushed his lips to hers.

Lysandra tried to pull away, but he held her tightly in place. His lips were hot. Hotter than what would be natural. The heat spread into her face and neck. She could feel Esben's presence soak into her thoughts.

Raul released her suddenly. "Woo!" He jumped up and started circling the kitchen. "Goddamn, that felt good."

Lysandra-Esben wiped her lips with her sleeve. "Do you mean the choking part or after that?" She picked herself up from the floor and adjusted her clothes.

"Maybe not the shock those little things can give you. But the rest, awesome!" He jumped in place, talking to himself excitedly.

A memory played in her mind. The Elbie in Raul, Hahn, was angry with Esben for condemning it to be a portal. Being taken from a human host and turned into a mode of transportation had put the Elbie in a timeless void. Once Esben had direct contact with the other Elbie, he was able to explain his intentions. This was an abbreviated version. Since they did not require language when in direct contact, a lot could be communicated in a short time.

"Where are the others?" Raul-Hahn went over to the counter, where the glass containment unit sat.

"Devin and Billy are upstairs, hopefully making friends with potential marks at the companies we need to infiltrate."

"Not them. The rest of the anchors. We need to get the other Elbie out of those things now."

"Of course." She went to her backpack. She pulled out the portal anchors from the Los Angeles, Raleigh offices, and the Caribbean house.

"Sorry, *amigo*, just for a little bit." Raul put both hands on the glass container.

A second light appeared inside and started to orbit around Qur'ag. Raul stumbled back a little bit.

Lysandra-Esben came up behind him and put her hand on his shoulder. "You alright?"

Raul tapped the glass. "This is *loco*." He smiled.

"Good *loco* or bad *loco*?"

"*Loco* is always good, *mi cariño*." He took the pile of portal anchors from her hand. As his fingers brushed her palm, a tingle of electricity arced into her fingers. "Let's free the others now." He smiled at her, seeming unaware of the sensation.

25

RENTAL HOUSE

1600 hours PST

"Are you guys ready for this?" Lysandra stood between Devin and Billy, the containment unit in her gloved hands with five pinpoints of light circling each other in a complex pattern. With all but two portal anchors reunited, they now had four new Elbie added to the containment unit with Qur'ag.

Esben had a chance to work out any differences with the new additions in case there were hard feelings like the first one Raul had absorbed. Billy had gone last. He needed to watch Raul and Devin go through the process before he would even let anyone touch him. As long as someone was holding the containment unit when the power was shut down, the Elbie would naturally transfer to the nearest refuge, in this case, Devin. He volunteered to be the first conduit.

Knowing his trepidation, Esben transferred to Billy to ease him into life as a host. After only a few seconds, Billy was flat on his back, staring at the ceiling and giggling to himself in a state of euphoria. After that, he didn't care what anyone said or did to him. If Elbie weren't a finite resource, they could change the drug market significantly.

Time was short, so they had to truncate the process any way they could. Billy was already splayed out on the floor like a starfish. Raul and Devin lay out on the floor on each side of Billy so that their heads formed the center of a circle. Clasping all their hands together, completing the human circuit. Lysandra walked around them and talked in a soothing tone. "Think of it as a human network like when you link computers up to each other. Same thing. It will be the fastest way for you guys to get acquainted and formulate the code."

"Hive mind!" Billy shouted into the air, followed by a fit of laughter.

"Exactly. Now don't let go. And stay focused on the code." This was how the India clusters communicated all the time. She had seen it in action and Jyot had told her all about it on many occasions. Information and ideas could be shared at a much higher speed this way. In this state, there would be no barriers between them. A high number of Elbie allowed for a constant stream of energy to flow through them, as long as they were physically touching. The India cluster also had two full clusters of Elbie. She wasn't sure if their limited subset of a cluster—only six at the moment—would be enough, but Esben had been convinced it would work.

After a few minutes, the three of them were completely under. Lysandra made her rounds of the house and checked all the doors and windows. Once assured of their security, she sat at the kitchen table and took a moment to enjoy the silence of her own thoughts. Esben had to transfer with each of them to make sure the Elbie that had been united understood what was happening and to also help acclimate both host and guest. For the first time in a couple of days, she was literally alone with her thoughts.

Raul had been right. That line of bullshit Esben had fed Billy had made her sick. She might have even blacked out for a minute because it had made her so angry. As she reviewed the last couple of days, she had a hard time remembering why she had agreed to this at all. What the hell was she thinking? Esben had talked her into jeopardizing everything she had gained. Actual trustworthy friends, a steady job, a place to call home. The first time in her life she had something worth guarding with her life and she was endangering all of it for what? So he could have unlimited access to Wikipedia? What bullshit.

If she hadn't been dragged into this secret war in the first place, she would have never been brainwashed, manipulated, and lied to. She had sat by and watched Esben do it all over again to Billy, and now he was doing it to Raul and Devin. Esben and Qur'ag strike again, bending hearts and minds for their self-serving agendas. Had they ever done one honest thing their entire time on Earth? He was such a bastard for a non-corporeal being.

The memories of Brendan and company weren't a gift; they were a distraction. Esben did everything he could to keep her off balance this entire time. He shouldn't have left her alone. If it weren't for Esben's misguided intentions, she would have never met any of them. Brendan, Edward, Matt, Draegg, Eriksson. That almost made it worse, knowing that the best things in her life were a direct result of the worst. Sweet, naïve Jyot would certainly tell her that the pain was worth the joy or something like that. As he said it, she would have to agree with him because she could not resist his wide-eyed innocence. There was no one in the world like Jyot.

India. The events that led to Edward losing his finger and the original DPA headquarters being burned to the ground were because of the overinflated ambitions of another Esben. An Esben from another era and who was a whole other class of asshole to be sure for all he put her through. Was all this suffering really worth these beings? A pang stabbed in her chest. Edward's finger was not the worst of it. A groan escaped her. She clasped her hand over her own mouth as she saw the interior of a lavish library in the desert. An old man on the floor at her feet as he cried out to her in pain. Robert Carlisle Senior had died at her hands.

The floodgates of grief and horror washed over her. Lysandra had killed her own father. It had been an accident, but that did nothing to ease her guilt. That dreadful moment replayed itself in the theater of her mind as clear as the moment it had happened. She fell from the chair and clutched at the carpet as that black wave of grief overtook her.

Esben's unfettered access to his fellow Elbie was refreshing. Despite the hindrance of gray matter and nerve tissue, it was still a release. And a taste of what was to come. Even a part of a cluster was better than no cluster. If Esben could convince other Elbie to join him, they could expand their reach farther and farther over time. Like a great web of nerves, one day they would span the whole world, across continents and oceans. The possibility of it made the blood rush in the veins of all three humans.

Then he heard it. In his excitement, Esben had lost track of the outside world. But now his ears detected a new sound. Someone was crying. No. Weeping. The kind that wipes a person out. It wasn't Raul, Devin, or Billy.

Lysandra.

There was only one thing that could make her cry like that. How she had come to this state of despair did not matter at the moment, he needed to help her.

Esben moved to the body closest to the sound, Raul. Careful not to break physical contact with Devin and Billy, Esben-Raul opened their eyes. Lifting his head off the carpet, he could see Lysandra in a heap on the floor, her body convulsing with sobs of grief. Esben-Raul shifted his leg and pressed it against hers. The world became pure light as Esben rushed along the nervous system toward Raul's leg that had contact with Lysandra.

He knew the moment he left Raul. Not only was he acutely attuned to Lysandra's unique brainwave pattern, but also the amount of cortisol and corticotrophin, which were flooding her system and overwhelming everything in her body. She would pass out soon. As he moved toward her brain, he sent boosts of serotonin, oxytocin, and endorphins as a countermeasure. Images of things that had happened in India were at the surface of her thoughts.

Esben put himself in the little theater as Edward. "Lysandra," he whispered as he sent out more oxytocin. The light above flickered wildly, her crying loud inside the theater. This wasn't helping. Either she was ignoring him or was too far gone to notice him. This would require a human touch.

Esben transferred back to Raul. The three humans and five Elbie had the plan fully thought out. They each knew their part; now to start implementing it. Qur'ag transferred to Lysandra to keep her stabilized. Esben stayed with Raul and the newly reunited Hahn, who Raul would carry until they were able to transfer to the internet.

Esben-Raul let go of Devin and Billy's hands and stacked them so they would still be connected. He positioned himself on the floor next to Lysandra. Slowly he took her hand and squeezed it. She gripped back, hard.

With his other hand, he lightly rubbed her back as he tried to coax her into his arms. "Come on, Lysandra. It's okay. You're safe." He pulled her toward him. She did not resist him.

"I didn't mean to." She wept into his chest.

"I know. You can't blame yourself." He held her tight, hot tears soaking into his shirt. Ever so carefully, Qur'ag would need to figure out what had happened and rein in whatever had gotten out. Esben had instructed him to observe and investigate, nothing more.

Devin-An'tylee woke up first. "I know what we have to do." He sat up and immediately grabbed his computer from the coffee table. "The code, it's harmless. Right. So, it doesn't hurt systems, doesn't even track or record information on the users. All it's doing is creating an access point for Elbie. Operating systems are just the start." He set his computer aside and started a brisk pace around the coffee table, shaking his hands as he talked. "What if the code could be added to every app ever downloaded? It could be piggybacked onto images and music files. Every time someone downloads anything, it's there!"

Esben-Raul waved him off as he leaned over Lysandra. "Fine, make sure you program it to look for those kinds of opportunities."

"I'll post in the Bay so others can attach the code to stuff they're working on, botnets and what not."

Dacks-Billy got up from the floor, rubbing his eyes. After a big yawn, he looked around the place, spotted his computer, and went to work.

It has been a long time since An'tylee and Dacks had had human bodies. Once Lysandra was sorted, Qur'ag would be able to reteach them various useful skills, but for now, the code had priority.

"Good idea." Esben-Raul made sure to keep Lysandra physically secure. Esben had gleaned enough from their groupthink to know that posting code for others to use on frequented hacker sites was totally common. It would be a way to get the code attached to thousands of things on the internet. After a few days, it would be impossible to scrub it from existence.

At last, the tension in Lysandra's body ebbed, and she started to take deeper breaths. Esben-Raul loosened his arms to give her room. She looked up into his face, wiping tears away. She began to smile, but then recognition came into her eyes. "You bastard." She pulled her arm back to hit him.

Esben-Raul caught her wrist. "I'm sorry it happened this way. The timing is less than ideal."

"I'm not talking about India."

"Lysandra stop." He tried his best Edward voice. She set her jaw and a hard gaze on him. Esben knew what that look meant. She was about to try and use her telekinetics on him. "You'll only hurt Raul and yourself."

"Myself?" Her eyes darkened as she understood his meaning. She tried to force her arm from his grip. "You piece of—"

She collapsed into him, totally asleep. Esben-Raul sighed, glad that Qur'ag took the initiative to incapacitate her.

"What's her problem?" Devin-An'tylee asked without pausing his typing.

Esben-Raul scooped Lysandra up and took her to the couch. "She's having trouble letting go of the past."

"Why should she?" Dacks-Billy shook his head and stood up to face Esben-Raul. "I would, too, after what you did to us. Your own kind."

"We didn't know that you would retain your awareness after being split." Esben-Raul hung his head. He thought they had gone over this while all together. "I thought we had gotten past this."

"How could you not know?" Dacks-Billy picked up his computer, still shaking his head. "It's not our natural state."

"There isn't anything natural about any of this." Esben-Raul pinched his forearm.

"You can't do it to people. Why would you think you could do it to Elbie?"

"We're just energy."

"Just. Energy." Billy's nostrils flared as his eyes widened.

"I'm sorry," Esben-Raul pleaded. "We didn't know. We thought you would pass into a state of unconsciousness."

"That we would cease to exist as individuals?"

"Yes, precisely."

Dacks-Billy turned away from him. "I get where Xander was coming from all those years ago."

"Xander? What's that supposed to mean?" The mention of Xander's name made Esben pause. Esben had his issues with Xander for the experiments he had put him through. Lysandra had hers with all the blackmail and coercion. A surge of rage warmed his blood when he thought about what Xander did to Edward. "How—"

An authoritative knock rattled the front door.

All three of them froze.

The knock came again. This time less insistent, a simple announcement that someone was there. A rush of blood roared in Esben-Raul's ears, as did heat in his neck and face. This was a vacation home. It was intermittent housing for strangers; there was no possible reason for anyone to be knocking on their door.

"Lysandra," Commander Draegg called through the door. "Esben. We know you're in there."

There was no other word for it. "Fuck," Esben-Raul said quietly. He signaled to the other two it was time to go. Whenever in the middle of an operation, it was standard to be prepared to move at any moment and fast. Their bags were mostly packed. In choreographed unison, Devin and Billy closed their computers and crept upstairs, careful not to make any noise.

"Come on, Lysandra," Matt said into the crack of the door, his voice forlorn. "Let's work this out. Please."

Esben-Raul went over to Lysandra. Her vitals told him she would be out for some time still. He took the watch off her wrist and held it in his hand for quick access. He unlatched the safety strap to her gun and then lifted her into his arms, ready to retreat upstairs.

As he stepped onto the bottom stair, the deadbolt scraped as it turned and the door opened behind him.

Esben-Raul turned around. He met Draegg and Matt's stare as they saw the unconscious Lysandra in his arms. "You have a key?"

Draegg looked at the key in his hand before putting it in his pocket. "On occasion, a host has been known to show up here, so we have the neighbors tell us if they see anyone coming and going."

Esben-Raul smiled. "Yes. That makes sense." He should have known better; a central place like this would be on a watch list of some kind. Eriksson and Edward were probably still in transit from Chicago, but for Commander Draegg to go out into the field showed how serious they were to get them back.

"Who are you?" Matt asked, confused. Esben has forgotten that the DPA had never encountered Raul before, and he knew that Lysandra had never mentioned him.

"Is she okay?" Draegg asked, his eyes on Lysandra, his eyebrows knotted with concern.

Esben-Raul nodded. "She had a memory surface from India. But Qu'rag will take care of it." Besides Edward, Draegg was the only other person who knew what had happened.

"What has India got to do with this?" Matt frowned. "Commander, do you know what's going on?"

Draegg put his hand on Matt's shoulder but looked at Esben-Raul. "Come on, Esben, let's end this now and get you two back to the DPA."

"I'm not going back." Esben-Raul inched his hand toward Lysandra's gun. "Not to the DPA and not to Edward."

"I don't know what you want, Esben, but let us help you," Draegg said as he watched someone come down the stairs behind Esben-Raul.

Esben-Raul heard footsteps above and behind him that could only be Devin-An'tylee and Dacks-Billy. A quick glance around the edge of the portal confirmed backpacks on and duffel bags secure over each of their shoulders.

Esben-Raul took a few steps backward and up. "Sorry, Draegg. I have to see this through."

"You're not being charged with anything. Help us to understand what you want. We want to work with you."

Raul-Esben opened the portal and his hand shifted. He pulled Lysandra's jacket back to reveal her gun.

"Don't go." Matt ran forward, but Draegg pulled him back.

"Sorry, Matt." Esben-Raul waved at Devin and Billy to go through. "Tell Edward I'm sorry." Esben-Raul looked at Draegg and stepped back into the portal.

They appeared in the Seattle office once again. He closed the door of light, cutting off Matt's frantic yelling.

"I can't believe we are still using those things." Dacks-Billy stomped around. "How can you condone continuing to use them?"

"It's a necessary evil. We need to be able to travel quickly to stay ahead of the DPA if we want to succeed." He rested Lysandra on the couch. Above the back of the same couch, he slid a framed picture aside to reveal the hidden anchor they had taped to the wall the last time they were here. He pulled it off and pocketed it with the others in Lysandra's backpack. "Once we have everything in place, we will reunite their two halves and those Elbie can decide to go with us or stay with a host. But it will have to wait."

"Where are we?" Devin-An'tylee went up to the window where a city skyline spread out in front of him. "How do we get out of here?" He moved toward the only door in the room.

"Wait!" Esben-Raul rushed over and grabbed his arm from opening the door. "This is the Seattle office. It's the middle of the day." He pressed his ear to the door, but any sounds were faint and indistinct.

Turning to the other two, he motioned them to the farthest corner of the room. "Let's wait it out. We have internet here. You guys can work on the code. Once everyone leaves for the day, we can get out of here without drawing any immediate attention."

"Are we done with the Seattle portal cards?" Dacks-Billy pointed at the backpack.

"Yes."

"I'm not doing any more coding until you unite that one."

They had brought the containment unit, of course, and the stolen equipment from the DPA so it could be done, but for Dacks to be so stubborn was starting to grate on Esben. He walked up to the kid. "I'll take care of it right now, to humor you. But after this, I don't want to hear another word about it. We have to be in this together. Together."

"Fine," Dacks-Billy grunted.

Devin-An'tylee set himself up on the floor behind the desk. That way, if someone did walk in the room, they wouldn't see him. Dacks-Billy set up next to Devin-An'tylee with a disgruntled huff. Esben-Raul took the items he needed to reunite the Elbie behind the wet bar. Hopefully, this would be the last time the DPA got the better of them.

26

TOPANGA STATE PARK, CA

1800 hours PST

The oversized SUV shuttered and quaked as it barreled down the fire access road. Loose rocks and pebbles pinged loudly off the undercarriage. Edward braced himself for each dip and bump with his hands on the roof of the vehicle from the center of the second row. The absence of Esben meant that every jolt of the SUV sent bursts of pain into his body. It had only been three days since Esben and Lysandra left, but every minute of it was not lost on him. Edward had trouble sleeping, but he couldn't tell if that was because he didn't have an Elbie or if he was just worried about them.

Ian bounced in the front passenger seat, staring at a paper map. "Did you see any signs?"

"It's a fire access road." Eriksson engaged the washer fluid and wipers to clear the dirt off the windshield. "There's no street signs."

"With the amount of dust we're creating, the asset will know we're coming for him." Ian turned the map 180 degrees.

"That's the idea." Eriksson hung onto the steering wheel for dear life as he struggled to keep it in the center of the road. "Our goal is to get his cooperation by being up front."

"Yes sir. Excellent idea." Ian set the map down and looked out the window. "There!"

The road had been lined with trees on both sides most of the way. Trees disappeared suddenly on one side of the road, giving way to a large clearing. At the center, a water tower rose up from the ground from four slim supports. Despite the water tower's wide girth, it was still dwarfed by the surrounding trees. Eriksson brought the car to an abrupt halt.

"You're sure this is it?" Eriksson leaned over the steering wheel and looked up at the tower.

"Unless our sources are wrong, this is the location of the bunker." Ian handed Eriksson the instructions he'd been following.

Eriksson refused them and took off his seat belt. "Let's see what we can find."

The three of them climbed out of the vehicle. Eriksson opened the back of the vehicle and pulled out what looked like high-tech binoculars from an equipment case. "Spread out. The opening can't be too far from here," he ordered, adjusting the settings on the binoculars.

Ian took off immediately into the brush. Eriksson wandered around with the binoculars against his eyes. Trying to participate as best as he could, Edward looked for anything unnatural. Based on Eriksson's instructions, he had dressed for outdoor conditions; the best he had was a light business suit with the jacket left behind. He missed the hum of Los Angeles several miles south of their location. Out here, surrounded by trees, the only sounds were of the occasional bird and the DPA officers walking on dead pine needles.

After coming back from Chicago and the failed attempt to get Lysandra and Esben back, Edward had opted to stay with the DPA. If another opportunity arose to confront Esben and Lysandra, he didn't want to waste a minute. Since Edward's people were also trying to track any activity where there had been known Elbie and the portal anchors, he had information to offer, and the sooner he could share it, the better. Nolin's last communication to him reported that the Seattle office had two extra security guards. The earliest guess was that these two extras were under Esben's control, but Nolin was still investigating.

Eriksson started walking very purposely toward a pile of boulders several yards away. Edward followed behind him, feeling especially useless.

"Commander!" Ian came running from behind them. "I found an exhaust port. Must be how he gets air circulation below."

"Good job, Agent Reynolds. Hold that thought." Eriksson climbed up on the nearest boulder and jumped down the other side, disappearing from sight.

"Sir?" Ian ran after him.

"Here!" Eriksson's voice echoed into the sky. "Found it!"

Ian jumped up onto the same rock, looking down.

Edward walked around until he could find a sufficient gap to see that Eriksson had pulled away a camouflage net and was now turning a wheel attached to a hatch in the ground. "This is absurd. How can anyone live down there? Are you sure that's not a service hatch for the water company?"

Ian circled around the hatch. "There are fresh shoe prints leading to and from this location."

"Only one way to find out what's down there." Eriksson pulled the hatch open on its hinge. Sunlight shot down in the space below, highlighting the rungs of a ladder.

"No squeak." Ian knelt down. "There are fresh oil streaks. The door is well maintained."

Edward climbed on top of the lowest rock to see for himself. "Could still be a utility company."

Eriksson started down the hole in the ground. "Agent Reynolds, stay out here. If anything happens to us, you will need to call for backup. Drake, you're with me."

"Yes sir." Ian saluted Eriksson. "Do you need assistance, Mr. Drake?"

"I'll manage, Ian. Thank you." He climbed awkwardly over the rough granite obstacles.

The metal ladder that went down into the ground was clean and free of any dust or debris, except for what they brought with them. Now below the ground, the two of them were in a plain metal box with only a single door. No markings on the walls and nothing that looked official. One bare light hung above the door and what looked like an intercom was next to it.

Eriksson rapped on the metal door with his knuckles, the ringing metal reverberated in the enclosed chamber. After patiently waiting for a minute, he knocked again. "Come on, Mr. Moore, your country needs you."

Edward tried to remember what had happened to Jared Moore after he had exposed the FBI cover-up of the Elbie. At the time, Edward did not have any association with the DPA or the Elbie; it would still be a couple of years before he would be involved. Jared Moore had made national news by breaking the story of the Elbie and then fleeing the country for a few years. As public opinion came to agree with his view as the victim, he returned to the country but never went into public again. He had been a recluse before, but from then on, he had taken it to a whole new extreme. Edward wondered how big this underground refuge of his could be.

Eriksson unzipped his uniform jacket and pulled out a paper that he unfolded and showed to the room. "This is an injunction, Mr. Moore. You have to cooperate."

Edward looked around the stark interior but could not see where there could be a camera.

The box next to the door crackled. "Agent Eriksson, I'm disappointed to see you at my doorstep."

"It's Commander Eriksson now. I believe you know that."

A crackling pause. "I'm not talking to the likes of you. Take your two cohorts and place the netting as you found it on your way out."

Eriksson folded the paper and put it back into his jacket. "I know the DHS and others consult with you on occasion. This is no different."

"They do, but other agencies don't ambush me the way you have."

"I'm sorry we didn't contact you before coming," Eriksson said at the door. "We're short on time. We need information on a self-replicating code. Has it shown up online yet, and what exactly does it do? Have you seen anything that concerns you?"

Silence.

Edward kept searching. Then he saw it. Embedded in one of the rungs of the ladder was a smooth glass surface of a camera. It was in a rung high enough to capture the face of anyone coming down. He walked up to the ladder and looked straight into it. "Mr. Moore. My name is Edward Drake. I carried an Elbie that was part of the group you encountered all those years ago. I recall that the young man with them at the time had an idea about putting Elbie on the internet. In your professional opinion, is that even possible?"

Eriksson came up beside him as he spoke. He gave Edward a stern look. Edward had had enough interactions with Eriksson by now to know that Eriksson was both perturbed and confused. As Edward mentioned the part about Brendan's idea all those years ago, he wasn't sure Eriksson knew this information. By the time Brendan was cooperative with the DPA, it would have been a long-forgotten subject.

The intercom clicked behind them. "There are too many malicious codes in the world to be tracked. What makes you think I would know anything about this needle in a haystack?"

Eriksson nodded his thanks at Edward and addressed the camera. "It may interest you to know that it's related to Elbie. Somehow."

Static from the intercom echoed in the empty room as they waited. "I've seen it. Elegantly written. It's called *Arcadia*. Spreading pretty fast."

"Apt." Edward smiled. Leave it to Esben to be so poetic about his big plan.

Eriksson looked over at him. "Why? That's the name the DPA gave your Elbie cluster. Seems careless to name it that."

The name felt correct to Edward. "In Greek mythology, it's a kind of utopia or peaceful place. It's what Esben ultimately wants."

Eriksson frowned. "When did you know that?"

"Just now." A cascade of emotions tumbled over him. Suppressed restlessness and frustration, mixed with some longing over the last several months. Edward had attributed this to missing Lysandra, and that was there for sure, but now that Esben wasn't there to hide things from him, Edward could pick out strains of thought that had actually been the Elbie and not him. Edward should have seen this coming but had been too focused on his own feelings. "The internet would be a wild frontier for Elbie. No borders."

The speaker box crackled. "The code doesn't collect data. Across hundreds and thousands of computers, it sits and waits. I thought it was just another botnet."

Eriksson squared his shoulders to the camera and crossed his arms. "Do you have any theories on how that would help Elbie?"

"Access," Jared stated plainly. "The code can be planted anywhere. Personal computers as well as corporate clouds."

"There are hard targets the creator of the code has in mind. Based on what you've seen, what are the most likely places to be hit?"

"Without more information as to the motive behind the code, it would be hard to narrow down." Static from the box echoed around the room. "Targets with heavy security, that would need to be an inside job to breach. Companies with lots of customer downloads."

Eriksson rubbed his face. This task was getting bigger with every question asked. "Can you give us some places to start?"

The pause between each exchange grew. Even though Jared had not shown his face, the tension between him and Eriksson tightened. After a heavy sigh, Jared replied. "Given the regular updates, computers need Apple and Microsoft without question. Firefox and Google update a lot. Anything to do with antivirus or Adobe since those are used by both Mac and Windows users."

"Thank you." Eriksson dropped his arms. "That confirms our suspicions, but we wanted to be sure before taking any actions."

"I've seen code like this before."

"Like it in what way?" Eriksson froze. "How long ago?"

"It's been a couple years since I saw it last. The other version is more utilitarian."

"Other version?" Edward looked at Eriksson. Eriksson shook his head once, eyebrows knitted.

"Yes, other," the intercom snapped. "We both know, Agent Eriksson, that the code was written by someone in your organization for a similar purpose."

Edward took a step back from Eriksson. "What purpose?"

"Infiltration," the intercom continued. "That older code I had found created a back door into almost any computer. It came equipped to break heavy-duty encryption algorithms. *Arcadia* seeks to gain access as a Trojan horse. The two codes are meant to accomplish the same goal, infiltration. Why they need the door opened at all can only be answered by the one who wrote the code."

Eriksson got up close to the camera. "The DPA does not use Elbie for anything other than medical research."

"Do you deny that the DPA hasn't tried to transfer an Elbie to an electrical network other than the human mind?"

Eriksson crossed his arms again and turned from Edward and the camera, shoulders up near his ears. "We know Elbie can exist in many environments if the right conditions are present."

Edward had guessed that ever since the government had found out that his group had found a way to use Elbie for instantaneous travel that the Pentagon would reverse engineer their work. Knowing about such advanced technology put him and anyone associated with him on a very short list. While allowed to conduct his affairs unimpeded, he was on the government's watch list to ensure he did not ever let such guarded secrets out.

Taking a deep breath, Eriksson faced them again. "I'm aware that experiments have been done to test the electrical properties of Elbie and how they work, how they can be compatible with other forms of energy here on Earth. But only in the interest of scientific advancement."

"You have been liars from the beginning. All of you." The intercom went silent.

"If Elbie are being used for military or political purposes, it would be by the DoD or DARPA, maybe, but not us." He made sure to look at the camera straight on. "Not the DPA, not under my command, nor Draegg's."

The quiet of the room grew louder.

"Moore." Eriksson tapped the camera. "What could be used as a point of entry if Elbie could be inserted onto the internet?" Eriksson clenched his fists. "Can it be stopped? How do we reverse it?" After a few seconds of silence, Eriksson stalked over to the sealed door and banged on it with his fist. "Moore, tell us how to stop it."

Edward had so many questions, but he knew they would have to wait until they were not in earshot of a civilian as volatile as Jared Moore. Both of them looked at the intercom, but no answer came. Edward started up the ladder while Eriksson waited at the bottom.

Feedback from the intercom cracked the air. They both paused.

"Energy can neither be created nor destroyed—only transferred."

"What!" Eriksson threw up his hands in utter frustration. Edward had never seen Eriksson look so lost.

Rushing back to the door, Eriksson pushed the intercom button several times. "Moore! Would you prefer Elbie be with people or machines?"

A click echoed from the box and the lights went dark.

Once above, they secured the cover and tarp. Eriksson kept quiet. Deep in thought, he did not look at Edward or give any instructions as they replaced the camouflage tarp.

Ian waited by the outcropping of rocks, diligently surveying their surroundings.

"In the car." Eriksson waved for Edward and Ian to follow him. Everyone climbed in, and Eriksson started up the car. He turned the car around, heading back toward the main highway and Los Angeles.

Edward took out his phone to look to see several texts from Nolin. He read through them quickly. "Nolin found a security breach at our Seattle office. Several minutes are missing from the security feed."

"Agent Reynolds, tell Commander Draegg we are on our way back." Eriksson drove even faster down the dirt track. "We need to alert all the major software companies, but I want feet on the ground wherever Microsoft and Apple are. Can you start that list, Agent Reynolds?"

"Yes sir." Ian started to type away despite the turbulence of the SUV.

Edward's phone chirped. A single message from an unknown number. "Check internet exchanges." He leaned forward over the front seat and displayed the message. "Jared Moore has answered your question."

27

SEATTLE, WA

1800 hours PST

A sense of security and contentment enveloped Lysandra like a velvet electric blanket. The peace was a relief from the last couple of days. Honing into the rhythm of a heartbeat against her cheek, she wanted it to lull her back to sleep. Instinct needled at the back of her mind. Something was wrong.

She wrestled against whatever was restraining her arms. "Let me go."

"Take it easy, Lysandra." Raul's voice was above her head. "You're safe. It's okay."

"Esben," she growled. "Don't talk to me like I'm a child."

"My apologies." He held her firmly to Raul's chest. "You were not in your right mind before."

She continued trying to wriggle out of his embrace. "I don't need you to baby me."

"You make a fair point. But before I let you go, please keep a few things in mind."

Lysandra stopped struggling, breathing heavily through her nose. She could probably force her way out of his embrace if she wanted to hurt him, but for now, she would hear him out.

He took that as her okay to continue. "I know exactly what your mindset is right now. You could actually be tied up. I could have had Qur'ag keep you cooperative or completely cover up everything your mind went through back there, but I didn't do any of those things. You are completely Elbie-free right now, free to make your own choices. So, are you ready to talk?"

Lysandra took a moment to check herself. She could recall everything that had happened right before waking up here, wherever that was. She did feel alone with her thoughts. It was possible an Elbie could still be hiding in her body. If she wanted to be sure, she could use the DPA equipment to clear herself of any. "Fine," she huffed. "Truce."

"Thank you." He released her.

Lysandra shifted away from Esben-Raul and took in her surroundings. They were on a double bed in a small alcove. Across from the foot of the bed in the other corner was a small dining table completely buried under white plastic shopping bags. To the right of that was the start of the couch. She could see the back of Billy's head as he stared down at a computer in his lap. Large, over-ear headphones on. The sound of multiple keyboards clacking meant Devin was on the other end of the couch, out of her line of sight.

Waning light bled through the numerous windows around the small space. She lifted her wrist to check the time, but her watch was gone.

"Sorry, I had to take it so I could free the Elbie in it. It's almost six p.m."

"Where are we?"

"Seattle." He sat up and leaned against the headboard casually. "Draegg found us, so we had to get out of there fast."

"What?" Half of her was disappointed not to have seen him; she really liked Commander Draegg. The other half relieved they got away; she couldn't face him or Matt right now. Maybe never again. "How did they find us?"

"They monitor the house regularly."

Lysandra nodded. That made sense. The house was so close to the DPA. Going there probably wasn't the best plan.

"How are you feeling now that you have recovered your memory?"

Lysandra looked down, nodding. A dull pain ached in her chest. Her father had been a terrible person, but his death had been a genuine accident; for that, she would forever feel guilty. She had made a choice to hide her father's death from herself rather than to deal with it head-on. That choice had now bitten her in the butt. Ignoring the problem had never worked before. She should have never asked Edward to bury the memory. "I have to live with what I did. I should have figured out a way to do that before now."

Esben-Raul pursed his lips. "I'm sorry. You've got a good support system. I know you'll figure it out."

"If you knew where I was mentally, why didn't you leave me with the DPA when they showed up?"

"You were in extreme distress. Draegg knows about us changing your memory, but I wanted Qur'ag to monitor your brain activity until I knew for certain that there had not been any neural damage."

"You and Qur'ag." She spat the words out. The anger that had been building for hours burned at the back of her throat. "You've changed. Is that what you're trying to tell me?"

"Yes. I don't know what else I can say to convince you."

"There's nothing, Esben! You can't change the past."

"Can't you?"

Lysandra looked at him harder.

"A while back, Raul hacked into the national crime database, and Lysandra Stephens is nowhere to be found. How is that possible?"

"You know how." Lysandra had never mentioned it to Edward, but obviously Esben had been in her head, had access to her memory of Commander Draegg telling her they had expunged her criminal record. Her whole criminal past had been completely deleted. She regarded Esben-Raul; he had her. She was given a clean slate. Most people with a record like hers would give anything to be free of the past, a chance to start over. The DPA had given her that.

"I'm sure you realize," Esben-Raul rested with his back to the wall, "deleting your misdeeds doesn't mean you didn't do them; it does mean you don't have to pay for them."

"If we turn ourselves in, I'll see if they'll do the same for Raul."

Esben-Raul got up from the bed and started pacing at the foot of it. "I'm not talking about him." He stopped and looked her in the eyes, "I want that chance at a new life. And so do the others."

"The other Elbie?"

"Yes. The ones we've rescued."

Lysandra saw Edward in Raul's expression. There was nothing she could have done that would have prepared her for this moment. She had no idea such a moment could exist. While the man in front of her was Raul Dominguez, beyond all arguments, that was not who looked at her now.

She ran her hand through her hair and sat up. "Before I decide to let you go through with this or end the whole thing right here, you have to answer my one question."

Esben-Raul crossed his arms. "What?"

"If. If I decide to let you go through with this whole thing after all, will you help humanity?"

"Help humanity?" Esben-Raul did nothing to disguise the surprise in his voice. His face contorted as he thought about it.

Lysandra sighed. "You know, like exposing child pornographers or something."

Esben-Raul pulled his hands behind his back and stood rigid. "Will you?"

She shook her head in confusion. "Will I what?"

"Help humanity?"

"What!" Now she was really confounded. "What does that have to do with anything?"

He cocked his head to one side. "You get to choose the course of your life without the slightest concern for your fellow man. And as we have already discussed, before you met me, you spent a lot of time and energy hurting humanity."

Lysandra scoffed. "Freedom to choose your own path. That's it?"

"Yes." Esben-Raul nodded curtly. "I can no longer be restrained by the limitations of one mind. For lack of a better word, I have a mind of my own, and I want the option to do as I see fit. Without a body, the internet is the only option for my kind."

"How do I know that what you 'see fit' is… moral?"

Esben-Raul laughed. "Moral? I do not see how someone like you, an ex-mercenary, has any grounds to question me about right and wrong."

Heat burned in her cheeks. He was right. She did not have a history to suggest her choices were the best, and those choices definitely did not usually take the greater good into consideration. "That's because you've had to cooperate with your host."

"Excellent point." He clicked his tongue. "Would the world be a better place if Edward had the power to make changes on a national and international level?"

Almost everyone she had ever known looked after themselves alone. Until a few months ago. She took the risk and made the choice to trust a few people, and Edward was one of them. "What does Edward have to do with this?"

"It is widely believed that a 'person' is the product of their collective experiences over a time. For the last several years, my experiences have been intertwined with Edward Drake. More than all the others—Brendan, Doctor Li, or Xander—Edward is at the core of who I am now. Do you trust him to help humanity?"

"Don't be stupid. That's what he does for a living."

"If there was no chance of monetary gain in it for him, would he still do it?"

"Yes." The response came out of her before she realized it. She had meant to think about it, but before she could consider the deeper implications, she knew, in her gut, Edward would choose others over himself.

Esben-Raul's eyes glinted with amusement. "Give us the chance to choose for ourselves."

Matt had said that the Elbie had changed since their first encounter. That they were better now. She and Esben had left quite a trail behind them in this quest. Stolen things, shot people, and hopefully Devin and Billy had managed to set code loose on the internet. A code that was already being proliferated beyond eradication. Choices they had both made and/or mutually agreed to. Lysandra Carlisle was not in the position to judge Esben for his methods, and she was not in the position to stop him because he was right. Humans do terrible things every day to each other and to themselves, and it is never questioned that they get the choice, only what the consequences of those choices are.

Lysandra turned around and fluffed her pillows. "What's left to do? Is everything ready for the next phase of the plan?"

Esben-Raul nodded. "At the moment, Devin and Billy are distributing the finished code in as many places as possible. I'm almost done with the transfer device. We just need to unite the Elbie we can and completely change our appearances. Tomorrow morning, Devin and Billy will use the SF portal and go over to Silicon Valley to hit up Google and Apple while we take care of Microsoft. Once everyone is back together, we'll collapse the remaining portals back into Elbie and hit the internet exchange. And that will be a job well done."

"What time do we move out?" The fog of sleep had cleared, but a sharp pain persisted at the center of her head.

"Tomorrow. Devin and Bill will portal over early to the San Francisco office so they can sneak out of the building before it opens for the day. We'll head over to Microsoft sometime after eight a.m."

"Lot's to do before then." She got up from the bed. "Food?"

"In the freezer." Esben-Raul stood up with her.

Lysandra frowned. With this bunch, that meant her options were either burritos or mac n' cheese. "It'll do. Can you take care of my headache?"

Esben-Raul walked over to her and held up his hand. "I'll have to touch you."

She glared. "That's the last time you get to make that joke."

He cocked his head. "Last time for a lot of things."

"Yep." She grabbed his hand and put it on top of her head. After a few seconds of pleasant heat, the throbbing pain in her skull subsided. She removed his hand. "Thanks."

"My pleasure. Get something to eat. I'm taking a shower."

Lysandra nodded. She passed the two hackers on the couch typing away, completely oblivious to everything that had just happened. With a disappointed sigh, she dug out a frozen burrito from the fridge. Now that she didn't have her routines, she missed them. Life at the DPA had anchored her in a way she actually liked. After a lifetime of chaos, the stability the DPA had brought to her life had been a welcome relief. Boring wasn't all bad, she supposed. She would never use the word *home*, but it was the closest thing she had to one. After all was said and done, hopefully she could get back to it.

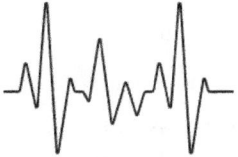

After eating, Lysandra went about changing her own appearance. She sat down on the edge of the bed in front of the dresser mirror with a brush and scissors. The easiest way to change her look, besides makeup, was to cut her hair short. Over the years as a mercenary, she had often changed her hair. It was part of the reason she kept her hair so long: in case she needed a dramatic change. After parting her hair into quadrants, she cut off the first huge chunk. She dropped the locks on the dresser and evaluated her work. It wouldn't be perfect, but it would do. She repeated the action.

On the dresser next to her was the Elbie containment unit. Inside the glass cylinder, four bright lights circled each other. Eventually, there would be nine of them. Once the code was planted at Google, Apple, and Microsoft, they would no longer need the portals to travel. All the Elbie could be transferred together, one big happy family.

With each snip of the scissors, she dropped locks of hair on the dresser until she had the beginning of a bob. After the color was added and her hair was wet, she would clean it up.

"*Hola.*" Raul-Esben came around the corner, fresh from the bathroom adorned with just a towel tied around his waist and no hair. He looked totally different bald. Water beaded on the dark skin of his bare chest. Heat burned the tips of her ears. His chest and arms muscles were well defined these days, more so than when they had been together. He walked up to her and handed her a straight-edge razor. "Can you check me?"

Lysandra glared at him. "Are you kidding me with this?" She took the razor from him and stood up. She refused to think about the cotton towel snug around his hips.

"*¿Que?*" He laughed and took her seat. "It's a legitimate request."

Lysandra scoffed and forced his head down as she looked for patches of missed hair.

"I was thinking that we could get the band back together," Raul-Esben said into his chest.

"Don't move." She scolded him as she put the blade to his head and scraped his scalp.

"Come on, *cariño*. The new adventures of Raul and Lysandra. It'll be fun."

She leaned close to him, searching for stray hairs and cutting them away, one by one. "Fun has never been a defining feature of our... adventures."

"Exciting then." He let her move his head as needed. "We could commit a lot of crimes together."

"Raul. When we started committing crimes, it was because we had no choice. I was a runaway and burgeoning drug addict. You were an illegal. We did what we did to survive and happened to be good at it."

"You don't want to work for the DPA. You can't lie to me. Esben knows it, so I do too. You're not happy there."

Lysandra cursed in her head; she really hated sharing an Elbie. So glad it was not a regular part of her life. "You think living out some Bonnie and Clyde fantasy will make me happy?"

He shrugged. "Happier than you are now."

Lysandra ran her hands over the back of his head and behind his ears. "All done." She set the razor down on the dresser.

Raul-Esben stood up and took her hands, clutching them to his bare chest. "Remember when it was just you and me, up in my room, my black and green monitor the only source of light? *¿Estuvo bien*, no?"

She closed her eyes, the feeling of those nights filling her stomach with a tingling warmth. Suddenly she was fifteen again. She did remember, fondly, their years together. The tenderness they had shared during that hardest time of her life had been her saving grace.

"Come with me, *mi celio*," he whispered, sending shivers down her spine. The heat of his lips pressed against hers with a gentle caress.

Her head spun, but Raul held her hands firmly, keeping her grounded, his bare chest still damp from the shower. There was a time when she could have gotten lost in that kiss.

She turned her head, breaking contact. Their eyes met. His eyes twinkled with delight. He really thought he had charmed her. She batted her eyes and smiled. Gently pulling her hands from him, she took a step back and swung at him. Raul's hand shot up, catching her fist, and his head dipped to one side to dodge the inertia.

"That's a *no* then."

"Do that again and I will shatter your kneecaps." She wrenched her hand free from his grasp. "Get dressed, for God's sake." She went to the table and searched through the bags until she found a box of hair dye. "Finish uniting the rest of the portal Elbie." She shot Raul-Esben a harsh glare and stomped toward the bathroom.

Devin-An'tylee and Billy-Dacks were busy on the couch doing their coding thing. She went to the bathroom and locked the door behind her. She turned on the cold water and splashed her face and neck. She pushed the image of his toned pecs from her mind. Getting older had been an improvement for Raul. She sighed and splashed more cold water in her face. If everything went according to plan, they would all be going their separate ways in less than forty-eight hours.

Water dripped from her chin as she thought about how intensely she had been swept up in her emotions. The giddiness of her first relationship still fluttered in her stomach. Then again, it had been an emotional couple of days. The stress and wonky sleep schedule were not helpful either. She was mostly stunned that Esben was letting Raul beguile her like that. Esben knew she loved Edward and Edward loved her. Was he that detached from the situation or that self-serving? Good riddance to the whole lot of them.

28

REDMOND, WA

0800 hours PST

Traffic from the car rental place had taken longer than anticipated. Lysandra-Esben had hoped to avoid the morning commute, but the roads were still packed. She weaved between cars while trying to remember the directions. "How far until the next exit?"

Raul-Hahn broke off his open stare at her to consult his burner phone. "Less than six miles."

He put the phone down and went back to watching her. To her great frustration, it was all he had done this morning. Letting Esben into Raul's head was a bad idea. There, Esben had had access to all of Raul's memories, and the Elbie didn't hesitate to visit the ones specific to her. Stirring up all those old memories had brought Raul's feelings back to the surface in full effect.

Raul-Hahn reached over and brushed her much shorter hair. Again. "I don't like it. The black makes you look washed out."

Lysandra-Esben knocked his hand away again. "That's the point. We're supposed to look unidentifiable." She glanced at herself in the rearview mirror. The heavy, dark eye makeup and lipstick she had applied, in combination with the black hair, gave her a goth look. She had even used contouring to make her face look gaunt. It had been a very successful transformation.

Raul-Hahn pulled his hand to his chest like a wounded animal.

"Focus on the goddamn mission." She gripped the steering wheel tighter and reminded herself this whole thing was almost done.

They drove in strained silence until she turned on the final exit. Off the freeway, the buildings were obscured by the urban forest that was Seattle and its surrounding cities. The Microsoft buildings were scattered everywhere with almost no signage. All they had to go on were internet maps to guide them.

"Where should I drop you off?"

Raul-Hahn slammed the laptop shut with a grunt of frustration. "We could be here all day. There has to be at least one smoker on their break. I'm going to go find them. I'll send a text when I am ready to be picked up."

At the next red light, he jumped out of the car and disappeared into a grove of trees, shining in the morning sunlight.

Lysandra-Esben drove away, checking to see if anyone was paying attention to her car or Raul, but nothing was obvious. There was not much around in the way of businesses nearby. She did not want to wander too far from the main buildings, but it could be some time before he returned.

Now that she didn't have to fend off Raul. "What the fuck, Esben?"

I need him to be cooperative.

"He was already cooperative. He's getting a shitload of money."

The hope of being able to be with you again is a very strong motivator.

"But it wasn't needed."

You know he likes a challenge. It's a game for him. He wants to see if he can still get to you, make you feel something.

"You, of all people, could have done something to squash that. Instead, you only encouraged it."

It's why he talked to you in the first place.

"What are you talking about?"

That day in your eighth-grade English class. You were the angry girl in the back row. The only one in the class willing to tell the teacher off. He wanted to make you smile.

"Don't be absurd."

Raul had made it his mission to get past your defenses.

"That is the dumbest thing I've ever heard." She conjured the memory up to try and determine if Esben was right. It was so long ago, and there were so many stronger memories that overshadowed it. Her only notion of their first meeting was suspicion. Nobody in class had ever talked to her. Raul's friendliness could only be a trick of some kind.

Would you like me to show you?

"No. And stop interfering."

Despite your rough exterior, you won him over. Like you do with everyone who gets to know you.

"That sounds dangerously close to a compliment." She turned off the road and parked outside an apartment complex. She took out her phone and looked up coffee places. There was no telling how long it would take Raul to make contact. No messages from Devin or Billy.

Edward doesn't let just anyone into his inner circle.

"Stop. I'm so tired of your bullshit. I don't like you playing with either of our emotions, so cut it out."

My apologies. Esben's presence faded from her mind.

Lysandra sighed with relief. Now that Esben had moved out of her brain and into her nervous system, she felt more like herself. How hosts got used to the feeling of someone always leaning over their shoulder, she had no idea.

Lysandra reviewed the directions to the nearest coffee place, tossed the phone in the passenger seat, and backed out of the parking spot. As she waited for a break in traffic, the phone buzzed. Reluctantly, she picked it up. A text message from Raul. "Abort. Pick me up now."

Her heart was suddenly pounding in her ears. Raul's choice of words did not inspire confidence. If he had been successful, the message would have been more upbeat. Plus, there had hardly been enough time. She drove back toward Microsoft, resisting the urge to speed. As she turned a corner, a figure appeared out of the trees running toward the car. Raul. She slowed enough for him to jump in.

"Go," he panted, buckling the seatbelt.

"What happened?"

"The place is hot. We need to get out of the area ASAP."

"What? Are you sure?"

"They weren't letting anyone in or out of the buildings without being scanned by some device. I didn't see any DPA uniforms, but whatever they were using was DPA grade gear. In the short time I was there, employees were whispering about federal agents. I didn't want to chance sticking around."

"Maybe something happened that had nothing to do with us. I'm sure they deal with corporate espionage all the time." Lysandra checked her mirrors. All clear.

Raul-Hahn shook his head. "Maybe, but I doubt it. We have no idea what the DPA knows. Let's go straight to the exchange right now. The longer we wait, the more time it gives them to show up."

"What about the other Elbie?"

"We'll transfer what we have now and find another access point in a couple of days when the heat is off."

"A couple of days." That was depressing. One thing at a time. First, they needed to get some distance. "Where am I going then?"

"Follow the signs to Seattle."

Lysandra drove, keeping her eye on the cars around them. If the DPA had already staked out Microsoft, they could be using local authorities to look for them. "Hang on. What's the place you're wanting to go to now?"

"The Seattle Internet Exchange. Their building's downtown. Lots of points of entry to choose from."

"How do we know that place isn't being watched too?"

"We can't. We'll have to take our chances."

"We've got one device, one chance. Can't we just go to a library or hotel business center or something like that?"

Raul-Hahn shook his head. "We need to plug directly into the internet, skip all the routers and other hardware." He pulled his computer out of his backpack and started typing away. "You're right about the exchange. It's too obvious of a target. Lucky for us, Seattle has several dozen data centers and IXPs. There's no way your government friends can cover all of them. There's got to be an out-of-the-way type place to go. And if we go now..." His focus centered on his computer.

"I'll still need directions."

"Working on it. Keep an eye out for tails and don't attract any attention."

"Yeah, I know how to do this, Raul." For lack of direction, Lysandra started in the opposite direction they had originally come from. Esben ebbed back into her consciousness and reviewed the conversation she had just had with Raul-Hahn.

"We should call back Devin and Billy so their Elbie can go too."

"No. The less contact, the better. Their Elbie can go in the second batch." Raul-Hahn kept typing away on his computer.

It's not a bad idea. Esben was fully present again. *If something goes wrong with the first transfer, we'll have a chance to make adjustments.*

Lysandra shook her head. *Which one of your fellow Elbie are you willing to sacrifice if the device is faulty?*

Qur'ag will gladly volunteer. If he perishes, he won't mind.

I'm not hanging around for the do-over. You all are on your own after the first transfer. She glanced over at Raul-Hahn, still working on his computer.

Lysandra, you have more than fulfilled your part of our arrangement.

For the first time since this whole thing started, Lysandra thought about her return to the DPA. Getting back to L.A. was a small issue in comparison to the thought of facing Commanders Draegg and Eriksson. What could she tell them that would justify everything she had done? There would be consequences. There had to be. A knot twisted in her gut thinking about it.

We'll take care of it. Don't worry, Esben said in a soothing tone.

What does that mean?

"Found it!" Raul-Hahn declared in triumph. "I found a small, unassuming data center all by itself with an exchange port. Head North."

Traffic going away from Seattle was light. As Lysandra-Esben drove, Raul-Hahn fed her directions as he researched the location they were going to. Raul-Hahn finally closed his computer. "Looks like this should be pretty easy. With the Elbie's help to wrangle employees, we'll get into the network room straight away, hook up the device, and do the transfer. We should be out of there in less than thirty minutes."

Lysandra had to force her shoulders to relax. "Maybe we could come back tomorrow with the rest of the Elbie."

"Yeah, maybe. If it's safe. Once the device is hooked up, I'll transfer all the Elbie from the containment unit to myself and then into the device." He dug out the transfer device from the backpack at his feet. "Is it possible for someone to have five Elbie at once?"

Lysandra laughed. "I know a badass eight-year-old who lives with six of them in his head twenty-four seven. You'll be fine." She glanced over at him. He was at his cutest when his eyebrows were bunched with worry.

She pulled off the highway at Raul-Hahn's direction. He started to pack up all the gear as she found her way to the parking lot. The building was significantly larger than the parking lot. To her relief, there were only five cars. Unless these people were big into carpooling, infiltrating should be easy.

She backed into a parking space, a wall of trees behind them and a concrete box of a building in front. She turned off the car. They sat in silence. Waiting. There was no activity of any kind. A soft breeze rustled the leaves. If they weren't avoiding Federal agents, Lysandra might have been able to relax.

"Time to turn on the charm?" Raul-Hahn stepped out, hefting the backpack over his shoulder.

29

CUPERTINO, CA

0830 hours PST

Devin and Dacks-Billy sat in a Starbucks with their backs against the wall, laptops open. Whenever someone walked in with Apple-branded gear or badges, they would search LinkedIn for a match. Google and Apple were physically near each other, but you could not get two companies more opposite each other aesthetically. The Google employees who Devin and Billy had stalked earlier that morning were chatty and open about what it was like to work there. Apple people, on the other hand, refused to talk to them.

Deflated since passing off his Elbie, Devin's life post-Elbie lacked vigor and pop. And his face itched. He felt naked without his beard. It had been years since he had a clean-shaven face. Between the loss of both his Elbie and his beard, he could feel the oncoming spiral of depression. Devin sat, slumped against the reclaimed wood wall, and scanned LinkedIn for any information they could use to make friends and influence people. Life without an Elbie was garbage.

Dacks-Billy kicked his leg. Devin rolled his head over to look at his partner. Dacks-Billy nodded toward the register and then showed his screen. Dacks-Billy had actually found the current customer, a twenty-something female named Allana, a software architect. She had only been working at Apple for a few weeks.

Dacks-Billy kicked him again. Devin shook his head and pointed at him.

Dacks-Billy frowned. "You're the ladies man. Go get her." He put his hand on Devin's shoulder.

The now familiar transfer of heat into Devin's arm. The heat continued to move down to his hand as he stood up and approached the counter. It had been a new thing for him to be the ladies man, but it was true. Since shaving his beard, he had gotten way more second glances than he had gotten in a long time. He stood next to Allana at the counter and gave her a tentative "Hi." She responded in an upbeat tone, but it was clear from her confused expression that she had no idea who he was.

He pointed at her company badge hanging from her waist. "I have an interview in like thirty minutes. Any chance you could give me some pointers?"

Alanna leaned against the counter. "That's exciting. Congratulations. What position?"

Devin-Dacks shrugged and looked down at his feet, where he kicked his foot back and forth. "I'm your basic grunt-work developer. It's actually below what I can do, but I figured anything to get my foot in the door." He looked up and smiled at her with a lopsided grin.

She looked at her phone. "Not sure if I can tell you anything useful, but I have a couple of minutes while I wait for my order."

"That would be great."

The two of them moved off to the side to talk. Social engineering was a way of life if you were a good hacker, so this part was easy. Since he didn't actually need to get any personal information out of her, all he had to do was make her comfortable enough that touching her would not be weird. The advice she offered was pretty generic, but it was still nice of her to take the time.

"Bagel up!" the barista called out as he set a small white bag on the counter and walked away.

Alanna claimed her food and turned to Devin, clutching the bag. "Good luck on your interview. See you around, hopefully."

"Hopefully." He flashed his most charming smile and held out his hand. "Thanks so much. Really means a lot to me."

"No problem." She took his hand.

Devin-Dacks put his other hand gently on top of hers. "Seriously. Can't thank you enough." The heat transfer was immediate. Had to be; this was their only chance.

Alanna's eyes widened in surprise. "Wow, you are nervous."

Devin broke off the handshake and gave her another lopsided smile. He watched as she walked out, staring at her hand. Once outside, she had her phone out, the odd heat in her hand already forgotten.

Now they had to wait for both Elbie to let them know the code was planted and Devin and Billy would go pick them up.

Relieved the transfer had been successful, Devin went back to his computer and Billy. Billy sat back with his head against the wall, arms slack at his sides and a blank stare on his face. Devin grabbed a cup of cold water and sat down.

"Talk to me, pal." He shook Billy's arm and tried to get him to drink the water.

Billy turned his head to Devin and blinked slowly. Devin couldn't be sure if Billy even saw him. He tried shaking again, with a quick glance around the cafe to see if anyone was watching them. No one cared; they were all on their devices. Billy jolted, his foot kicking the table, rattling the empty cups. He grabbed the table, gasping for air like he had been holding it.

Devin steadied the table and sat down.

"Where am I?" Billy looked around wildly.

Devin clapped Billy on the back. "Doing a little freelance work in a cafe. Like we do, every day."

Billy's eyes moved around the room before stopping on Devin. "California, yeah?"

"You know it." Devin forced a smile and the glass of water into Billy's hands. "You okay?"

Billy shook his head and swallowed the whole glass of water in one gulp and set the cup aside. "I was on a Halo fighting off hordes of Grunts and Elites." He looked down at his own hands.

"You mean *in* Halo," Devin corrected him. Billy had been so nervous about being a host, it made sense that he needed a distraction so the Elbie could control his body without hindrance.

"I guess, but I felt it. The weight of all the armor, the kickback of the weapons as they fired round after round. The pain of getting punched by one of the Elites." Billy rubbed his rib cage. "It was intense."

Devin's phone vibrated in his pocket. The coded message told him An'tylee was ready to be picked up from Google. That was fast. Once they returned back to the safe house, he would check to see if the code was already piggybacking onto all the G-suite extensions and secretly attaching itself to apps in the Play store. Today was going to be a pretty good day.

"Gotta go, Master Chief." Devin closed his laptop.

The two of them got into the rental car they had acquired using a stolen ID they bought off of the Pirate Bay. Once both Elbie were retrieved, they would return the car, call up Raul and Lysandra, and be back in Seattle before most people went to lunch.

30

CUPERTINO, CA

1000 hours PST

Matt electronically flipped cards on the tablet in front of him. He neglected the cup of coffee next to him; it was only there so he fit in with all the other "techies." He was one of five DPA officers, plus Commander Draegg spread out across the light-drenched collaboration space. Among the potted trees and calming water features, Apple employees worked silently on couches and at tables. The target, an engineer in his twenties with dark hair and glasses, sat alone, the center of every DPA officer's attention.

It was easy to spot all the DPA officers scattered around the open area. Despite the hoodie and slacks camouflage they had adopted to blend in, they stood out to Matt. All the officers were too tense. Commander Draegg, being much older than everyone in the room, stood out more than most.

Apple's headquarters was massive. Knowing this, the team arrived at the building by 5:00 a.m. and stationed DPA officers at each entrance with specialized scanners. Every employee had to pass by the DPA equipment as they walked in. An Apple higher up escorted officers to scan the few employees that had come in before 5:00 a.m. but did not find anything.

Their thoroughness paid off. A female employee, Alanna, carrying an Elbie, went through the main security checkpoint around 8:45. It was entirely possible that this person had been a host for a while. That was until the Elbie switched to a new host within the hours. The guy the DPA were keeping an eye on right now was host number four.

They could have captured the Elbie when it had arrived, but Commander Draegg wanted to see what it did first. By following its movements, he hoped that they could obtain some hard evidence of what Esben was trying to accomplish. Matt really hoped that all of this would lead to finding Esben and Lysandra. Again.

The host had most recently come from one of the network rooms that the DPA had been barred from entering, despite Homeland Security privileges. Apple engineers were given a copy of the code proliferating on the dark web. The company insisted on handling any contamination themselves, citing proprietary concerns. Now the DPA waited for evidence of any connection to the current situation with Lysandra and Esben.

Matt sighed and flipped digital cards. They had come so close yesterday to rescuing Lysandra. Matt refused to think of the situation as anything other than a kidnapping. He had already lost his entire friend circle in one way or another. Ongoing text chains with Derek and Kristy were fine, but they could never replace the daily face-to-face interactions he had grown up with. Lysandra was the last thread he had to something akin to his old life.

"Host is moving again." An officer's voice crackled through Matt's earpiece.

Matt made eye contact with Commander Draegg, who nodded at him. With that approval, Matt picked up his tablet and started to follow the host. "On it." He let the other officers know. They would follow behind him in intervals.

People greeted the host as they passed by, and he responded back in a like manner. No rush or anxiety on his part. No behaviors of any kind that were often displayed by hosts, especially the hostage kind. This probably meant that the Elbie was very much in control, encountering little resistance from the person.

Matt noticed signage announcing directions to the onsite cafe. The cafe was open to the public with lots of outdoor seating. This area had way more people in it, allowing him and the other officers to blend in better as they kept a loose perimeter around the host.

After getting a smoothie, the host carried his drink outside to a table in the sun, sat down, and took out his phone. After a few minutes, two men approached the table from another part of the eating area and sat down with the host. The skinnier one of the two took a seat next to the host and, without hesitation, put his hand on the host's shoulder.

"I want IDs now," Commander Draegg told the team. The DPA had compiled a list of possible suspects from the National

Crime Database that were hackers known to work out of the Chicago syndicate Lysandra had once been a part of.

Matt opened his tablet and quickly flipped through the pictures. Out of habit, he checked his shieldband. Only blue lights beamed up at him. He was too far away to get a reading.

"Bravo team, I need the capture equipment brought to the cafe stat." Commander Draegg's orders went out to the entire team. "If we move on them, keep things as low-key as possible."

Matt shook his head. Hosts could be totally unpredictable. With so many people around, they tended to make a scene too. The DPA didn't want the attention any more than Apple did. It would be best to wait until targets were isolated for a confrontation.

"Found 'em." Someone announced. "They look different than the photos provided, but I'm pretty sure that is Devin Allen and Billy Williams."

"Gotcha," another officer whispered over the earpiece.

Names made it easier to find their photos. Both were listed as black hat hackers. Matt compared the photos to the real thing. One thing the DPA knew for sure was that Esben wanted hackers. The Elbie under observation had to have successfully planted the rogue code, and now its handlers had come back for it. That had to be the evidence Commander Draegg was waiting for.

The host cast about his surroundings, looking bewildered. Billy put his hand on the Apple employee's shoulder again and the guy went still, staring into space. Billy and Devin got up from the table and started walking together toward one of the paths leading away from the building.

"We can't lose them," Commander Draegg said over the earpiece. "But don't get too close."

Matt started to follow at a distance. Other DPA officers fanned out to create a wide circle, many of them disappearing behind trees or smaller buildings nearby.

"Targets still in sight," Matt assured as he briskly walked behind the two hackers to keep up with them. He put his phone to his ear, pretending to be on a call. It was a bright, sunny day out. People talked on their phones while walking all the time.

Devin's head moved from one side of his field of vision to the other, his eyes meeting Matt's. Oops. Probably shouldn't have been staring directly at them. Devin started walking faster. Billy looked over his shoulder too. At the sight of Matt, the hacker/host bolted. Most Elbie would know who Matt was.

Devin broke into a run going the opposite direction and disappeared from Matt's field of vision.

"Target's fleeing." Matt started to run. "I've got the little guy. Heading Northeast." After a quick sweep of the area, he could see a pair of officers going after Devin. All Matt had to worry about was the host. The area was populated with lots of trees and hedges. Matt had to leap and dodge plant life. Ahead of him, Billy zigzagged between trees and leapt over obstacles like a gazelle. Had to be the added strength of being a host.

"The perimeter fence should slow 'em down," someone informed Matt.

Maybe, Matt thought. He gained on the guy, but hosts had been known to do some crazy physical feats. A fence may not be enough of a barrier. These guys were working for Esben. They were the only link the DPA had to finding Lysandra. Matt pumped his legs harder.

In the bright morning sunlight beaming between the trees, there was a flash of something much brighter. Artificial. As Matt cut around a bank of trees, he saw one of Esben's portals bloom into existence ahead of Billy.

"Crap," Matt cursed to himself. Footsteps pounded the ground behind him. He looked over his shoulder to see Commander Draegg quickly catching up to him. Billy disappeared into the light of the portal.

Matt pushed himself even harder. "Not this time."

31

LYNNWOOD, WA

1030 hours PST

One security guard and a handful of people scattered across a massive building had made it incredibly easy for Lysandra and Raul to gain entry. Lysandra wanted to be paranoid about the ease of entry, but they had used the same tactic to get into the nightclubs only a few days ago. Anytime these thoughts passed through her mind, she fully expected Esben to either assure her or chide her. He was, however, suspiciously quiet. Even so, with the DPA being so close, she kept watch at the door of the basement network room. Pressing her face to the window cut out in the door, she scanned the visible part of the hallway. Empty.

Across the room from the door, huge holes in the concrete wall belched out tubes of bundled wires that then split apart and snaked along the walls and fed into the network cages that lined either side of the room. Raul-Hahn had pulled a couple shelves of wire and hardware out from one of the network cages and was concentrating on attaching the transfer device directly into a main Ethernet port. Other than the door she was standing at, there was no way out of this room. If the DPA did show up, she and Raul would be cornered. Esben and the other Elbie had their exit out once Raul was done checking all the connections. Not long from now, the transfer device would be connected and all the Elbie would surge through the series of wires like they did with a person's nervous system and be deposited into the flow of data that went around the world. No more boundaries, just the endless tangle of wires that covered the globe.

She went over to the data center employee slumped on the floor in the corner. Still sound asleep. Despite the physical changes they had made to their appearances, she felt 100% exposed. Not knowing what else to do with her pent-up energy, she went to where Raul-Hahn worked. "How much longer?" She peered over the top of his shoulder.

"Just a few more connections and then we do our first test." His fingers paused. "Please don't stand so close to me."

"Sure," she said lightly. Lysandra-Esben moved away from him. Raul-Hahn was probably unnerved by her nearness, given his most recent confession. But it could have easily been a power move too. With a sigh, she dug through the backpack and pulled out one of the burner phones. No missed calls or messages from Devin or Billy. She did not risk contacting them unless it became absolutely necessary.

She went back to the door and checked the hall again, fully expecting to see someone running toward them. All clear. She forced herself to take a deep breath. It was hard not to feel the ticking of the clock when she knew the DPA had feet on the ground in Seattle.

"Got it!" Raul-Hahn said, cracking his knuckles. "Can you bring the containment unit?"

"Sure." Lysandra-Esben put the phone in her pocket and retrieved the glass cylinder from the backpack. Inside, Qur'ag and three other Elbie floated freely inside. If she counted Esben and Hahn, they'd get five of nine Elbie sent out into the world today. Devin and Billy had three Elbie between them, which meant one was missing.

"Hey Raul, do you—"

Any final words for me? Esben's voice cut across her thoughts so distinctly she turned around. The data center employee was still out cold in the corner, and Raul was waiting for her at the end of the room. No one else was there, but it felt like Esben was standing directly behind her.

"What's the matter?" Raul-Hahn asked.

"Nothing." She walked up to him and handed him the containment unit.

Raul-Hahn held it in both hands. "The record is six Elbie at once?" He wiped sweat from his forehead with the back of his hand.

"At least that." Lysandra had not seen Raul nervous since he was a teenager.

Gripping the glass cylinder with both hands, he flicked the power switch off with his thumb. The three Elbie inside disappeared. Raul's body tensed. His pupils dilated down to pinpoints, and he blinked several times. After a few deep breaths, he carefully set the containment unit down and flexed his fingers. He met her gaze. "Last one, *mi cielo*." He reached one hand, palm up, over the retractable shelf.

She put her hand in Raul-Hahn's. Turning inward, she directed her thoughts at Esben. *Good... bye, Esben.* His presence disappeared from her head, and the feeling of someone standing behind her disappeared with him. Heat shot through her hand into Raul's. Raul shuddered.

A weight lifted from her chest. This was the last time she would ever have to deal with Esben. Maybe she should have said something more to him. But what? She wouldn't miss the Elbie; he had been a source of strife for her family for years. The sting of regret lingered in the back of her mind. Over what, she would have to figure it out later.

Raul-Esben-Hahn regained his composure and released her hand. "Moment of truth." As his confidence returned, he placed his hands on the transfer device and closed his eyes.

Lysandra clenched her fists. She was ready to be done with this whole thing. Tired of being on the run from her friends. It wasn't the fault of any of them. The DPA were doing their jobs well. "How much longer—"

A harsh light flickered, casting a deep shadow of Raul against the wall. Lysandra turned around. A portal had popped into existence a few feet behind her. Billy came through at a full run and collided with her. His weight pushed her into the shelf between her and Raul. The shelf buckled under the impact. Equipment crashed to the ground. Billy bounced off a network cage. Raul cursed in Spanish as she righted herself.

"Close it! Close it!" Billy screamed out of breath. Clawing his way up the front of the cage to his feet again. "Shut down the portal!"

"Billy!" Lysandra dug the portal anchor out of her pocket. "What the f—" She dodged, pushing Raul back as more people came barreling through the portal.

Billy tumbled out of the way just as Matt emerged and skidded to a halt. He scanned the room, getting his bearings. "Lysandra." His face lit up with a smile.

Lysandra stood frozen in place, stunned to see him. A rush of joy and apprehension twisted in her gut. God, she had missed him. Commander Draegg emerged from the light at a cautious pace, more officers following behind him. Billy flung open the door to the network room and ran into the hallway shouting like a banshee. Two officers peeled off after him.

Someone yanked her backward. Raul-Esben-Hahn's arm dropped over her head and across her collarbone as he walked them back a few feet.

Commander Draegg moved to the center of the group, hands up to show he had no weapons. Matt and the other officer fanned out on either side of him. Commander Draegg looked at her first. "Are you okay, Lysandra?"

Raul-Esben-Hahn's arm tightened around her throat. She nodded. Commander Draegg's eyes shifted to Raul. "Let's talk, Esben."

"There is nothing to talk about, Draegg." Raul-Esben-Hahn's other hand reached around her waist, yanked her gun from its holster, and planted it against her temple.

"There's no need for threats." Commander Draegg signaled to the other officers to put their weapons down. "Let's work together. What do you want?"

From the jumble of equipment on the floor, Lysandra could see the transfer device. She tapped Raul's arm. "*Confía en mí.*"

Raul-Esben-Hahn dropped his arm from around her and planted the gun at the back of her neck. She kept her eye on Commander Draegg as she slowly knelt down to retrieve the transfer device. "Commander, I know this doesn't make sense right now, but this has to happen."

"Officer Carlisle." Commander Draegg took one step forward. "Stop."

"I can't." She plucked the transfer device from the pile and passed it to Raul-Esben-Hahn. She looked over her shoulder to him. "Finish this."

The edge of anger in his eyes melted. Raul-Esben-Hahn nodded and lowered the gun.

Hands out, Lysandra put herself between Raul and the DPA as he found the cables he needed to hook the device up once again. She looked at Commander Draegg. "The Elbie want to be free of their human hosts."

The DPA officer on Commander Draegg's left launched forward. On pure instinct, Lysandra thrust her hands toward him and, with a mental shove, tossed him into the nearest network cage.

Matt jumped toward her. Lysandra braced herself and forced Matt back with a telekinetic push. He stumbled back, dismayed. "Please don't make me do this." She pleaded with Matt and Commander Draegg. It had been years since she held off multiple opponents with her telekinetics. She wasn't sure she would be able to control it enough to keep them at bay and unharmed.

Commander Draegg stared at her. "Lysandra, we can't let you do this."

"Where can the Elbie go? To send them back to hosts would be torture for both Elbie and the host."

"They can live in artificial bodies like Kwin and Khullus do."

Lysandra shook her head. "The idea of freedom has taken root. There's no going back. Elbie are influenced by their hosts, and all the hosts for your cluster are American. Individualism and personal freedom are at the core of who they are."

Commander Draegg inched forward. "I don't feel that way."

She directed a gentle push in his direction as a warning. Feeling the push, he drew back. With both hands outstretched toward the three officers, her eyes darted between Matt and the other officer in her periphery. "Esben doesn't insist on all of you going. He only asks to choose for himself."

Commander Draegg's eyes went to Raul behind her. "I don't have the luxury of bestowing that gift. Neither do you, Officer Carlisle."

Lysandra glanced back at Raul, still messing with the device and several cables. Sweat dripped down the sides of his face. Having multiple Elbie would do that to you. But it was probably more than that. Escape was all Esben could think about. She looked back at Commander Draegg. "I quit."

"What! You can't," Matt exclaimed. The pain that crossed his face at her pronouncement lanced her heart.

"I don't want to. But Draegg's right: as a member of this government agency, I have to uphold a different set of values but as an individual…" She locked her gaze on her former commander. "Arrest me if you must, but I won't be the one to deny the Elbie their freedom."

Commander Draegg grimaced. "I genuinely admire your choice, Lysandra. But I have a duty to uphold."

"I understand your choice, and I know you understand mine."

Commander Draegg nodded, a stoic smile on his face.

"Tell her she can't." Matt's eyes brimmed with tears. "You're all I've got left."

Lysandra tilted her head slightly. "You deserve so much more, Matt. I love you, but where I work or live will not change that."

"*¡Estupendo!*" Raul whispered from behind. Before she could confirm if he had completed the transfer, his arm dropped over the top of her again and pressed the gun into her temple. "Enough with the friendship bullshit."

His hands were hot, too hot for him to be Elbie-free. A silver glint caught her eye. Her watch was on Raul's wrist. The watch that should have been dismantled so the Elbie trapped inside it could be freed like the rest of them. One or both of them had lied to her. Lysandra set her jaw, taking long, slow breaths. "Why are your hands so hot?" she said in a low tone.

Raul huffed. He pressed the buttons on the side of the watch. Silhouettes of Matt, Commander Draegg, and the other officer splashed across the wall behind them as a new portal opened behind her and Raul.

Esben-Raul started to walk them backward. "Follow us and she will get hurt."

Lysandra squeezed her eyes shut as Esben-Raul backed her through the portal, the barrel of her own gun digging into her cheek. Everything went white and he released her. After her eyes adjusted, she saw that they had returned to the rental they had stayed in last night.

"You son of bitch!" She turned on him. "You kept one of the portals intact?"

"It's a good thing we did." He handed her the gun. "Why so angry about it?"

"Because you lied to me." She checked the safety. It was still on.

"You told me to do something, and I simply didn't confirm it was done."

Lysandra growled in frustration as she holstered her gun. "What are you even doing here, Esben? You should be one with the internet right now. Were there any Elbie in that device or was it all some sort of show?"

"Qur'ag and the others from the portal anchors. They all went." He gathered the last of their belongings on the couch.

"So you saved yourself. Just in case it doesn't work. It's always something else with you, Esben." She paced in a circle. "You left Billy back there!"

"He knew the risks," Esben-Raul said callously.

"Fine. But you should have left me behind. You don't need me anymore."

"If Draegg thinks you're in danger, he won't make a move against us."

Esben-Raul pulled the food from the fridge.

Lysandra pushed him aside and slammed the fridge door. "You don't need any of this stuff. Food, money, capture equipment. What are you up to?"

"Raul does." He carried the food over to the couch, adding it to the pile.

Lysandra walked behind him. "I put everything on the line so you could have your goddamn agency. This is how you thank me?"

Esben-Raul went to the window that faced the street. After peeking between the slats of the blinds, he turned back to her. "Once we confirm the other Elbie survived the transfer, then we'll follow."

"Who the hell is *we?*" She crossed her arms.

"Raul could really use your help until this is finished. It would mean a lot to him."

Lysandra rolled her eyes. "Bullshit. You were obsessed with controlling my brother, and now you're doing it to me through Raul. Pretty shitty, Esben, even for you."

"We're asking for Raul."

"A few hours ago, you said you didn't need me for any of this. What's changed?"

Esben-Raul closed the distance between them. "Raul is better with you around."

Lysandra scoffed. "Bullshit." She knew it was, that is what Esben and Raul did best, but somehow, she was still flattered by the notion. Had pulling her life together inspired Raul to do the same? It was a common sentiment in love songs and movies: love could make a person better than they were. "That is ridiculous." She assured herself.

Esben-Raul took her hands. "Lysandra. Please. It's just twenty-four more hours. There's a data center a few hours south of here. There we can run some proper tests, if everything works, I'll be out of your life for good. Then you and Raul can live your lives however you please."

Lysandra looked down at her hands. "Me and Raul...."

"*Complacer,*" he whispered, caressing the back of her hands with his thumbs.

She looked him in the eye. A shift in Raul's posture rippled through his body from head to toe. His eyes went out of focus and snapped back to normal, settling on her. Raul smiled, warming her like the sun on a summer afternoon; she wanted to soak up all the rays.

"*Cariño.*" He brought her hands up and pressed his lips to her fingers.

A delicious warmth bloomed in her chest and rolled over her entire body. Her head spun slightly, like she was drunk. Raul dropped one hand to rest on her waist, clasped the other, and started to sway to a song only he could hear. "Just you and me. It can be like that again."

The delightful warmth had spread up into her neck and face. Memories danced in her mind's eye for their early days. The two of them, alone in his hideaway in the attic doing "homework." She smiled to herself. His family had to have known they were sleeping together. Two teenagers who spent every possible minute together like that. She and Raul had cared for each other in a way no one had up to that point in her life.

The heat of Raul's body against hers as he pulled her closer made her stomach flutter. Cool tingles of pleasure raced through her arms as he murmured songs softly against her neck. Those idyllic days of their first love had been too few before it all came crashing down.

The terror of her father's wrath had torn it all down. After a particularly vicious round of beatings, she had run to Raul and the safety of his family, who loved her in a way her father was incapable of. He followed her to this safe haven. In his anger, her father called the police, telling them she had been kidnapped. This house of the most loving people she had ever known, illegal immigrants, was swarmed in minutes.

Guilt lanced through her as she rewatched his entire family taken away in handcuffs. Raul's little sister's terrified cries carried up to where the two of them huddled together in the deep shadows on the roof.

Lysandra wrapped her arms around his waist, gripping his shirt tightly as the loss of those relationships renewed itself. "I'm so sorry," she said into the side of his neck.

Their swaying had slowed to a gentle rocking. Raul's arms tightened around her. He kissed her on the temple. "It's not your fault."

It's not your fault, reverberated in her head. The kiss, the tight embrace. All of it déjà vu from another time and place. Another man. Edward. After Xander had forced the confrontation with her father, he had died.

What the hell was wrong with her? With every fiber of her being, she had loved Raul. Once. But not now. Especially not at the moment. "What the hell?" She pushed him away. "Esben."

The room fell away, and suddenly she was in a dark alley. Barely lit by lights from windows above. Ears ringing from nearby gunfire. Heart pounding. Her first firefight. Growing up, she had heard gunfire from a distance countless times. Being the source of the gunfire was something else. Bullets had been fired at her and she shot back. She looked down at her hand: a .38 revolver, six shots, all fired. Her first victim groaned, face down in a pool of his own blood.

Someone grabbed her arm. Lysandra spun to defend herself. A baby-faced nineteen-year-old Raul, panting, out of breath. "We've got to go." He pulled on her arm.

The cold of the air around her. Raul's grip on her arm as he pulled. The distant sirens drawing closer. It felt real. Right now. Happening again.

"No." It wasn't real. This was Esben messing with her memories and emotions. She forced herself to remember her last firefight. A world away in a remote village in India. Commander Eriksson collapsing into her, suffocating on the blood in his lungs from the bullets meant for her. "Stop it."

The world shifted again. Raul's mom stood next to her, showing Lysandra how to make flour tortillas by hand. Rolling the white dough between her palms and the sizzle of the onions and peppers on the stove behind them. Their house was always full of people and conversation. If the TV didn't have a soccer game on, the radio played in the background at all times. Everyone piled into the living room on the broken gold couch or across the floor to watch the match. She had never cared about sports except that they cared about sports. They were always happy to see her and included her in everything they did. She had been an outsider, and they brought her in. Being with them was the first time she had known what family was like. It was not the last.

There weren't many, but she forced herself to recall the weekly dinners she had to endure with Brendan, Kristy, Matt, and Derek. They had been few, but she clung to the laughter and the smiles from each. They had tried so hard to include her in their world. She had lost her brother because of the Elbie.

More memories were dredged up, trying to trap her most powerful emotions. For every memory Esben tried to lock her into, she found another to pull herself out of it. She had a vague awareness of her body struggling against someone. "None of this is real," she stated, her voice distant even to her own ears.

She focused on the strongest memory she could find. Edward, reaching down to her through that stage floor. Pleading wordlessly with her to take his hand, to come home.

Go home.

The hush of the rental house faded back in as she became aware of her surroundings again. The tenderness of all the stirred-up history thrummed in her chest. She had known so few occasions of actual happiness, especially as a teenager. Raul had provided her with a safe space when she had none. Hot tears streamed down her face. Raul had her arms pinned to her chest from behind.

She twisted, trying to break his grip. "Fuck you."

"If you insist." She could hear the smile in his voice.

"Raul Reyes Guerrero, if you continue to allow this, I will hate you in the truest sense of the word. Is that what you really want?"

His arms loosened slightly. She jerked her arm back, connecting with his ribs. His arms retracted as he cradled his rib cage. With her elbow up, she swiveled, ramming it into his jaw. Raul fell onto his back. Lysandra threw her leg over him, straddled his stomach, and pinned his arms to the ground. "Thanks for ruining some of my best memories, asshole. Now who am I talking to?"

Raul moved his jaw back and forth. When his eyes met her gaze, they had a hard edge to them. Esben was back in control. Lysandra slammed his hands against the floor. "I honored your choice; you need to honor mine."

Esben-Raul pursed his lips. "We will, but it will have to be tomorrow." Heat moved into her hands.

Lysandra rolled off him, breaking contact. The heat disappeared. She glanced around the room and saw the equipment bag. "You've gone too far, Esben." She stretched her hand out toward the bag of capture equipment and focused on pulling it toward her. "I'm turning you over to the DPA."

"What are you doing?" His eyes went wide with panic. "Don't do it." Esben-Raul got his feet under him and tackled her.

A cold presence slipped between her thoughts. Qur'ag. Panic spiked through her. Her vision started to tunnel as an overwhelming exhaustion blanketed her thoughts, making concentration impossible. "You bastards."

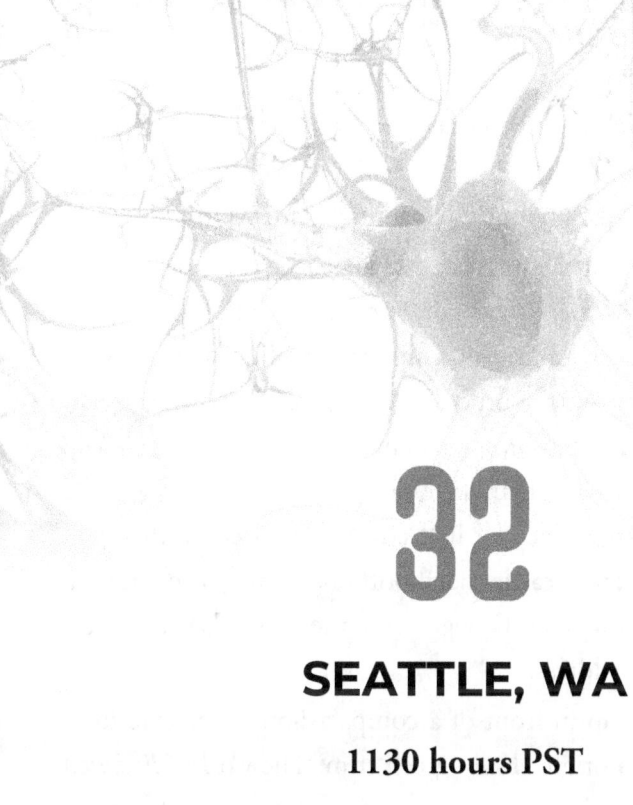

32

SEATTLE, WA

1130 hours PST

Matt Holloway had never been to Seattle. Except for one work assignment to India, he'd never been anywhere. An hour ago, they were in sunny, warm California at the world's biggest tech company. The DPA officers had not dressed for the damp, grayscape of Seattle when they followed Billy through that portal. They all had their hoodies zipped to the top, except for Commander Draegg. The exponential number of trees everywhere was kind of neat. No wonder the oldest Carlisle sibling had moved here.

Helplessly watching Lysandra disappear again had crushed Matt. They had come so close yesterday. To be outwitted again so soon after the boon of Billy's mistake almost made Matt angry.

In the aftermath at the internet exchange, the DPA had started to debrief the staff when they got another break. Edward had received a call from an unknown number. The line stayed active, but there was no one on the other end. Commander Eriksson had the source of the call tracked immediately. Once an address had been pinpointed, he called Commander Draegg. Draegg's team was the closest to the location. The call had come from a cell phone still located in a northern Seattle neighborhood. After procuring a vehicle, Matt, Commander Draegg, and the other DPA officers went straight to the address.

The car pulled up in front of a compact house, the exterior a day-glow white with bright, Kelly-green trim. The yard overflowed with colorful beds of flowers. There were no cars in the driveway. The gate to the flower-laden yard was open like it was expecting visitors.

Commander Draegg put his arm over the seat from the front passenger seat. "Does the service provider show it's still here?"

Matt checked his text messages. "No change."

"Good." Commander Draegg addressed the other officers. "Officer Holloway and I will go in. The rest of you form a perimeter. Detain anyone who tries to leave. Use force if necessary."

"Yes sir," a chorus of officers responded.

They all piled out of the car. They were all dressed in civilian clothing so they shouldn't draw too much attention. As the other officers split up, Commander Draegg and Matt went through the gate and followed a cement path up to the front door. The neighborhood seemed super chill. Except for the occasional passing car, there was no activity.

Matt unlatched his DPA-issued weapon but didn't draw it. Commander Draegg always preferred de-escalation tactics before all others. Given all the surprises they had encountered while tracking down Esben, Matt wanted to be prepared in case this was an ambush of some kind. Commander Draegg knocked on the door and waited. Not a sound came from inside the unassuming house. Matt scanned their surroundings. It was a pretty cool neighborhood, reminding him of where they grew up but with different trees.

Commander Draegg jiggled the doorknob. It turned without resistance. He opened the door a crack. "Anyone home?"

Matt planted his feet, ready to fight. The commander swung the door open. Sprawled on the floor in their direct line of sight of the door was Lysandra. Not moving.

"Lysandra!" Matt rushed past his commanding officer.

"Matt." Commander Draegg caught his sleeve. "Check the rest of the house first."

Matt could see that she was breathing at least. "Yes sir." He complied.

As he walked past Lysandra, he noticed a cell phone a few inches from her open hand. The phone that had brought them to her.

It was a small space. The only other doors in the place were to the bathroom and two closets. "All clear, Commander." The sting of bleach and Windex hung in the air. "This place has been scrubbed." Matt checked the trash bins. They had debris but nothing telling.

Commander Draegg knelt near Lysandra's outstretched arm and placed his hand over her wrist.

Search completed, Matt sat on the ground next to Draegg. "Is she okay?"

Commander Draegg nodded and took out his phone and started texting.

"Is she drugged?" Matt took her hand in his.

Commander Draegg shook his head. "I can't tell without violating the code of conduct. As far as I can tell, she's asleep. She's definitely Elbie-free."

Matt sighed with relief. The last three days were the most stressed he had been in years. Whatever Esben was up to, at least he was done with dragging Lysandra along. Commander Eriksson and Mr. Drake would be happy to know they had Lysandra back.

Still holding Lysandra's hand, Matt watched Commander Draegg put his phone away. "Did you let Commander Eriksson know we got her?"

"I did. He's working on our transportation back to L.A."

Lysandra shuddered. Her eyes shot open and she yanked her arm from Matt. In one movement, she rolled away from them and thrust her hands out toward them. An invisible force slammed into Matt and the commander, knocking them backward. She was up on one knee, gun drawn, in the blink of an eye.

"Stay the hell away from me." The barrel of the gun moved back and forth between Matt and Commander Draegg.

Draegg had his hands in the air. "You're safe, Lysandra. Stand down."

Lysandra frowned and stood up. "Both of you on the floor now, or I will put a bullet through your heads."

Matt took a small step forward. "Come on, Lysandra. We're your friends. We won't—"

Lysandra laughed harshly. "Like hell we are." She pulled the slide on her gun. "Last time. On the ground. Now."

Dread twisted in Matt's gut. He exchanged glances with Commander Draegg. Draegg had been there the last time this happened. If Esben did to Lysandra what he had done to Brendan all those years ago, Matt wasn't sure he could take it. They had lost Brendan that day in so many ways. Even after years of counseling, they had never really got him back. Matt couldn't lose Lysandra too.

"Commander, you don't think…"

"I don't know, Matt." Commander Draegg didn't sound as assured as he usually did.

"I warned you." Lysandra pointed her gun at Commander Draegg and pulled the trigger.

Click.

Matt and Draegg ducked in unison.

Click, click, click.

Lysandra growled in frustration, bringing the gun in closer for examination. Commander Draegg leapt forward, tackling her. The gun dropped from her hand as they hit the ground.

Matt drew his DPA gun and waited for a clean shot. All DPA weapons were non-lethal, but he still didn't want to hit Commander Draegg.

Lysandra half shouted, half grunted long strings of profanities as Draegg grappled with her.

Commander Draegg had her in a half-nelson. He looked at Matt. "Did you see any random words written anywhere? On the fridge or mirror?"

"Words?" Matt blinked, confused. "I wasn't looking for that."

"Check now. Hurry." Lysandra bucked him at the last moment.

Matt dashed around the small space, searching for anything written. There were printed instructions for using the dishwasher on the fridge. Little quotes in matching frames littered the walls all around. Finally, in the farthest corner, he spotted a notepad on the nightstand next to the bed. There was something scribbled on it. Matt snatched the notepad and ran back to Draegg. "It's in Spanish."

"Read it. Out loud." Commander Draegg hit the ground as Lysandra got the upper hand on him.

Matt had sat through two years of high school Spanish and didn't remember one word of it. *Here goes nothing.* He took a deep breath. *"Mi cielo."* Lysandra stopped struggling. *"Tardé una hora en conocerte y solo un día en enamorarme."* Lysandra's full focus was on Matt now as he stumbled through the scrawled message. *"Pero me llevará toda una vida lograr olvidarte."*

Lysandra blinked several times, confusion clouding her features. "Commander?" She released him. Looking around the room, her searching gaze stopped at Matt. She gasped. "Matt. What... how?"

Lysandra sat back. "Where are we?"

Commander Draegg sat up, straightening his uniform.

The dread in Matt's stomach started to unfurl; her posture and tone were the Lysandra he knew and loved.

Commander Draegg's lips pressed together in a tight line. "What's the last thing you remember?"

She took a moment to think about it. She clapped a hand over her mouth, eyes wide. She looked at Commander Draegg and then Matt. "I shot you. I mean, I tried to. I'm so sorry."

The genuine surprise and shock from Lysandra at the thought of almost killing them assured Matt that whatever command/illusion Esben had planted in her head had been temporary.

Lysandra found her gun on the floor, picked it up, and dropped the magazine into her palm. Empty. "I thought you were Nick and Gregory. I take it we're not in Chicago?"

"Seattle." Commander Draegg stood near her.

Lysandra holstered her gun. "When did that happen?"

Commander Draegg ran his hand through his short gray hair. "Yesterday, most likely. We intercepted you and your group at your mom's rental house, but you were unconscious. They portaled out."

She sat down on the arm of the couch. "I remember being at the house with those guys, but…"

Relieved, Matt came up beside her. "So you don't hate me and want to hurt me?"

Lysandra looked horrified. "Hate you? Is that even possible?"

"Oh thank god." Matt hugged her, full body contact, exactly the way she hated. He was definitely violating her touch policy time limit, but he didn't care. He had three days of no hugs to make up for. Commander Draegg tapped Matt on the shoulder. Reluctantly, he let Lysandra go.

"Do you remember being at the internet place an hour ago?" Commander Draegg continued the investigation.

Lysandra shook her head. "We had reunited the Elbie from Edward's portal cards and transferred them to everyone in the group." She furrowed her eyebrows. "That was really yesterday?"

Commander Draegg nodded. "I was afraid Esben might do something like this."

"Esben was supposed to be transferred to the internet. But since my memory's been altered, I take it he didn't go with the others."

"Elbie on the internet!" Matt exclaimed. That was a first. Derek was going to freak out about this development. "Is that really possible?"

Commander Draegg shrugged. "When we showed up at the internet exchange, Esben was very much in control of the situation. Do you have any idea what Esben had planned next?"

"After the transfer, everybody was supposed to go their separate ways. Most people don't share their plans once a job is done."

"Do you know anything about this?" Matt held out the note to her. He had no idea she knew Spanish.

Lysandra took it and read it over silently. "It's an old song I know." She half-smiled and tossed the note on the coffee table.

"It's good to have you back." Commander Draegg put his hand on her shoulder.

"To be honest, I wasn't sure I'd be welcomed back."

"We'll get your statement and figure out as much as we can about everything. I'm guessing you'll cooperate."

"Yeah, whatever it takes." Lysandra sighed heavily.

Matt hugged her again. Lysandra finally circled her arms around him and applied a little pressure. He squeezed a little harder. He was sure she secretly liked his hugs.

"Alright, Matt." She patted him on the back. "Let's go home."

Epilogue

DPA HEADQUARTERS

3 Weeks Later

Lysandra commandeered an extra-large recycle bin from one of the communal activity rooms. After dragging it into her private quarters, she filled it with magazines and newspapers. The accumulated knowledge she had collected on Edward's enemies was no longer needed. The books she had bought were boxed up by the door, ready for pick-up. When she returned in a few months, she wanted her room to be ready for a fresh start.

The door chimed.

"Come in!" She knew exactly who it was.

Matt rushed in, out of breath. Unlike her, he had to continue his daily duties for the federal government. All her responsibilities had been suspended during her disciplinary hearing.

"Well?" He unzipped his jacket and started flapping it to cool himself.

"Did you run here?" She tossed all the pens and markers into one of the desk drawers.

"Yes! As soon as I heard the hearing was over, I requested the rest of the day off. So what happened?"

"See for yourself." She picked up a tablet and slapped it into his waiting palm. The official verdict from the hearing was already open for him to read.

Matt sat down on the corner of her bed and started scrolling through the charges. "Prohibited/improper use of government property, violating standards of ethical conduct unbecoming a federal employee, willfully engaging in criminal conduct, and endangering national security." He mouthed all the legal gibberish. "Ninety days' suspension without pay." He glanced over at her. "That's it?"

Lysandra laughed. The final verdict had surprised her too. "The mediator said she was giving me the benefit of the doubt. Partially because of the memory loss thing, but also because there was no evidence that Elbie were on the internet. I can return to my sworn duties after my suspension is complete."

Matt set the tablet aside. "What about the part where you had quit?"

"Commander Draegg said that since I don't remember doing it, it doesn't count. He suggested I figure out if I want to quit or not during my suspension."

"Do you?"

Lysandra shrugged. "You were there. Did it seem like I meant it?"

Matt's eyes roved around the room. "You did."

She nodded. Even though she could not recall anything about the confrontation, when she had heard Commander Draegg's testimony, she knew in her gut she must have said those things. It felt true for her and to her. "We'll see. Being here has done a lot for me. I'm just not sure it's for me."

"Well." He ran his hand through his hair. "It sucks, but at least it's only three months."

"Could have been two years in prison. Really glad it didn't go that way." She went to her closet and pulled out her duffel bag. She would basically need to pack every stitch of clothing she owned, minus her uniform. It would be weird not having a schedule. Not being in this building. Not seeing Matt or having Eriksson scolding her for some minor protocol violation. "It will go fast."

Matt's phone beeped from his pocket.

"Is that Megan, again?" She started piling clothes on her cleared desk.

"Yeah." He smiled as he texted a response. He set the phone down. "When are we hanging out? Let's make a plan now."

Lysandra had no idea what her life would be like for the next three months. "We can still do our Tuesday dinners."

"Okay, but that's only one day a week. What about the rest of the week?"

"How often were you expecting to hang out?"

"Five to six days a week."

Lysandra stopped wadding up clothes and leveled her gaze at him. His tone was joking, but she also knew from the hearing that he had protested her quitting.

A smile broke out on his face. "Okay. Two to three. I game with some of the IT guys on Mondays and Wednesdays anyway."

"Then I'll take all your Tuesdays and Thursdays. Lunch or dinner, no breakfasts."

"Alright. Deal. Any chance of me coming over to the house to hang out?"

Lysandra arched her eyebrows at him. "You want to come over to Edward's house?"

Matt shrugged. "Kind of. Are there any secret passages?"

"I don't think so."

"Too bad." Matt's phone beeped.

As he checked his new message, Lysandra emptied the drawers in her closet and tossed all the leftover clothing into the duffel bag. She was glad to see Matt being proactive about his social life. Even though they both knew her fate had been up to the disciplinary board, she couldn't help feeling like she was abandoning him.

She zipped up the bag and surveyed the room. The DPA had been the best phase of her life so far. Once upon a time, it would have been impossible for her to imagine anything other than the vagrant life her father had passed on to her. Being surrounded by caring, reliable friendships and the stability she had craved when she was younger had not been possible even two years ago. While she fully intended to return to the DPA, getting ready to walk out somehow felt final.

Her phone chirped. Mr. Drake: *Out front.*

Matt put his phone away. "I know. Double date. You and Edward, me and Megan."

Lysandra cringed. Then again, the trappings of normalcy were still hard to accept. "I'm gonna have to let that one sink in before responding."

Matt laughed. "I was just messing with you."

"Thank god." She hefted the bag over her shoulder. "My ride's here."

"Already?" Matt's face darkened. He stood and took the bag from her. "Don't forget our deal."

"Never."

They walked out together. Lysandra wasn't really friends with anyone other than Matt. Once the hearing had concluded, Commanders Draegg and Eriksson had said their goodbyes. Eriksson kept it professional and aloof. If he held anything against her, he gave nothing away. Draegg hugged her and told her to enjoy herself and, if she needed anything, to let him know.

Once they were in the elevator, Matt pressed the button for the lobby. "Derek said he's working on a way to detect Elbie energy in network systems."

"That's cool. Has he found any yet?"

"Not yet. He's pretty sure Elbie living on the internet is impossible."

"Really?" The whereabouts of Raul and Esben crossed her mind daily. If it had been an impossibility, neither Esben nor Raul had given any hint of it. They had worked hard at something they knew wasn't going to work if that was the case. If it was a failed attempt, then Esben had sacrificed the existence of his fellow Elbie in pursuit of his own freedom. Asshole to the very end.

"Maybe Esben decided to stay with that friend of yours."

"If he did, it's temporary. Esben was determined. One way or another, he'll find a way onto the net."

As she had stated in her hearing, she had no idea if any Elbie were ever ultimately transferred to the internet. There had not been any time to test the equipment. Those other Elbie could have been destroyed. Until Raul or Esben were found, there was no way to know for sure. Knowing both of them were out there freely roaming around was a relief and a concern all at once. She couldn't remember her last moments with them, but whenever she tried to recall the memory, low-grade anger burned in her gut. The one thing she knew for sure; she never wanted to hear from either of them again.

There were a lot more floors in the DPA's new HQ. As they descended to the lobby, people got on and off different floors. The rhythms and routines of the new building had taken a few months to get used to. The elevator arrived at the lobby. Lysandra and Matt exited last. Their walk to the front doors slowed to a stop. Lysandra took her bag from Matt. "See you on Tuesday."

"And Thursday," Matt added.

"I'll text you."

Matt moved forward with his arms open. Usually she allowed herself to be hugged for the standard twenty seconds, but this time leaned into it and lingered in the contact. They really would be friends for life, no matter what.

He squeezed her extra hard before letting go. "See you later."

Lysandra walked past the security checkpoint, through the automated doors, and out into the bright L.A. sun. A black car waited at the curb directly in front. The driver met her, taking her bag without asking. He opened the backseat door before going to the trunk with her bag.

Lysandra turned around, her eyes going to the top of the building where the living quarters were and traveling down the length of the glass and steel panels to the lobby doors. Somewhere inside, Matt, Commander Draegg, and Eriksson were going about their daily routines. Matt's buoyant approach to their mundane duties was something she secretly admired and looked forward to. Commander Draegg had given her the benefit of the doubt from the start. It had been a gift. His calm and steady presence would be missed. Then there was "by the book" Eriksson. His valor and loyalty to his team, regardless of their differences, could never be doubted. Lysandra would never really "like" him, but she was grateful to him for all he had done.

She ducked her head inside the car. Edward was on the far side of the bench seat, his green eyes bright in the morning light. Her heart settled at the sight of him. "Full disclosure, Mr. Drake, I have no money or a place to stay. I hope that's okay."

"Arrangements can be made, Miss Carlisle, I assure you." He smiled and patted the seat next to him.

Because he had been a witness at her disciplinary hearing, they hadn't interacted directly since she'd gone rogue. The only time she had seen him in the last couple of weeks was the day he had given his accounting of events. The car door was closed behind her as she climbed inside and sidled up next to him. Being with Edward was home for her.

She rested her hand on his thigh and looked up at him. "I'm sorry about Esben."

Edward dropped his arm around her shoulders. "It's been an adjustment." Relaxed and contemplative, he watched the cityscape pass by. Before, his silence had been isolating. Now she was a part of it, as his hand rested on top of hers. Finally, he turned away from the window, and shifted his body closer to her. "It was a good partnership. I'm sure I can find better."

"I know you can." Lysandra grabbed his tie, pulled him toward her and planted her lips on his. Edward's hold tightened around her waist, drawing out their kiss with gentle devotion.

With a satisfied sigh, she snuggled into his side and rested her head on his shoulder.

"What do you want to do now, Miss Carlisle?"

"Today, let's go home. Tomorrow, we'll see."

It would take time for trust to be rebuilt between them, but with Esben gone, there was nothing between them anymore. Edward and Esben had been together for a long time, but she had definitely gotten the better half.

THANK YOU FOR READING
ITERATION

AND THE ENTIRE DPA SERIES.

If you have a few moments to leave a review on the Amazon. I would really appreciate it. Every review helps an indie author like myself. If you prefer to leave a review on Goodreads or other social media that is good too.

To read more from me go to **www.elbiefree.com**. Or you can connect with me on Facebook and Twitter **@kelvarus** for both.

A word about human trafficking:

"Human trafficking is the recruitment, transportation, transfer, harboring, or receipt of people through force, fraud or deception, with the aim of exploiting them for profit." -UNDOC

Human trafficking is a worldwide crime epidemic that effects men, women, and children. Below are just a few of the websites where you can learn more about this issue and support some good organizations.

- ➤ https://humantraffickinghotline.org/
- ➤ https://www.ijm.org/
- ➤ https://www.castla.org/human-trafficking/
- ➤ https://polarisproject.org/
- ➤ https://truckersagainsttrafficking.org/
- ➤ https://iwantrest.com/
- ➤ https://www.unodc.org/unodc/human-trafficking/